DRAWN
from
MEMORY

LAURA HATOSY

Published by Scrap Paper Press

PO Box 3021

Wakefield, MA 01880

Cover design: Lynn Andreozzi

Editor: Michelle Hope

Proofreader: Brooke De Lira

While inspired by real events and characters, some details have been fictionalized to suit the narrative of the story the author wanted tell.

ISBN: 979-8-985-64081-6

Library of Congress Number: 2022902553

Printed in the U.S.A.

For Chris and Mom

Copenhagen, Denmark
September 28, 1943

Chapter One

THE SOLDIER DIDN'T STAND a chance.

Pulling the memory from him was like easing open a well-oiled door. I just had to picture what I wanted to erase—his image of me, a sixteen-year-old girl in Tivoli Gardens with a sketch pad under her arm and a bleeding orange cat at her feet—and poof! The German's eyes became unfocused, and his mouth hung open.

My ability worked best on the stupid, so it didn't say much for this guy's intellect that I could pluck the last few minutes from his mind as easily as picking a flower in a garden. Still, some strength drained out of me. I staggered to avoid treading on the stray at my feet. My smirk disappeared. It was no time to get smug.

It wasn't as if the soldier were alone.

Thankfully, the other one was distracted by the effect I'd had on his partner. He called out to him and waved a hand in his face. The dazed soldier would recover in a second or two, but I wouldn't be around to see it. I scooped up the stray and fled the park despite my wobbly knees.

I plunged into City Hall Square and snatched the bright-red ribbon from my dark hair to better blend in with the throng of afternoon shoppers. I chanced a glance behind me. No sign of them.

I slowed to catch my breath and wished I could've taken a picture of the befuddled looks on their Nazi faces.

A powerful hand seized my arm and yanked me to a stop. For a second, my heart stopped too. I wrenched my elbow out of my assailant's grip, ready to make a run for it again, but when I caught sight of his face, my panic evaporated. It wasn't a soldier, just another sixteen-year-old, with a face I recognized.

"*Pokkers*, Gideon!" I hurled myself into the shelter of a doorway, dragging him with me and knocking into an old woman. Gideon mumbled an apology on my behalf, whether for shoving her or my swear, I couldn't be sure. I clutched my chest until my heartbeat regained its usual rhythm. "You nearly scared me to death!"

"What are you doing, Rachel?" Gideon asked once the affronted old woman had shuffled off. "You can't run through the streets—" His words cut off. The second soldier appeared at the entrance to the square. The German scanned the area. I crammed myself deeper into the doorframe, cowering behind Gideon. When the soldier sprinted in the opposite direction, I let out the breath trapped in my chest.

Gideon gaped at the disappearing uniform and slowly turned back to me. "What did you do now?"

"Why do you always assume *I've* done something?" I thrust the cat in his face. "Why don't you ask what *he* did?"

Gideon noticed the orange stray for the first time.

"The soldier did this?" Gideon pointed to where the cat's ear had been torn away. Blood ran down the side of its head.

I cradled the cat back under my arm, careful not to jostle its injury. "They were throwing rocks at the poor thing in the park." I'd been sketching the new Ferris wheel when its pitiful cries had carried over from the other side of the lake.

I didn't mention erasing the soldier's memories. No one knew about my ability, but if anyone suspected, it would be Gideon. His memories had been the first I'd pulled, and I didn't know what I was doing back then.

"And you had to rescue it, right?" Despite the serious tone of his voice, his lip quirked up ever so slightly, which was practically beaming for Gideon. The girls in our class assumed he was some deep, brooding mystery by virtue of his disheveled hair, heavily lidded dark eyes, and the natural tendency for his mouth to turn down. In truth, he was just perpetually grumpy.

I stroked the stray's mangy back, trying to soothe it as we walked. It struggled, not knowing any better. To relieve the cat's fear, I pulled the memory of its trauma. It came easily enough—the cat's mind was only marginally simpler than the soldier's. It hissed, and its hackles raised. It didn't recognize me anymore and swiped its claws, leaping out of my arms and darting away.

"Ow." I dabbed at the scratch.

Gideon tipped my chin to examine my neck. "So, a soldier chased you through the city because you rescued a little cat?"

"Well, *no*," I said. Any hint of Gideon's amusement disappeared. "They aren't the only ones who can throw rocks."

"Rachel."

I'd forgotten how much I hated when he glowered at me like that. "Relax, Gideon. If you don't let up"—I pointed to the clenched muscles in his jaw—"you'll crack a tooth."

He grabbed my elbow again, more gently this time. "Let's get you out of here."

We crossed the square and surveyed the streets for Nazi uniforms. The cobblestones were the only gray and the patina on City Hall's copper spire the only green.

"I just gave them a taste of their own medicine," I said. We ducked onto a side street to avoid the crowd.

"If my memory of your handball game is correct, you hit your mark."

"Hit my mark?" I smirked again. "Not sure if he was named Mark, but yeah, I hit him squarely enough." My aim *had* been good.

"Rachel, Denmark is occupied by people who hate us. You need to be more careful."

"You sound like my father." Actually, Papa would probably applaud my rescue effort. "Well, maybe not like *my* father, but someone's."

When we reached a corner at the main thoroughfare, Gideon looked both ways twice, but I crossed without looking. Strict gasoline rationing made for little traffic, except for the armored cars that could be heard from blocks away.

"You never think things through," he said.

"What's that supposed to mean?"

He poked a finger at the tiny scar on my cheek. "The Swan Incident." I could *hear* the capital letters, giving the event more gravitas than it warranted.

I rolled my eyes at him, ready to hit *him* with a rock. "I was seven, Gideon." One of the baby swans in the park had gotten stuck in a metal grate. I freed it and presented it to its mother. She left the scar on my cheek for my trouble. Who knew swans were so vicious? "That was a long time ago."

"Exactly. Times have changed." At a cross street, Gideon held out an arm, blocking me like a tollgate. He checked both ways before emerging back onto another cobblestoned boulevard.

"I won't give them the satisfaction of changing me." I brushed some cat hair from my puffed-up chest.

"They'll have the satisfaction of throwing you in jail or, worse, carting you off to one of their labor camps."

My pace faltered, but only for a second. "Quit trying to scare me, Gideon. That hasn't happened to any of us yet."

"We've been lucky so far."

He was always so gloomy. Sure, Jews in the rest of occupied Europe had been sent away, but this was Denmark. After more than three years of German occupation, the Nazis hadn't dared to make a move against us.

Unlike Jews in the rest of the Reich, my father still owned his bookshop. Gideon's father continued to teach at the university. All us kids went to school every day. We didn't even have to wear the yellow star. Our king, Christian X, had threatened to wear one too, if we were forced, and the Nazis backed down.

"King Christian will protect us," I said. Gideon didn't have a comeback for that.

We dodged a streetcar at the corner, hopping over the metal rails embedded into the cobblestones. As we passed the Dagmar Cinema and its guards, Gideon lowered his head. Before the occupation, my older sister, Annalise, had used every bit of her spending money at the theater, giggling over silly American romances. Now, it featured only Nazi propaganda films. Gestapo headquarters loomed behind it like a tombstone.

The youngest, thinnest guard—a Dane—tipped his cap every time he saw me, his cheeks reddening, his eye contact fleeting. This time was no exception.

"Hello, miss," he said.

Gideon stiffened. Soldiers rarely spoke to us like that. I returned the hello, but not the smile, giving him the steeliest regard I could muster instead. I wasn't usually the kind of girl boys blushed about, especially when I went everywhere with my prettier sister. Still, his attention wasn't welcome.

I hated all these men, but I especially despised this shy Dane. Once we were occupied, Danish Nazis, though few, had stood by while the Germans executed members of the resistance at the old army barracks at Ryvangen. The Germans rewarded their betrayal with jobs and extra rations.

"Oh, look. It's Heinrich's little girlfriend," an older German soldier said in his own tongue, deepening the red in Heinrich's cheeks. "The Danes are as sweet as their *wienerbrød*," he continued, butchering the pronunciation of Denmark's famous pastries. He ran his eyes over me, making me appreciate my thick wool coat. I hugged my sketch pad to my chest like a plate of armor. Gideon's firm hand gripped my elbow, and neither of us talked until we rounded a corner.

"Do they think because they can't speak Danish that we can't understand German?" I kept going on into Gideon's silence. "I don't do anything to encourage Heinrich. I hate the freckled traitor." I hoped Gideon would agree with me on something, but he stayed quiet. "Don't you?" I asked.

"What choice does he have?" He jerked the collar of his coat up around his neck. "Besides, he wouldn't even notice you if you kept your head down."

"I can hardly make myself less adorable, Gideon." I pushed him in the side to show I was kidding. I tugged a small knit cap out of my coat pocket and drew it over my head, tucking my brown hair under it. "Better?"

He scanned my face as though he might say I was still too adorable for my own good, but he pulled the cap over my eyes instead.

"Hey!" I bumped him in the side again and adjusted my hat. "Even if I sashayed down the street like Annalise, it isn't fair they—"

"You can save the philosophy lesson. Normally, I'd agree with you. But now..." He glanced up at the old Iversen factory in front of us. It used to produce shoes, but for the last two years, it had made engine parts for the Reich. The smokestack belched fascist fumes into the blue Danish sky. "We don't live in a fair world anymore." Gideon squeezed both fists, cracking all his knuckles in one terrific pop, like a chicken's neck snapping.

I shuddered and brought my shoulders up to my ears. "Do you have to do that?"

He stretched out his fingers in a show of surrender. I hated the sound but couldn't help smiling at his old habit. He had been cracking his knuckles since we were little and, combined with the sight of the old Circus Building we passed, the sound brought on a tiny ache in my chest. Did he remember all the Saturdays we spent inside as kids? For months, he'd used his new job in an electronics repair shop as an excuse for never spending time with me. That was when he bothered making excuses at all.

"Despite that disgusting compulsion of yours, I've missed you. It's been a long time," I said.

The annoyed wrinkle in his forehead disappeared, and he focused on his shoes. He didn't answer my unspoken question.

"Why isn't Gideon friends with me anymore?" I had asked Mama a year ago.

"It isn't natural for boys and girls to be best friends forever," Mama had explained. Annalise nodded in a worldly way I resented. What did she know? She was only a year older than me.

"That's dumb. Why not?" I asked. Mama cleared her throat.

"He'll want to spend time with girls he...likes." Mama fiddled with one of my colored pencils.

"I am a girl." I ruffled my skirt as if to accentuate the distinction. "He likes me."

"Not that way, dear."

The silence between Gideon and me hung in the air like the smoke from the factory. I hoped Gideon would crack his knuckles again so I could yell at him some more. The edge of a cheerily wrapped package peeked out of his coat's front pocket.

"What's this?" I asked.

"An old toy train. I rewired it myself."

"Who for?" I asked.

He gaped at me as if I were crazy, an all-too-familiar expression on his face. "Your mother invited me to the party."

Party? I blinked at him.

"Erik's birthday?"

My little brother's birthday party. I'd completely forgotten.

"*Pokkers!*"

With five siblings, remembering birthdays proved difficult in my family, and it wasn't like there would be cake to
look forward to. At four years old, Erik didn't remember
a time when birthdays meant cake, before the war and
rationing.

Back at the apartment, chaos reigned. Two of my
younger brothers, Anders and Hans, at seven and eight,
relished their role as the big kids and chased the
four-year-olds. Mrs. Olsen's herd of dogs next door
howled at every new arrival. My baby sister, Birgitte,
wailed as she bounced from one cooing neighbor to the
next, miserable with anyone but my mother. Erik, the
guest of honor, shot through the crowd to reach us. His
words poured out in one great flood.

"Rachel! Gideon! You're late! Did you see what I got?
Mrs. Madsen says it matches my hair." We hardly got a
glance at the gift, the golden-maned stuffed pony Mama
had made from fabric scraps, before he scampered off to
the platter of smoked herring on the dining room table.

Gideon crossed the room and placed his gift on Mama's
piano. Papa scooped it up before my mother saw it on her
most prized possession.

A familiar wave of exhaustion washed over me. My
ability came in handy, but I'd collapse into a heap if I
didn't draw the images I'd pulled soon. How many times
had I fallen into a near coma before I'd figured that out?
I hurried into the kitchen, hoping for a quiet place to
sketch, but Mama was washing dishes with some of the
other mothers.

I tried to slip out unseen to find another place. "Rachel,
you're here. I need your help." I hoped she wouldn't want
me to lay out more herring, with their accusing dead
stares, but she pointed to a glass of water instead. "Could
you bring that to your sister in your room, please?"

Annalise wasn't in the living room captivating the
guests with her charm? There could be only one reason.

"She's elevated?" I whispered to Mama. *Elevated* was
one of our code words for my sister's condition.

"She's been in bed all day," Mama said.

"Is she really sick or just afraid she won't dazzle the whole room?" I asked. Mama pursed her lips, pretending not to know what I meant. Four-year-olds weren't my sister's preferred audience.

"Just bring her the water, please."

Movie posters covered our bedroom walls. All of them featured Cary Grant, Annalise's favorite actor. Before the occupation, she had flirted shamelessly with the Dagmar Cinema's manager, so at the close of every film, he gave her the poster. They had started on her side of the room but overwhelmed mine long ago.

I weaved between my easel and Annalise's smaller upright piano—not as good as Mama's in the living room—to bring her the water in our bed. I didn't know where we would put Birgitte when she was old enough to be moved out of Mama and Papa's room.

"All right, who are we ignoring today?" I asked.

Purple bags hung beneath her eyes while the rest of her skin was green. Her jet hair hung limp. She hadn't curled it this morning.

"Oh, Annalise. I'm sorry." I slid the stack of fashion magazines out of the way to sit beside her and passed her the glass. "Here I am saying you're too vain to come out, and you're really sick."

"Good." She gulped at the water. "I'd rather they think I'm vain than weak."

With our mother busy with my younger siblings, it often fell on me to care for Annalise, so I recognized her symptoms. If she skipped a meal, as she sometimes did to maintain her already-perfect figure, she would shake, sweat, and go pale, but when she was nauseated and thirsty, like she was at that moment, she had eaten too much sugar.

I narrowed my eyes at her. "What did you eat, Annalise?"

"Nothing." She fidgeted with the fringe of the blanket and wouldn't meet my gaze. I wasn't only an expert on her symptoms. I could tell when she was lying too.

"Annalise…"

She slapped her thighs with both hands. "Fine. Willem brought me one of those little chocolate tortes from Muller's bakery."

"You know you can't have that!"

"I don't care. Mr. Muller is a genius! How he makes something so delicious during rationing I'll never know."

"Annalise…"

"I'll hear nothing against Muller's tortes." She waved a hand in front of her queasy face. "Totally worth it." She sipped her water. "And it's not like I could tell Willem I couldn't eat it."

Annalise had insisted on keeping her illness a secret. She had given Papa's best friend, Uncle Stellan, the cold shoulder for a month once for mentioning it.

"Did I hear *Gideon* out there?" she asked and jutted out her chin toward the living room.

I palmed my face. It wasn't just her transparent attempt to change the subject that annoyed me. It was the new subject itself. My sister developed romantic theories regarding everyone, so when Gideon and I drifted apart last year, she determined love had caused the distance. No matter how many times I explained to her we had only ever been friends, I never persuaded her.

"He's here, but—"

"Aha!" The conversation—ridiculous as it was—brought a little bit of normal color back to her cheeks.

"And what does that prove exactly?"

"If you didn't like him, you wouldn't be in here avoiding him." She took another long sip of water, grinning at me over the top of the glass. She blinked at me several times, her big brown eyes round and mocking.

"That makes no sense," I said.

"Love never does, Kitten." She said this as if the lesson had been a hard one for her.

Annalise *played* at love enough—she'd inspired a lovesick proposal at fifteen and collected admirers like beads on a string—but I doubted she had any firsthand insight into the concept.

"You watch too many romantic movies." I moved to return to the party to convince her of my indifference, but this backfired.

"Running back to your boyfriend?"

I was too tired to argue with her. The party made quiet corners scarce, but I needed to find one and draw so the drain on my energy would pass. I left her to drink her water and wiggle her eyebrows.

Out in the living room, Papa was having his own argument with one of the neighbors.

"Listen to reason, Niels," our neighbor, Mr. Madsen said to him. "Get your family out of Denmark. While you can." He gestured wildly—a common characteristic of people who argued with my father. In contrast, Papa's long, lean body barely moved.

"I have a business to run," said Papa. "Margrethe has her piano students, and the children have school. This isn't Russia or Poland." Papa was right, of course. What happened in the rest of Europe could never happen in Copenhagen. Half the people in the room were Christians, the other half Jewish. No one considered that strange, not like those backward places.

"You're right." Mr. Madsen placed a hand on Papa's shoulder. "Denmark is filled with people who would risk death to protect you." Somehow, the idea of dying to defend his infuriating friend calmed him. "But Hitler is crazy, and you don't know what he'll do next."

"I will concede this point," Papa said, his eyes twinkling. "Hitler's insanity is a rich, unpredictable tapestry." Unlike his friend, Papa was enjoying the discussion. His eyes didn't sparkle like that when everyone agreed.

"The rumors..." Mr. Madsen gave Gideon and me—the youngest in earshot—brief consideration. "What they're doing to Jews in the east, Niels..."

Mama appeared with the baby, finally quiet on her hip. She shot a dirty look at Mr. Madsen.

"Enough about the war. This is a party," she said. My mother indicated the roomful of children. Despite her desire to keep it from me, gossip about Germany's hard labor camps and forced deportations abounded at school. People had even died. King Christian would never stand for it here. Papa patted her arm in agreement, and the conversation seemed to be over, but I couldn't leave it at that.

"We can't let them bully us out of our own country, Mr. Madsen," I said.

Mr. Madsen's eyebrows arched high and knitted together as if I'd said something crass rather than an opposing point of view. Would he have disapproved if Gideon had spoken his mind? Mama regarded Papa with no small amount of recrimination. This is *your* fault, the look said.

Papa believed girls should express themselves. "Everyone has the right to be rude about their opinions," he had said, much to my mother's chagrin. My rude opinions pertained to the war, while Annalise's regarded the state of hemlines, but by Papa's definition, the Abramson girls were both decidedly modern.

"It's our home too. Right, Papa?"

My father covered his mouth to hide his pride from my mother, but before she could chastise him, someone crashed through the door. We all jumped. My father's best friend, Uncle Stellan, stood in the threshold, his policeman's uniform drenched at the armpits and down the center of his back.

Had he been chasing criminals? I couldn't make sense of the state of him. Neither could Papa.

"Stellan, you know better than to make so much noise. You'll set off—" The dogs next door began their howling again.

"The Nazis...They..." Uncle Stellan bent, resting his hands on his knees, and gulped air.

"What have they done?" Papa's voice was as tentative as a toe checking a frozen river before attempting to cross.

"They've seized the temple records," Uncle Stellan said, still wheezing. He shut the door behind him, muffling the sound of the neighbor's dogs. "There's to be a roundup in two days."

Mama stepped in front of me as if to block me from the news.

"How like you, Stellan," said Papa, any remaining mischief vanishing from his eyes along with his color, "to settle a perfectly delightful debate so succinctly."

Chapter Two

LESS THAN AN HOUR later, I caught Annalise shoving a set of pin curlers into the suitcase I had packed for her.

"We don't have room," I said. I ripped them out and flung them on the bed.

"You get to bring your sketch pads and pencils." She stuffed them back in. "I get to bring my curlers."

Annalise didn't know how badly I needed my sketch pad and pencils. I had picked the wrong day to use my ability. I'd missed the opportunity to sketch the memories before we had to flee. I could barely keep my eyes open. I couldn't tell her that, though.

"Fine, but the magazines go," I said and heaved out the pile she must have crammed in when my back was turned.

Annalise stared at the magazines as they joined her collection of sheet music. She would have to leave it all behind.

"How long before we can come back, do you think?" Annalise asked. My eyes swept the room. I mourned my paints, my easel, and even the lumpy bed I'd had to share with my sister most of my life. I swallowed, not wanting Annalise to sense the lump rising in my throat. I couldn't believe this was happening. The king was supposed to protect us.

"We'll be back when the war ends, I guess." The lump bobbed back up as soon as I said the words. It could be years.

And that was assuming the Nazis lost.

"Who do you think he's talking to out there?" she asked. I shrugged, unable to swallow the lump this time.

Uncle Stellan spoke on the phone in a hushed voice in the living room, but I couldn't make out what he said.

The rest of the apartment was quiet. All the guests had left. The Christians had gone to spread the news. The Jews had gone to pack. Gideon had slipped out without saying "I told you so."

I latched our suitcases shut and hauled them into the living room while Annalise finished dressing.

Uncle Stellan hung up. He clipped a curt nod at my father—one part relief, one part secret—and they hauled a trunk to the door.

Papa passed the set of shelves without taking a single one of his books.

Mama emerged from her room with Birgitte over one shoulder and a large handbag over the other. A pair of wool socks hung out the opening. She tucked them in and zipped it. She stopped and eyed the kitchen from the threshold.

"We have to leave the dirty dishes, Margrethe," Papa said from the doorway.

"There's an entire sink full, Niels."

"Someone will clean it up. We have to go. Now."

I knocked on our bedroom door to hurry Annalise. She emerged and threaded her arm through mine.

Mama herded my brothers out, pausing only to slide her hand over her mother's piano.

I prayed Birgitte wouldn't wail when the eight of us squeezed into the back of Uncle Stellan's police van. Mama cooed in her ear and had to cover the baby's mouth when she let out a delighted giggle instead.

We slipped out of Copenhagen like criminals on the run. Uncle Stellan drove us to his summer cottage in Rungsted, an hour up the coast. Despite Papa's elbows and Hans's kicking feet, I fell asleep before we left our block, only waking up when we arrived.

The red paint of Uncle Stellan's fishing cottage had faded nearly to pink from the years of salty air, and the thatched roof reminded me of my brother Anders's hair first thing in the morning. The two-room cottage couldn't hold our large family, so Uncle Stellan enlisted Glen Lund, his next-door neighbor and an old school chum of Annalise's, to host Papa and the boys.

I fell back to sleep on the couch as soon as we got inside, despite the bustle of our hectic arrival. When I woke up, a blanket covered me, and everything was dark and quiet. The exhaustion from using my ability had dissipated, but my stomach churned. What would happen to us? No one was awake to ask.

A framed picture of Uncle Stellan's family hung beside me. His girls were the same age as Anders and Hans. Their smiling faces, blonde hair glinting in the sun, made me ball my hands into fists. Christian families like theirs would spend the rest of the war in their own homes, comfortable and safe, while we had to hide like hunted animals. Where was King Christian? How could Papa have been so wrong? I stopped my hand before I swiped the picture off the wall.

I needed some air.

Out on the front steps, I inhaled the crisp night, hoping it would soothe me. Shadows materialized a few feet away, their muffled whispers not understandable but recognizable enough. I crouched to eavesdrop behind a shrub close to where the shadows stood.

"Anything else?" That was Papa. I recognized his voice, but not the anxiety in it. "What did the resistance say?"

The Danish resistance fought the Nazis from within. They smuggled downed British pilots out of Denmark. They distributed an illegal newspaper covering stories such as the German defeat at Stalingrad, which the Nazis had censored out of their papers.

"The Gestapo broke up our meeting." That was Uncle Stellan. "They've been all over us since we blew up the Central Building." The Central Building had produced war materials for the Nazis before the resistance blew it up. But Uncle Stellan said *our* and *us*. Was he part of the Danish resistance? His job as a police officer would afford him access to supplies and information.

We all quietly cheered the resistance's illegal activities, but we also mourned when several of them were caught and executed behind the German barracks. That could have been Uncle Stellan. His family was in just as much danger as us.

"What's the plan?" That was Papa again.

"Maybe two nights." Surprisingly, that was Glen, the man who owned the cottage next door. His fishy-smelling clothes and his crippling shyness hardly gave him a heroic air, but apparently, he was part of the resistance too.

"How many Jews?" Papa asked.

"Almost eight thousand," Glen said.

"Eight thousand? How will you get to them all in time?" Papa asked.

It sounded like a rhetorical question, but someone answered him.

"We will, Mr. Abramson. Don't worry." My hand clamped over my mouth to stifle my sharp intake of breath. I knew the voice of this other member of the resistance, the group that printed an illegal newspaper and blew up factories. That had some kind of plan for saving the Danish Jews. Whose members were occasionally shot in the park.

It was Gideon.

Their voices hushed, and I couldn't hear more. Uncle Stellan said, "Mother Country," the resistance farewell, and all but Gideon returned to Glen's cottage. His shadow faced away from the house and me, a bicycle propped against his hip.

"You can come out of there now, Rachel," Gideon said.

I startled at the sound of my name in the dark.

"The moon is so bright, you can see Sweden from here," he said.

I stepped out from behind the bushes. "You're in the resistance."

Gideon didn't turn around. He stared at the dark bump across the strait.

"That's why you've been so distant lately."

I had *told* Annalise it hadn't been anything romantic. She would be disappointed. He turned, and the moon lit half his face silver.

"I didn't want you involved. You'd only get into more trouble." He tugged on his earlobe, turning back toward the water. "You're awfully quiet," he said. "I expected some of that Abramson righteous indignation."

"I'm too proud of you to be angry," I said. His shoulders relaxed. "But you're right. It isn't very fair. You get to go off and fight for the resistance." I slammed my shoulder into his. "Girls never get to do anything brave."

"Yeah, like lucky Friedrich Lang." Friedrich, the grocer's son, returned from fighting Nazis in Poland, his empty sleeve pinned to his shoulder.

I winced. "That's true." I wrapped my arms around myself. "I hate not knowing what's going on. What's happening?"

"We're leaving."

"Where to?"

Gideon jerked his chin across the water.

"Hundreds of Danes all along the coast, mostly fishermen like Glen, are ferrying Jews across the strait."

I had taken the boat trip before. It took less than an hour. I wasn't comforted by the thought, though.

"But the Germans patrol the coast," I said. I shot a hand in the direction of the water through the trees. I lowered my voice. "They could be down there right now.

"Fishermen have built secret compartments in their boats to hide people for the crossing."

"But the dogs..." My heart rate picked up at the thought of the German's beloved shepherds snarling at our hiding places.

"The resistance has been trying to come up with a solution to that problem for years." His voice dropped to a conspiratorial whisper, and I leaned in closer to him. "Every captain has a cloth with dried rabbit blood on it."

"That will attract the dog's attention! Why would you want to do that?" I hated how much my voice sounded like a childish whine.

"Because of what else is on the cloth."

"What?"

"Cocaine." He had a smug expression. "It kills the dog's sense of smell temporarily."

I let out a sigh. "Brilliant," I said.

"The Coast Guard and police are helping. They have hundreds of Christian volunteers. Even some Jewish ones." He stood a little straighter, which made me stand straighter too.

"Like you?"

"I'm escorting families from their hiding places to the boats. Not everyone has a friend with a summer cottage on the water, you know."

My blood ran cold at a sudden thought. "What about Birgitte?" My baby sister could have given us away today. How could we hide her?

"A doctor will give her something to make her sleep," said Gideon. I gnawed my lip. "I know your mother won't like it, but it'll be perfectly safe, Rachel."

The resistance planned every last detail to save us. I wish I could have helped. What good was my ability if I still needed rescuing?

Chapter Three

I HELD UP THE sketch and compared it to the view out our window. There was something off about my version of the copse of trees near the water. I crumpled it up and tossed it in the trash.

Glen said it would be only two days, so I resented the third I spent sketching landscapes.

Mama sighed and took the drawing out of the bin. She smoothed the paper without taking her eyes off me. She opened her mouth to say something, but Glen and Gideon's arrival distracted her.

Gideon didn't bother with hellos. "You leave tonight."

"Finally." I flounced onto the sofa.

Mama ran into the bedroom to pack, leaving my crumpled landscape on the table. Gideon picked it up.

"It's kind of lopsided," he said. I snatched it out of his hands and balled it up again.

"Are we really leaving?" Annalise said, coming out of the bedroom. She had a fresh dusting of powder on her face. She must have applied it when she heard the boys come in.

"You leave tonight," Gideon said again.

"What about you?" I asked him.

"My parents leave tomorrow, but I'll be here a few more days to help with the evacuation. I'll meet them in Stockholm later."

"It's brave of you to stay behind," I said.

"It's what I have to do. It'll only be a few days."

"Will you stay with your brother when you get there?" I asked.

"Alec?" Gideon asked.

Of course I meant Alec, the one who already lived in Sweden. Not Ezra, who had been dead and gone for nine years. Gideon still seemed to forget sometimes.

That was probably my fault.

"It'll be nice to have a friend in Stockholm," I said. We were headed there too, to a cousin of my mother's. "Please be careful." Annalise stood chatting with Glen, but her eyes darted to where I had laid a hand on Gideon's arm. She arched her eyebrow at the sight of Gideon and me sitting on the couch that had been my bed last night, a tangle of sheets mussed all around us. How could she think about that at a time like this? I pulled away. I rubbed my ears, hoping they hadn't gone red.

Gideon shifted his weight on the sofa, getting ready to leave. I resisted the urge to grab his arm again.

"I'll be back to take you all down to the boat at midnight." His eyes scanned the room, and he leaned toward me as if about to impart a secret. My eyes went to Annalise. What would she make of that tender look in his eyes?

She hadn't noticed. Although still chattering on at Glen, she filled a glass with water at the kitchen sink. She took a big sip.

Her sugar levels must have spiked again. For a second, I wondered if she'd stowed away any of Muller's tortes in her suitcase with her curlers, but her pleading eyes met mine, and my mind shifted to excuses I could make to get her out of sight before everyone noticed how sick she suddenly looked.

"Rachel?" Gideon asked.

"I'm sorry," I said. Annalise's skin had gone green. "What did you say?"

"I asked if I could talk to you for a minute."

"We're already talking," I said to Gideon without looking away from my sister. She was getting greener by the second. I had to get her out of here.

"For once, could you *try* to make it easier for me?" Gideon rubbed the nape of his neck.

"Easier?" I could ask her to help me pack, but my suitcase sat ready at the door. Annalise's fingers drifted to her temple, and she stumbled. Glen grabbed her arm, hoping to steady her.

Gideon continued to speak, too focused on his hands in his lap to notice how little I was paying attention. "Once we get to Stockholm, I hope you'll consider—"

I shot to my feet as Annalise collapsed.

"If the doctor says she can't be moved right now, we'll just have to wait until she's better," Mama whispered so she wouldn't wake Annalise in the next room. We sat in near dark. Mama worried a patrol would see the lights from the coast. Papa sat beside her on the sofa. Her eyes darted between Uncle Stellan and Papa when they remained silent. The look they shared turned my stomach.

"What?" I asked.

"If we don't go now, there won't be enough spots on a boat for us to go over together," Papa said. "And it's too risky to wait until after tonight. It won't be as safe here once the Nazis figure out what's happening."

"There's room for two in another boat in just two days," said Gideon.

"She'll be well enough to travel by then, but you and the other children have to go tonight," Papa said to Mama.

"I should be the one to stay to care for her." Mama wrung her hands. "I'm her mother."

Papa wound his arm around her and rocked her gently.

"Margrethe." Uncle Stellan sat beside her, his hands disentangling hers. "Think of your other children, Birgitte, Erik, Hans, Anders, and Rachel."

My mother flinched at each of our names, but I bristled for a different reason. "I'm not a child, Uncle Stellan." Gideon was the same age as me, and he was in the resistance. I turned to Mama. "I can help Papa with the others, and you can stay with Annalise." Everyone looked hopeful until Uncle Stellan spoke again.

"What about Birgitte?" he asked.

My baby sister was still nursing and would be inconsolable without Mama. Even if they did drug her for the trip across the strait, those few days while Mama waited for a boat would be unbearable.

"All right!" my mother yelled. She tore her hands out of Uncle Stellan's and buried her face in them.

"Annalise will need constant monitoring," Mama said, lifting her head. "We'll have to hire a nurse."

Papa worked so much at the bookstore, he rarely tended to his daughter's symptoms. He wouldn't know what to do. Mama and I could, but Mama couldn't stay. Uncle Stellan shared another one of those unsettling looks with my father.

"All the medical support is tied up for the rescue effort," Uncle Stellan said.

This was my chance. Uncle Stellan risked his life in the resistance. Glen put himself in danger for people he hardly knew. Gideon delayed his own safety to save others.

Girls never get to do anything brave.

The moment my mouth opened, Gideon mouthed a thousand little *noes*. It was kind of sweet that he thought he could stop me.

"I'll stay," I said. "You should both go. The others need you."

Mama mumbled about Nazis patrolling the coast again.

Gideon's lips were pursed shut, a hand raked through his hair.

I erased memories from my parents all the time, to make them forget a set curfew or an unwanted chore, but they were too smart for me to pull from both of them at the same time. I would have to choose.

Mama represented the real obstacle to my plan. Papa would follow her lead as he always did when it came to us kids. Plus, I wasn't a mind reader, and she had given me something to work with.

I did her a favor, pulling the Nazi patrol from her memory. I was sparing her, really. I visualized the gray-uniformed men and their German shepherds inspecting Uncle Stellan's bit of coastline and pulled with my mind. The image came, but it took some effort, not like that soldier back in Copenhagen. The results were the same, though. Her eyes clouded over, her mouth hung open, and she struck her forehead as if she had missed the obvious.

"Of course! Rachel is the perfect person to stay," she said.

Gideon crossed his arms over his chest.

I never had the chance to hold little Birgitte for this long. She was knocked out. The doctor who had administered the drugs was probably already on to another cottage.

Papa laced up Anders's and Hans's boots. Mama bundled up a very sleepy Erik. Anders and Hans had peppered our parents with questions about Sweden all night, fraying our nerves.

"Do they have streetcars, Papa?"

"Will we have to go to school, Mama?"

I kissed Birgitte's downy little head and handed her to Mama. She adjusted the blanket to cover more of her angelic face. Erik slept on the sofa, his stuffed pony clutched in his arms.

"Now, be sure to watch Annalise carefully. If she's extremely thirsty or hungry, she needs more insulin. If she gets dizzy and starts sweating, she needs something with sugar. There's plenty of juice in the icebox."

I knew all this already, but I would long for the sound of her voice in ten minutes, so I let her prattle on about how to sterilize Annalise's needles. She hugged me with one arm, squeezing the baby between us.

When Gideon arrived, he ducked into a corner, avoiding eye contact with Mama, who wiped her tears with Papa's handkerchief.

"I don't know why I agreed to this," she said. Gideon snorted, but Papa didn't hear and hugged me tightly.

"My little warrior," Papa said, and the bravery slipped out of me in a single cold rush.

Gideon stepped out of the corner, not to comfort me but to shield my parents from my contorted face.

I kissed Erik on the top of his head as I had with Birgitte. Unlike the baby, he woke up.

"Don't be sad, Rachel." He shot off the sofa and thrust his pony into my chest. "You take Jubilee." I hadn't realized he had named his stuffed pony after King Christian's horse. "He'll keep you and Annalise company."

"I can't take your Jubilee from you, Erik." I pushed the stuffed pony back into his arms, but he wouldn't have it.

"You must! How else will you remember the color of my hair?"

"I could never forget one hair on your head, sweetheart." I wiped my eyes and squeezed him. "Even in two whole days." But I took the pony anyway.

Maybe part of me knew.

Chapter Four

ONCE MY FAMILY LEFT, I distracted myself by sketching the image I made Mama forget. With just a pencil, I captured the exact steel gray of the Nazis' uniforms.

I finished and wandered into the bedroom, hoping for a long, diverting chat about the merits of Cary Grant with Annalise. She still slept, so I returned to the living room to pace.

At that very moment, the rest of my family was getting stuffed into a secret compartment in Glen's boat. It would be so dark. My brother Hans, who couldn't sleep without a light on, would be so afraid. And what if the dogs came? What if the special cloth with the rabbit's blood and cocaine didn't do its job? What if someone betrayed them?

I cradled Jubilee in my lap and fought the urge to run to the dock. My ability might have been able to help them if something went wrong. I couldn't sit here for one minute longer. No one would know if I snuck down and watched the boat leave. I checked Annalise again before I grabbed a sweater and slipped into the night.

The distance between the cottage and the shore stretched farther than I expected, with no path through the high grass and occasional shrub. A twig snapped a few feet off in the trees, then silence. The twig-snapper froze and so did I, each aware of the other's presence. I could only hear my own hitched breathing.

"Gideon?"

"Rachel?"

"Thank God."

"What are you doing out here?" He stepped out of the trees into the moonlight.

"I have to see them go."

"Why? So you can get caught?"

"You can't stop me." I quickened my pace past him toward the water, but he grabbed my wrist and lifted me at the midsection with his shoulder until I hung upside down. "*Pokkers*, Gideon," I said.

"Quiet."

"I insist you put me down." I slapped his back with an open palm.

"Put you down? Fine," he said, but didn't let me go. "That sweater makes you look seasick. You look terrible in green."

I slapped his back again. "That was not what I meant by *put me down*, and you know it, Gideon." I struggled to keep my voice to a whisper.

"If you and I get caught, who'll take care of Annalise?"

"You don't have to come."

"Yeah, right. And I'll have to face your mother and tell her I lost you. I'd rather face the Nazis."

"I just want to see—"

"They're already gone, Rachel."

Was it true? Gideon would lie to protect me, just like he had lied all those months to hide his involvement with the Danish resistance. I could use my ability on him—it wouldn't be the first time—but I didn't want to waste the energy. What if I needed it to defend Annalise? I couldn't risk it. I slumped like a rag doll and hung upside down over his shoulder, the fight gone out of me.

"You watched them get off safely?"

"I did, but I wanted to get back to you..." He slid me down along the front of him, our faces inches apart, and my cold hands draped around his warm neck. He took three quick steps back so they slipped from his shoulders and craned his neck away from me. "You and Annalise. I wanted to get back to both of you."

I stood on tiptoe and squinted toward the water. The trees blocked my view of the coast.

"They're going to be fine, Rachel." He covered his heart with his palm as if swearing an oath.

"How can you be sure?" I wiped my nose with the back of my hand.

"You should see the coordination that went into this," he said. He pulled me by my sleeve back in the direction of the house. "Everyone is helping. The Coast Guard, the police. Even the Swedish government."

"What is Sweden doing?"

"As soon as Glen crosses into Swedish waters, their navy will take your family aboard. There's a whole line of ships out there waiting. The Germans want Sweden to stay neutral, so the Nazis won't go after them once they're over the border." Gideon scanned the property. "Actually, the most dangerous part is what we're doing right now. Wandering around out in the dark," he said.

As if to prove his point, I tripped, grabbing his arm. I curled into him for heat as much as support. He shook me off, stingy with his warmth.

"You made me hurt myself, by the way," he said, rubbing his lower back.

"Don't try to cheer me up." I nudged him in the ribs.

He elbowed back, his lips still pursed tight.

"Glen let me in on the new plan," he said. "I can tell you about it if you can be reasonable and come inside."

I gave the shore one more look.

"You want to hear it or not?"

I turned back to the dim light of the cottage. "I'm all ears."

"No, you're all mouth."

"I guess you're feeling better," I said to Annalise the next morning. She lounged on the sofa. Even with curlers in her hair, she was as beautiful as the film stars she obsessed over. Hard to believe that, just the day before, her illness had delayed our escape. At the very least, she could have had the decency to look terrible. I swatted at her feet to make room beside her.

"I'm feeling fine." She plucked the curlers out, her hair bouncing into tight black springs. I folded my arms across my chest. "But," she said, cutting me off before I could complain, "I know it's important for me to rest up for tomorrow night, even though I might go crazy spending another two whole days cooped up inside." She adjusted a blanket over herself like a good patient. "When will Glen be here?"

Annalise had grown bored with my company. She liked a larger, more male audience. At least I had my sketchbooks and pencils to keep me busy. Without her piano, flirting with Glen was Annalise's only source of amusement. I took out one of the curlers she'd missed in the back, and she winced as a strand or two snagged.

"You don't even like him," I said.

"I happen to like Glen just fine." She patted the released curls on the side of her head, careful not to smudge her freshly polished nails. "Well, it's true he's no Cary Grant."

"No, he just risked his life to save our family. That's all." I shoved the curlers into their pouch and yanked the zipper closed.

Her eyebrow rose again. She took the curlers from me, probably afraid I would hurl them into the fireplace.

When they were safely away, she turned to face me and took both my hands. "I know you could be with Mama and Papa right now, safe and sound in Sweden, if it weren't for me. I don't blame you for being mad. If things were reversed, I'd be spitting nails right now." She set a hand on my arm, endangering her manicure. "You're a peach for staying with me, because as brave as I want to be, I'd be petrified waiting here without you."

She leaned over and kissed my cheek, and the tension in my shoulders softened. Annalise had that effect on people.

"Gideon says I shouldn't do things without thinking," I said. "But I didn't have to think. I had to stay with you." I squeezed her hands. "I'm glad you're feeling better."

She took a deep breath and grinned at the ceiling.

"You would have made Fafa proud, at least," she said and blew a kiss heavenward. Our grandmother believed all the world's ills came from overthinking a situation. She had been my hero.

And the only one to know my secret.

"I miss her," she said.

"Me too."

"I can barely picture what she looked like anymore," Annalise said. I fidgeted with the edge of her blanket and didn't meet her eyes. "I can still hear her play, though."

I couldn't pull that memory from Mama either.

I was seven when I pulled my first image—the face of Gideon's brother Ezra. I didn't even know what I'd done. I had only wanted to get that grief-stricken expression off my best friend's face. By the time my grandmother died, I'd gotten better at it, and Fafa's deathbed confession only made me bolder. Still, the images of Fafa at the piano—the one Mama still prized in our living room—were too numerous to erase.

"Do you think they'll have American movies in Sweden?" Annalise asked.

"I doubt they'll have *The Philadelphia Story*, if that's what you're getting at."

Annalise had been dying to see the Cary Grant romance since it was released in America three years ago. Her shoulders slumped.

"Maybe *The Great Dictator* will be playing," I said. Charlie Chaplin's satire about Hitler was a more important film than some screwball comedy of Annalise's. She wrinkled her button nose.

"They have to have *Casablanca*, at least," she said. "That's Ingrid Bergman's latest picture." I squinted at her, confused, and she continued, "Ingrid Bergman is from Sweden, Rachel. How do you not know that?"

"I don't know, Annalise. More important things have been occupying my mind."

"Ha ha, Rachel. I get it. *Occupying*. You're very funny."

Glen and Gideon visited later that day. Annalise appeared from the bedroom in a blue satin dressing gown looking like Hedy Lamarr, and rendered poor Glen speechless.

His pronounced Adam's apple bobbed in his throat. "Ha-ha-happy New Year," he said.

I'd almost forgotten Rosh Hashanah, the Jewish New Year. My family didn't go to temple, and there weren't enough rations to bake the traditional *challah*, but we would have lit candles and had a special meal. I wondered how they would celebrate in Sweden. Glen had assured us they made it across the strait in safety.

"Next year will be different," I said.

"It will be." Glen sat without moving his eyes from my sister. "The Hechts arrive tonight—" He broke off when Annalise sunk into the sofa beside him, curling her feet under her, grazing his thigh. He stared at her like a stunned animal.

I looked to Gideon to finish Glen's thought as he recovered from the brush of contact. "Who are the Hechts?"

"Lars Hecht is a member of the resistance," Gideon said. "He refused to leave even though he's Jewish, but we're getting his mother, wife, and child out of Denmark. They'll be traveling with you to Sweden. They've been hiding with my folks, but they'll arrive at Glen's tonight."

"How are your parents?" I asked. They were hiding in a church attic in the center of Rungsted.

"Packed like sardines. At least they will go tonight."

"They're lucky," Annalise said. "We have another whole day to wait." Gideon didn't look so sure.

"They'll be all right," I said. I knew how it felt to say goodbye to family, even if it would only be a couple of days. "If you need company, you could come back here." I rubbed his arm to comfort him.

His muscles tensed, and he stepped away. "I'll be fine." He shoved his hands in his pockets. Typical of Gideon to pretend he was okay when he wasn't.

"What's going on in Copenhagen, Glen?" I asked.

He pulled himself together, and his face lit up. "Oh, it's amazing, Rachel. The university and hundreds of businesses shut down so people can help out."

"That's incredible." Annalise rested a hand on Glen's shoulder. He blinked at her several times and dropped his eyes to his feet.

"It's like Papa said. King Christian isn't the only one who'll fight for us," I said. It wasn't just our king and our friends like Uncle Stellan. Practically the whole country had united to save us.

"That's not all," Gideon said, similarly pleased, but less willing to show it. "Word got out the Germans planned to ransack the synagogue like they did in Berlin, and a bunch of people—men, women, and children—moved everything out. Churches are hiding most of the stuff."

"For when you come back," added Glen, not lifting his gaze from the floor.

This elicited a happy sob from Annalise.

"My church is hiding prayer books. The...Haga..." Glen stumbled over the unfamiliar Hebrew. His face reddened. "How do you say it?"

"No idea. We don't go to temple much," Annalise said as she shrugged. She faced Gideon and me.

"The Haggadah is the prayer book for Passover," I said. She shrugged again. "You know where Ingrid Bergman was born, but you don't know what the Haggadah is?" Everyone laughed, even Annalise.

"So everyone got out of Copenhagen," Annalise said, her arms stretched out across the sofa's back. Glen's and Gideon's good cheer evaporated with one shared look.

"What, Gideon?" I asked.

"The roundup began in the city last night," he said. "Some Jews hadn't left, the ones who were too old or too—" He stopped short, hovering at the edge of forbidden territory.

"Too sick?" Annalise asked, her face ashen. She clutched the skirt of her dressing gown, her knuckles going white. "What are the Germans doing to them?"

"They're keeping them at Horserød," said Gideon. Horserød had been a summer camp before the war. After the Nazi occupation, it became a barracks, then a Jewish prison. "For now."

"For now?" I asked. I don't know when I had grabbed Jubilee. I hugged him to my chest as if the toy were Erik himself.

"They'll deport them to Terezin," Gideon said. Everyone had heard about Terezin, even blissfully unaware Annalise. Nazi propaganda called the Czechoslovakian ghetto Hitler's gift to the Jews. Photos of the idyllic country village circulated in Nazi newspapers. They claimed its thick walls kept the war out, not the Jews in. Prominent Jews from all over Europe packed their bags and chose to live there. If you believed the Germans, the place became a center of learning and culture.

We all knew a Nazi lie when we heard it. I shivered to think of our fellow countrymen carted off to who knew what kind of conditions. Glen pried Annalise's fingers out of the fabric of her dressing gown and into his own hands.

"They only caught a couple hundred people," Glen said. "Thousands of Jews escaped Denmark last night. And there are plenty of Christian Danes like me who won't stop until every one of them is in Sweden. I promise."

It was easily the most words I had ever heard the man utter.

"If—just for once—Gideon told me what he was up to, I'd know what to do." I paced the living room of Uncle Stellan's cabin, trying to ease the cramping panic rising in my chest. "But oh, no. God forbid he trusts me with any information."

We had spent the entire next day waiting for our departure time to come. When it finally did, Gideon didn't show.

Annalise grabbed my arm during one of my passes near the sofa where she sat and yanked me to a halt. "He's smart, Kitten. He'll be all right."

Sure, Gideon was smart, but he would never miss our meeting time. The thought of what could keep him got me pacing again.

"Maybe he saw a patrol and is waiting for them to pass," said Annalise.

"Well, we can't stay here forever. Glen is waiting for us on that dock." I ducked into the bedroom and snatched the dark-green blanket from the unmade bed. I wrapped myself in it, leaving only my eyes exposed. Gideon would marvel at my ingenuity, but then I remembered he had said I looked seasick in green.

It couldn't be helped. I turned off all the lights except for the single one over the kitchen sink.

"I'm supposed to sit in the dark while you go out there?" she asked.

"No matter what you hear, do not go outside." When Annalise opened her mouth to argue, I knitted my eyebrows together and pointed a finger at her. "I mean it, Annalise. I'll be fine." I had my ability, and she was still so weak. "I'll be right back."

I adjusted the blanket over my head and made my way along the hedge that separated Uncle Stellan's property from Glen's and led all the way down to the water. The trees lining the coast obscured the dock from view. It would provide plenty of cover for me to see what could be keeping Gideon.

As I approached, though, a stranger materialized from the trees.

He wasn't in uniform—just overalls and a flat cap—but I froze as if the Führer himself had stepped out of the trees. I tightened the blanket around my face, hoping he would mistake me for a bush. He wasn't fooled. He raised a finger to his lips as if I were shouting, not struck dumb. He pointed to the hedge. I lifted a branch and drew the blanket over my mouth and nose as I peeked through the space in the bushes.

I startled at the sight of a patrol making its way along the rocky shoreline. The branch I held jerked loose and flicked me in the face. I lifted it again, this time with more care despite my shaking hands.

A boat—no bigger than Glen's—sat moored at a dock three cottages down. No one appeared to be on it, but I couldn't be sure no one hid inside. A German shepherd howled. Four uniformed men boarded the boat and shined flashlights into all its dark corners. I waited for screams. For shots. None came, but my heart didn't slow until the patrol slipped out of sight around a bend. When I looked back to the trees, the man in the overalls was gone. I didn't go back inside until the barking faded into the distance.

The coast was literally clear.

When I headed to the dock again, now with Annalise in tow, I hoped Gideon would come out of the brush like he had the night my family left for Sweden. He would lead us down to the shore this time, not throw me over his shoulder like a caveman.

Annalise struggled through the tall grass with her large suitcase and her impractical open-toed shoes. I navigated better with my smaller bag and thick boots, wondering if the man in overalls would appear again.

From the edge of the trees, we could see Uncle Stellan's dock. Where Glen's boat was supposed to be, three shadows waited instead.

I slammed a hand into Annalise's chest to drive her back into the cover of the trees. On closer inspection, the shadows bore no resemblance to any Nazi soldiers I had ever seen.

The dark obscured their faces, but one was a heavyset woman. She clung to a matching child. The third person's shadow bent like the top of an S. They must have been the Hechts, the family we were escaping with. Maybe Gideon had brought them.

As if on cue, a twig snapped behind us, and I relaxed.

"It's about time you showed up. I was worried half to death—" I said, rounding on Gideon.

Only, it wasn't him. Their German shepherd was quieter than the one with the first patrol. I stumbled backward like someone had taken a stick to my knees. There were three too many soldiers for my ability to be of any use.

"Are you looking for me, miss?" One of the men tipped his cap in a gesture every bit as friendly as the freckled Dane on the streets of Copenhagen a few days before. "Because we've been looking for you."

Chapter Five

UNCLE STELLAN CAME TO visiting hours at Horserød every day with the same promises that we'd be all right. He reported back to our family, in Sweden, as often as he could. During our visits with him, we'd gather at the rough wooden tables in what used to be the picnic area, back when the prison had been a Copenhagen summer camp. For the last two weeks, hundreds of Danish Christians crowded past the gun turrets and barbed wire to check on their Jewish friends and neighbors.

"Rivka seems back to her old self, I see," Uncle Stellan said and pointed to the old woman we'd been arrested with on Glen's dock. We shared a bunk with Rivka as well as her daughter-in-law, Leah, and her eight-year-old grandson, Eli.

The old woman had pneumonia when she was brought into custody, but Uncle Stellan had gotten her some sulfonamide pills—we didn't ask how. From his work with the police department? Or in the resistance? I hoped it hadn't been dangerous for him to get. I couldn't bear it if he got into trouble helping us.

Across the yard, the volunteer doctor attempted to listen to Rivka's lungs with a stethoscope. She stuck an index finger into his chest and spoke to him with a rapid onslaught of words. I couldn't hear them, but Leah held her reddened face in her hands, and Eli giggled, no doubt at the colorful language his *bubbe* was using.

"She's a tough *alter cocker*," I said. The only highlight of the last couple of weeks was my nighttime Yiddish lessons with the tough *old fart*.

Rivka raised her voice, and I could make out the word *fakakta*. Leah's embarrassment transformed to horror, and she covered Eli's ears. I'd have to ask Rivka later what it meant.

"Did you hear the Larsens were released?" Uncle Stellan asked a little too loudly, probably to drown out the stream of Rivka's curses. "They have enough Christians on their family tree," he said.

It should have come as a welcome dose of good news, but it only made me see red. The Larsens kept kosher and attended temple every week, but because they could produce a Christian grandparent or two, they got to go home. We hadn't been to temple since Erik was born, and Annalise didn't even know what the Haggadah was, and we were the ones getting deported to a Czechoslovakian ghetto.

"Oh, that's wonderful, Stellan!" Annalise said. She had gone on a handful of dates with the eldest of the Larsen boys. "Isn't that wonderful, Rachel?" Annalise had been trying to coax a smile from me for days.

"You went to school with the youngest girl, didn't you?" Uncle Stellan asked me. I tried to ignore the past tense. I went to school. I didn't get to go to school anymore.

"Rebecca, yes. They live in Gideon's building," I said. The mere mention of Gideon tamped down Annalise's and Uncle Stellan's enthusiasm.

"Any word?" I asked. The dense black bread they served for breakfast in the camp spun in my stomach. If Uncle Stellan had good news about Gideon, he would have revealed it first thing, way before news of the Larsens. If the news was bad, though, he might have delayed the telling of it. If they had taken him out to that place behind the Ryvangen Barracks...

My stomach settled when Uncle Stellan shook his head. "No word yet, but we'll find him," he said. Gideon had been taken into custody, but Uncle Stellan hadn't been able to learn what they had done with him. He wasn't here with us at Horserød. "Most likely, he's been sent to Terezin with the others." Uncle Stellan was probably right. A transport had gone out the morning we arrived, and almost everyone who had been rounded up had been on it, but that spot behind the barracks haunted my thoughts.

"How about Glen?" Annalise asked.

The answer was the same as when she'd asked yesterday. "There's no word on a release yet." The Germans had arrested him with other Christians they'd caught during the rescue effort.

Uncle Stellan stared at his hands folded on the table. I assumed he was mourning our lost friends, but he had another worry.

"Your transport is tomorrow morning. This is my last visit," he said.

Transport was all anyone in Horserød talked about. Our bunkhouse buzzed with lurking, unknown dread. The moment had finally come. Some tension in my shoulders loosened. There's a twisted sort of relief when your worst fears come true.

"Terezin isn't like other ghettos," Uncle Stellan said. His eyes bored into us as though his intensity alone might reassure us. "The Nazis want to ease everyone's fears about their Jewish policies. Terezin is supposed to be proof the rumors are wrong."

"But the rumors are probably true, aren't they?" I asked.

"They've promised King Christian that won't happen to you," Uncle Stellan said. He didn't explain what *that* was—hard labor, disease, starvation. Take your pick.

"That's a relief," I said flatly. "The Nazis have done nothing but keep their promises so far." Annalise pinched my leg under the table. I stifled a yelp.

Uncle Stellan meant well, but our king had promised to protect us before. I had believed him. Yet we were in a prison camp on our way to a ghetto deeper into the Reich. How could he protect us a thousand miles away in Czechoslovakia if he couldn't do so in Copenhagen?

"You'll be given prominent status with war veterans and those who can afford to pay."

"Pay?" I asked. "People are *paying* to go to Terezin?"

Uncle Stellan nodded. "German Jews are giving every cent they have for the chance to go there."

"And it would be totally out of character for Hitler to go back on his word."

Uncle Stellan ignored my dig at the Führer.

"The king is insisting we get regular letters from every Dane in Terezin. You'll have to write me or one of the neighbors since your parents are outside the Reich in Sweden." I was happy my family had made it to Stockholm, but the gulf between us would grow even wider than ever. How long would it be before I saw any of them again? "You'll also receive a Red Cross parcel every month," Uncle Stellan said.

"Great," I said. Annalise elbowed me. Promises of a box of powdered milk and canned meat hardly made up for my exile into the unknown.

Uncle Stellan dropped a burlap sack onto the table, heavy with warm clothes, food, a fat envelope of Reichsmarks, and medicine for Annalise.

"You have to make everything last," Uncle Stellan said. "Terezin will be better than the other camps, but it won't be as good as it is here."

Good? Horserød was surrounded by barbed wire and armed guards who hated us. We ate nothing but bad bread and flavorless soup. I had been ripped away from my family and abandoned to the mercy of the Third Reich.

There was nothing good about it.

Early the next morning, we were led down the street to the train station. We chatted as if waiting to go to the theater or on an outing to the beach. Any illusion was shattered when the train arrived, though. Rivka wobbled in her tracks. Leah sniffled and tugged Eli in close. Annalise clutched at the fabric of her blouse over her heart.

When I imagined our deportation to Terezin, I hadn't pictured the *Orient Express*, but I hadn't expected we would be loaded into cattle cars like animals either.

Each car was thirty feet long. Barbed wire crisscrossed the small windows in their upper corners. Chalk numbers and letters covered the wooden slats. A crudely drawn yellow Star of David announced who the train was for, but the rest of the figures held no meaning for me. Did the code hold clues to our fate?

Dozens of soldiers, accompanied by their snapping German shepherds, swung the doors wide like hungry mouths waiting to swallow us whole.

A soldier called out, "There is nothing to fear. You will be given the opportunity to work for the Fatherland."

Not my Fatherland.

"In return," he continued, "we will protect you from the war." His voice was eerily calm, like how you would speak to a dog you were about to put down.

"What a load of *bubkes*," Rivka said.

I linked my arm with hers, and we stepped onto the uneven wooden ramp that led into the train's dark interior. I struggled to support her, balancing her suitcase and my own.

"Where are we going?" she asked.

"They're taking us to Terezin, remember?" I asked as if breaking the news to her for the first time. I leaned in close and raised my voice. "In Czechoslovakia."

Rivka covered her ear and glared at me. "I meant where within the car, you *schmo*." I flinched at the insult, although she had called me worse in the two weeks I'd known her. "There'll be more air by the window."

"Good thinking," I said. I should have known better. Rivka never showed any signs of her eighty-three years slowing her mind.

There wasn't much room. We would have to take turns sitting on the hay-covered floor. I didn't mind waiting. I preferred to stand over the others like a black cloud. Everyone sat, and Rivka grunted as she lowered herself.

"You all right?" I asked.

"Other than the deafness and galloping senility?"

I deserved that one.

The early-morning sun ignited the sky, but when the heavy wooden door rolled closed, darkness swallowed the car. Other than the small window, only wafer-thin shafts of light filtered in between the slats. A metal bar came down, engaging the lock with an ominous clang that reverberated through the cattle car.

I wanted my mother.

Eli began to cry, and Annalise mooed in his ear. He mooed back between hiccups. My sister clapped with delight and sang a song about a farm, which I recognized from our childhood.

The whistle blew, and the train lurched forward. I never got motion sickness, but my stomach lurched too.

While Annalise and Eli made up a new song about a cow on a magical adventure, I watched my lifelong home disappear out our little window. Copenhagen had none of the tall buildings of other big cities. Only church spires punctuated the skyline. My favorite, the black exterior of the Church of Our Savior's steeple glinted purple in the morning sun.

"What do you suppose Rebecca Larsen is doing?" I asked Annalise when the spire winked out of sight. "Do you think she's taking a stroll through Tivoli before going to school?"

"Stop it, Rachel." Annalise elbowed my shin. "Envy is bad for your skin."

A woman rocking in a corner moaned about the German shepherds tearing her apart, making Eli cry again.

She didn't even stop when Rivka called her a *kadokhes*, but I pulled her memory of the snarling dogs, and that quieted her. At least I had my ability. I could make everything a little less horrible for the people around me.

I took out a little sketch pad I kept handy. It was half full of memory drawings I'd pulled from inmates at Horserød. I drew before too much energy drained out of me, or I lost too much of the daylight from the little window.

We snacked on bread and cheese and took little sips of water from the canteen Uncle Stellan brought us the day before. We saved the dried meat and fruit for later. We didn't know how long we would be on the train.

"Kitten?" Annalise said. She grabbed my hand, and her fingers shook in mine. She needed insulin. I stood to block her from the view of other passengers. She prepared a syringe, and Leah and Rivka decided to "rest their eyes" just then.

Annalise measured it out in the dim, bouncing cattle car. She sucked in a breath when some of it spilled into the straw. Uncle Stellan had assured her she'd get a monthly supply from the Red Cross, but how could we depend on Nazi promises?

I was thankful it was October. The crisp fall weather kept the temperature in the train car bearable, although fear could make a person sweat just as much as heat. Someone had gotten sick, and the smells blended quickly in the cramped space.

After a couple of hours, a man made his way through the crowd to our little corner without making eye contact. At first, I assumed he'd come to get some fresh air, but instead of joining me near the window, he unzipped his pants.

Annalise shrieked, and I shot as far away as the crowd would allow. What was he doing? Rivka understood and smacked the back of his legs.

"You *yutz*, you'll get it everywhere. Wait a minute." She reached into her suitcase and unwrapped a large silver coffeepot from a mass of tissue paper. Filigree designs bordered its wide rim, and delicate legs curved from its bottom. Rivka stuck the lid back in the suitcase. She handed the man the pot.

"*Bubbe*," Leah said, "that coffeepot is silver."

"Well, we don't have a gold one, Leah. He'll have to settle for peeing in only silver," said Rivka.

This earned a laugh from our new friend, interrupting the sound of his stream hitting metal. The smell of urine mixed with the suffocating stench already in the air. I leaned my head toward the window to escape it. When the man finished, he squeezed past me to dump out the contents. The barbed wire screeched along the silver. He offered the pot back to Rivka.

"Leave it there for everyone," she said.

No one made eye contact when they came to use it, and I couldn't blame them. I hoped the Germans would let us out before I needed to go, but it was thirty-six hours and three trips to the coffeepot before the train stopped.

Chapter Six

THE DOORS HEAVED OPEN with a tooth-jarring rattle, and the sun shone into our unaccustomed eyes. We squinted, shielded our faces, and sucked fresh air like we were drowning.

I brushed dirty hay off my backside and made sure I had my sketch pad. Three new drawings adorned its pages. In addition to the snarling dogs, a man screamed the Nazis would take away his children, and another man wailed about the cousin they had shot in Warsaw. I had relieved people of their burdens, but I'd overdone it. I could barely keep my eyes open even though I had drawn the images.

"*Bubbe*," Leah said, "what about the coffeepot?"

Rivka snorted and flung a disregarding hand at it. "Leave it." When Leah opened her mouth to argue, Rivka asked, "Are you going to ever drink out of that thing?"

Leah wrinkled her nose, but she hooked the filthy pot with a pinkie anyway and grabbed Eli's suitcase with the same hand. "It's a family heirloom," she said when Annalise grimaced.

German soldiers held their noses as we passed. They yelled curses at us, peppered with phrases like *smell like pigs* and *animals they are*.

"They shoved all of us in a train for a day and a half with no plumbing," I said. The layer of grime covering me itched. "What do they expect?"

"They expect to shame us." Rivka walked with her back straighter than I'd ever seen it before.

We emptied into a walled town through a green door, set in fortifications ten feet thick. Armed guards stood on top of the ramparts. The newspapers had called this place a walled town, but it looked more like a prison.

Over the door read the words *Work will make you free* in German.

I whispered, "What a load of *bubkes*," under my breath. Rivka patted my arm.

The door swung shut. The few Germans in SS gray led us along the wall toward a distant threshold. Another larger group of soldiers dressed in unfamiliar olive-green uniforms joined us but remained at the outskirts of the crowd. The ones in gray seemed to like being in charge.

One of the SS officers noticed Leah's coffeepot and laughed. She hung her head down, shuffled along faster, and clasped Eli to her side.

"What a pretty pot you have there, madam," the German sneered at her, giving her a little push. Eli yelped as his mother stumbled, and she soiled her hand securing the pot, only making the soldiers laugh harder. One of them stuck out his hands to push her again. My entire body tensed, and furious heat bled into my face.

Someone yelled *stop* in Danish. Annalise clutched my arm, digging her fingers deep into my strained muscles, and shushed in my ear. It must have been me.

His eyes widened enough to show the entire circle of his blue iris. "Did we tell you to speak, Jew?" he asked. He took two steps toward me. I was too frightened to even back away. I had never been spoken to like that, had never seen any Jew treated that way, even at Horserød. It made me miss freckled, smiling Heinrich back in Copenhagen. "You're not in Denmark anymore," the officer said.

He grabbed my sketch pad from under my arm. Annalise's grip on my elbow—I'd have bruises by morning—prevented me from grabbing it back. He flicked through the pages and gritted his teeth at the drawings of the long food lines, the stark wooden barracks, the fence lined with barbed wire, and the machine-gun turrets, but his face went purple when he got to the pictures I'd drawn on the train. I lunged for the book too late. He ripped its pages to shreds.

The SS officer reached for the revolver holstered at his hip. Annalise jerked me back so hard, she fell backward to the ground, and I staggered, nearly tripping over her. The SS officer grinned, reveling in our terror, and eased his gun out. The fragments of the last sketch I'd drawn, the one of the man's cousin shot in the streets of Warsaw, whirled around my feet. Would that be my fate too?

Who would pull the memory of me being shot from Annalise?

One of the soldiers in the olive-green uniforms whispered into the German's ear. The pistol slid back in place. I huffed out the chestful of air I'd been holding.

The SS officer threw the remnants of my sketch pad at Annalise, making her duck behind her hands. He stalked off into the ghetto. The scraps of my drawings blew away in the breeze. I no longer cared.

My savior in green rolled his eyes. "Not very hospitable, I'm afraid." He was a little older than Annalise, and although his German was excellent, he had an accent. Czech? That would mean his homeland was occupied too.

"We're supposed to be extra polite to our Danish guests. M'lady." He bowed with flair Annalise would appreciate, along with a cleft chin exactly like Cary Grant's. He gave her a hand up from where she had sprawled.

"My name's Lukas. I'm with the Czech gendarmerie." His eyes never left Annalise. "You'll find we're a bit more...lenient than our German friends, but I'm going to have to keep an eye on *you*." He regarded my sister with one eye closed, half scrutiny, half wink.

We passed a spigot on the wall before entering the courtyard. Lukas turned it on. He stepped aside for Leah so she could wash both her hands and the pot under the gushing water. When she was done, Lukas himself dried the coffeepot with his handkerchief. She thanked him over and over.

Behind him and out of sight, Annalise laid the back of her hand on her forehead and mouthed, "Swoon." I took a deep breath for patience, but it was a relief to find a friendly face.

The little group of us rinsed our hands and faces of filth from the train. During Annalise's turn, her hands shook at the spigot. She needed food. Right away. We had been too nervous to eat much of our precious supply on the train. I may have been drained, but she was sick. Without a word, Rivka took her own suitcase from me so I could carry my sister's instead.

"Lukas, my sister—"

"Is feeling a little tired," Annalise cut me off. "Yes, Rachel, thank you." She glared at me, and turned to Lukas. "Could I have your arm, please?" Only my sister would ask a guard to escort her into her prison, but Lukas seemed only too pleased to accommodate her. He led us through the threshold and into the Terezin ghetto.

I couldn't believe what I saw. The densely packed buildings opened up into an attractive little park. Our fellow train passengers were seated at dozens of tables covered in white linen and set with china and silver. An orchestra, made up of uniformed officers and inmates together, played a classical piece I didn't recognize on a raised platform that looked like a stage.

"Maybe the Nazis were telling the truth," Leah said, her words lilting up as if asking a question. "Maybe it won't be so bad?"

"That would make for a nice change of pace," said Rivka.

I scanned the other inmates for Gideon but didn't see him anywhere. A weight pressed against my chest like Mama's piano had been laid there. If he hadn't been transported, it could mean he was...

Beside the orchestra, a man stood at a podium. He was over fifty and had a thick black beard to match his head of hair.

"Welcome to Terezin," he said. "My name is Samuel Tesler." He spoke with perfect German and flawless manners. "I'm a member of the Jewish Council." He petted the yellow star sewn on his sleeve as if he wore the badge proudly. "We manage the administration of the town." I scoffed at the word. Who did he think he was fooling, calling this place a town? At best, it was a ghetto. At worst, a labor camp. I wasn't sure which yet.

"Commandant Becker and I welcome you." Elder Tesler indicated a man in an SS uniform slouched in his chair. He laid a jovial hand on the Nazi's shoulder and patted it, giving me another reason not to like him.

Commandant Becker didn't smile or even look into the crowd.

"I know your journey has been difficult," said Elder Tesler, "but you're safe now. Enjoy your lunch." He gestured to the baskets of bread and giant steaming pots of beef (beef!) stew coming around. A photographer snapped a picture of the smiling elder surrounded by the abundance. Rationing was still so strict in Copenhagen, I hadn't seen this much meat in years.

The photographer stopped at our table and pointed his camera at Annalise. She held up a huge chunk of bread and smiled.

"How can you smile?" I asked her.

She tore the bread to pieces and popped one in her mouth. "Someone points a camera at me, I smile."

SS officers and Czech gendarmes circulated the tables with forms and pencils. The forms asked us to describe what skills or medical issues we had. Annalise, who hated discussing her condition with her own doctors, surprised me when she wrote *diabetic* on hers.

"I may need more medicine." She whispered so Rivka and Leah couldn't hear. "We don't know how long we'll be here."

The thought of counting on the Nazis for anything made me sick. Not too sick, though. I still finished my stew.

As our plates were cleared, a fleet of wheelbarrows full of parcels appeared, followed by the clicking photographer. We each received one enormous box, *King of Denmark* the only return address. People tore into the Red Cross parcels like children at Christmas. The photographer snapped a flurry of close-ups of their gleeful faces.

"There's canned salmon in here. Eli loves salmon," Leah said as if her son's preference was some kind of accomplishment.

"And soap!" Annalise said. She closed her eyes and breathed in its scent.

I was so absorbed in the contents of my parcel, I didn't notice a man approaching our table. I only looked up at the sound of slurping.

He was licking my plate.

He didn't look anything like the inmates serving us or those with the orchestra. His tattered clothes hung off his skinny frame. His unkempt beard did little to conceal his hollowed cheeks.

I bet the photographer hadn't taken *his* picture.

Why did we get beef stew on tablecloths when other inmates looked like that?

Annalise hadn't noticed the man, but she sure did when I handed my parcel over to him.

"What are you doing?" Annalise asked.

The man paused for the second it took him to understand. He clung to the box and flew through an archway that led to the main thoroughfare of the ghetto as if I were chasing him. Annalise stood as if she might.

One of the SS officers screamed, "Stop!" and took off after him. I tried to call back the soldier to tell him I had given the poor man my package, but Annalise pushed me back into my seat.

"Sorry," I said. She sat back down. "I just couldn't…"

"I know, Kitten." Her voice sounded understanding, but she held her own parcel a little tighter.

Elder Tesler reached our table, handing each of us a postcard.

"It's to let your friends know you're safe. Although maybe you shouldn't brag too much about eating *beef* stew," he said with a smile so infectious, Annalise mirrored the expression.

The front of the card had a drawing of the idyllic fortress placed in its bucolic setting, the word *Terezin* in a lavish font beneath. The backs were blank.

It made my chest ache to write to Uncle Stellan and not my parents, but he had been right when he said they wouldn't let us write to anyone outside the Reich. Annalise told him about the soap in her parcel and the pretty china at our luncheon. I didn't mention the cruel Germans ripping my sketchbook or the skinny man licking my plate. I didn't want to worry him. I kept it simple. I assured him we had made it there safely.

I told him we were going to be all right.

Then, they directed us to the showers.

Chapter Seven

THE SOLDIERS DROVE THE men out of the little park, down the main boulevard of the ghetto. The women and children crossed the railroad tracks to a pair of doors. *Brausebad*, German for shower, was written over both. SS officers queued us up outside. The more friendly Czech guards were nowhere to be seen.

The line didn't advance for long periods of time, but large groups entered together, so it moved quickly. After a couple dozen disappeared into the buildings, we arrived at an SS officer at the split in the line.

He waved some to the shower on the left and some to the one on the right. Rivka reached the fork first. She coughed, the only remaining symptom of her lingering pneumonia. He took a step back and motioned her to the left.

The officer dragged his eyes down Annalise, then up and down again. People were always giving Annalise a second look, even as tired and pale as she was. He motioned her to the left, me to the right.

"Why can't we go together?" I asked, pointing to my sister and Rivka. What earthly reason could they have to separate us in the showers? It was just to be cruel.

To prove my theory, the soldier grinned and pulled Eli's chubby little hand from Leah's. She screamed and grabbed for her son, but her wails only made Eli follow suit.

"It's okay," I said to Leah. It hurt to see them cry, and the guard's smirk made it worse. "We'll see them afterward." I didn't like it any more than she did, but it would only be for a few minutes. "Annalise and Rivka are with him."

My sister sang in Eli's ear as she led him away. He followed her but didn't take his teary eyes from his mother. Leah attempted a smile, but it was more of a grimace. I wore a similar expression as my sister's voice faded away.

When we neared the head of the line, a female inmate directed twenty of us to get undressed. In Horserød, they had shower stalls, but Terezin's showers were one large room. I hesitated to get naked in front of so many strangers, but I abandoned all modesty for a chance to scrub the filth and stink from the train off my skin. Leah pulled the new soap out of her Red Cross parcel. Since I had given mine away, I hoped she would let me use hers.

"These showers don't look as nice as that luncheon we just had." Leah covered herself with her arms. She was right. A crack splintered the stained cement floor. Once they loaded us inside, a large door shut with a clang. It reminded me of the cattle car door and sent goose bumps down my bare arms.

Leah and I stood directly beneath one of the rusty showerheads, dancing in place to keep warm. The windowless box got no sun. We looked up to avoid each other's nakedness, waiting.

The plumbing rattled, and the spigots at the other end of the room burst on first. A panicked scream echoed through the showers.

The water was really cold.

At the exit, we dug fresh clothes out of our suitcases. My old ones smelled so bad, they should have been burned, but Uncle Stellan had warned us to let nothing go to waste, so I shoved them back in my suitcase once I dressed in fresh clothes.

Another female inmate dispensed handfuls of patches to each of us as we emptied back into the street. She provided no instruction. She didn't need to tell us what to do with the yellow stars. Leah laid her suitcase on the cobblestone sidewalk to open it. She found a sewing kit and attached her star to her chest while I paced.

Normally, Annalise took forever to get ready, but I hoped she wouldn't make Rivka and Eli wait. When Leah finished with her star, she stood and set her needle and thread to my blouse.

"Please stop fidgeting, Rachel," Leah said. It wasn't my fault she'd pricked her finger. Her hands were shaking. The moment she finished, I paced again.

I ran my hand over the yellow star. It felt stiff on my blouse, like a dried-up stain.

A guard emerged from a building across the street. "You lot are supposed to be at the Sluice by now. Go on," he said.

Leah and I moved but lingered around a corner.

"I'm not leaving my son," Leah said to me and joined in my pacing. "What do you suppose the Sluice is?"

I had no idea.

"If Annalise is setting curlers in her hair while we wait out here with wet heads, I swear..."

The song about the cow and the magic carpet lilted into the street, and I spun on Annalise.

"It's about time, Greta Garbo." She'd wrapped her wet head in a scarf like a turban.

She ignored my disapproval. "It feels so good to be oneself again."

Leah knelt on the ground with her arms outstretched. Eli ran into them. Rivka's eyes caught on the yellow star affixed to my blouse.

"You all right?" I asked her.

She tugged at my patch. "This is *fakakta*," she said.

Rivka had explained to me what the word meant back in Horserød. She was right.

It was *fakakta*.

Leah urged Eli down the path, away from his cursing grandmother to the Sluice the guard mentioned. Out front, the pair of German soldiers from the train tossed a young man's yellow star between them, laughing at his attempts to get it back. I felt sorry for the poor guy, but I was relieved they were too distracted by him to recognize me.

"Do you see Lukas anywhere?" Annalise asked once we were inside. All the guards wore the same green uniform. She stood on tiptoe to see over the crowd.

"Focus, Annalise." I snapped in her face. "We need to figure out what's going on in that building."

"That's what I'm doing. Lukas will know." She continued to search.

We joined the line. In front of us, we could see several tables extending the entire length of the room. Czech gendarmes lined one side, and we filed past with our suitcases on the other.

"There." Annalise waved to Lukas at the other end of the room like they were greeting one another in Tivoli Gardens.

"Present your baggage for a security check," said the only SS guard stationed at the door. "We'll be looking for anything that could pose a safety risk." I let out a breath. We didn't have anything like that in our bags. The gendarmes rifled through the open suitcases on the tables, frequently setting items aside. The SS officer caught Annalise's eye, and he helped lift her luggage onto the table when it was our turn. Rivka and her family got into a shorter line on the other side of the building.

The Czech gendarme hadn't rummaged through our belongings long when he found my sister's fox cape. Annalise had rationalized the extravagance when packing, claiming it was her warmest coat. He set it behind him along with other furs, jewelry, candlesticks, and scattered stacks of money from other families.

"None of those things are dangerous." I pointed to the growing pile.

Without answering, he removed a white canvas bag with a red cross from my sister's suitcase. We both froze. He poked through it, making the glass syringes clatter. He eyed the table stacked high with the other items he'd stolen. My hands itched to snatch the bag out of his hands, but Annalise's steady voice stopped me.

"Please," she said. She reached her hand out, stroking his as she lowered the bag back into her suitcase. The gendarme licked his lips at her.

She smiled at him, and the insulin stayed. He must have liked the promise in her smile even in the ludicrous turban. I pulled the memory of it from his mind without thinking about how weak I already was. My knees buckled, and I braced myself on the table in front of me. It worked, but barely. He must not have been very bright.

He stole a pair of gold earrings I hadn't wanted to leave behind, and the envelope stuffed with money Uncle Stellan raised for us. The Nazis could have it all as long as they didn't take Annalise's medicine.

Or, at least, that's what I thought until he laid his hands on Jubilee.

"*Tag det ikke!*" I had forgotten my excellent German again. The guard jutted out his chin and placed the pony on the table with my earrings, all of our money, and Annalise's coat.

I snatched at Jubilee, surprising the gendarme. He jumped back and out of my way. The soft golden hair of Jubilee's mane slipped through my fingers as someone yanked me back. I expected it to be Annalise, or maybe somehow Gideon, but the hands that gripped me weren't letting go, even though I had stopped struggling.

"What are you doing, Jew?" A man of about thirty, short and squat with a bald and bumpy head, held me back by the wrists. He wore the uniform of a Czech gendarme, but he spoke perfect German.

"She wanted this stuffed horse, Commander Gruber," the guard said. He held up Jubilee carelessly by an ear.

"Since when are grown men afraid of stuffed animals?" I asked. Annalise grabbed my shoulder to silence me. The officer's nostrils flared, and his eyes narrowed.

"Do you think you're here to play, girl?" Commander Gruber asked. I didn't like the sound of his laugh, but at least he let go of my wrists.

I saw what he was going to do and tried to pull the memory of the white canvas bag from his mind, but I'd used up my power. The memory didn't budge, and I stumbled. I stared as Annalise's medicine joined Jubilee and all the other things that, until a minute ago, had been so precious. One of the officers had to push me to get me moving out of the Sluice and into the town.

I'd lost my sister's insulin. I may have killed her over a stupid toy.

"I'm so sorry."

She didn't answer. She just stared at the ground.

"I don't know what I was thinking."

Annalise was still quiet.

We followed the others in a daze through the ghetto to our barracks, but I hardly saw any of it. I would use my power. I would make that ugly, bald Nazi forget my face and steal it back. Well, not today, but tomorrow. *How could I have done this to her?*

"I'll fix this, Annalise. I will."

This got a reaction. "Rachel Abramson, you'll do no such thing." She grabbed me by both shoulders. "It's the Nazis that did this, not you, Kitten." The back of my throat burned. "It's not your fault," she said.

It was *a little* my fault.

"Miss..." a familiar voice called out. We turned to see Lukas, a half smile on his lips, a white tip of the canvas bag peeking out from under his uniform jacket. "I think you left something behind."

Chapter Eight

LUKAS LED US TO our quarters and chatted casually, ignoring my tears of joy. Not joy, exactly. Maybe relief. Or anger. Shame? I couldn't keep up with the twists and turns of the day.

"We can't thank you enough for returning *Rachel's* medicine," Annalise said. She winked at me to be sure I understood. After losing her insulin, I could hardly argue.

"Yes, thank you for saving it for me," I said.

"Anytime. I've never heard anyone talk to the Cauliflower like that. We're going to be friends, you and me." He looked at me conspiratorially but saved his winks for Annalise.

"The Cauliflower?" I asked.

"Knobbly head, skinny legs," Lukas said, waving a hand over his own thick blond hair. "He's the head of the gendarmes. He's Czech, but he grew up in Berlin, so he thinks he's better than all of us." I could tell by *us*, he meant Czechs and Jews alike. "He used to be a big shot at one of the camps in Germany."

He stopped in front of a large building, six stories tall. "This is West Barracks. All you Danes are in this building. You're lucky. It's not too crowded, and your families get to stay together."

Not ours. Our family didn't get to stay together. Mama, Papa, and four of my siblings were a thousand miles away.

"Thank you, Lukas," Annalise said before he took his leave. He clicked his heels and saluted her with mock solemnity. "Very promising," Annalise said to me but watched him disappear around a corner. She pivoted to face me again. "Don't look at me like that, Kitten. He got my medicine back." I couldn't argue with that.

A pair of chubby arms flung around Annalise's waist from behind. Eli hugged her tightly until Leah shooed him off, apologizing for him.

"Did you lose much?" Leah asked us.

I considered the envelope of money, the gold earrings, and, of course, Jubilee, but Annalise's white canvas bag had survived the Sluice. "Not too much," I said. From the distraught look on Leah's face, it would seem she had, yet her mother-in-law grinned from ear to ear.

"I don't see how you can smile, *Bubbe*," Leah snapped at Rivka. The old woman beamed up at me and laughed until tears gathered in the wrinkled corners of her eyes.

"Those *putzes* at the Sluice? They took the coffeepot."

We waited outside West Barracks for more than an hour for a gendarme to bring us to our room assignments. The Hechts got theirs before us, leaving Annalise and me alone on the street. My chin quivered as soon as they were gone.

"I promise to try to keep my big mouth shut, Annalise."

She laid her head on my shoulder. "You wouldn't even be here if it weren't for me. It's me who's sorry."

Since the SS officer destroyed my sketch pad, I dug around in my suitcase for another one. I drew Annalise's promising smile at the Sluice, and the drain on my strength slowed. I'd just completed the last pencil strokes when footfalls pounded behind us. No good news came with running feet. The runner dropped to his knees, and his head fell into his hands. It was the anguished *no* under his breath that I recognized.

Gideon.

Annalise and I bolted to his side and knelt in the un-paved street.

"You got caught." He held my face in his palm. "When I heard a train of Danes arrived, I hoped you wouldn't...Are you all right?" He looked between Annalise and me, stopping on me.

All right? Gideon was safe and right in front of me. I was too relieved to speak for a minute.

I rubbed his head like a genie's lamp. "You cut your hair." He never wore it short enough to expose the scar down the back of his scalp.

"You look so tired," he said and threw both arms around my neck. "Oh, Rachel, I'm so sorry. You were waiting, and I never came."

Warmth spread through me, beginning where his hand touched my face.

"We're together now, thank goodness." Annalise stood and shook a finger at me. "Someone has to help me control this girl."

"You think living here has given me some new insight?" Gideon asked, quickly forgetting his remorse.

"Enough, you two," I said. We brushed off our knees, and Gideon straightened. He'd somehow grown in the two weeks since I'd seen him. "I'm not that bad."

"No? Why don't we break open your Red Cross parcel?" Annalise cupped her hand to her ear as if listening to someone whispering. "What? Oh, that's right. You gave yours away to an inmate 'who looked hungry.'"

"She didn't." Gideon's eyes darted from Annalise to me as if they shared some inside joke.

"Don't talk about me like I'm not here." I tried to look stern, but I was too happy to have found Gideon so completely unchanged.

"You really gave your parcel away?" He struck himself on the forehead with the heel of his hand. "Of course you did," he said, answering his own question. "God, I missed you." He tugged my hair gently, and more warmth diffused over my scalp. "Rachel, you'll learn quickly. Everyone here looks hungry."

"Then, she practically had a brawl in the Sluice with the Cauliflower over that stuffed horse," said Annalise. Gideon's happiness dried up at the sound of the Cauliflower's name.

My sister did not notice the change in Gideon's expression and recounted the story as if from some safe and distant time, not an hour ago and a couple hundred yards away. My face burned. Losing Annalise's medicine was no laughing matter.

She finally noticed the dark cloud over Gideon's face. "It all worked out fine," she said. "We got it back."

He pointed his finger at me. "You *would* antagonize the most unpredictable man in the ghetto. People say he beat an inmate to death in the last place he worked." He watched me as that information sunk in. "Your impulsivity was dangerous enough in Copenhagen, Rachel, but here...here, it's suicidal."

A gendarme came to escort us to our room before Gideon could berate me even more. I was happy for the interruption.

Our room was smaller than our bedroom in Copenhagen, the set of newly constructed bunks the only furniture. No linens covered the mattresses, and when I sat on the bottom bunk, the wood shavings inside poked me.

"Ouch," I said. "It's like sleeping in a flower bed full of mulch."

"You'll be grateful," Gideon said and sat beside me. "Once you see how the rest of the ghetto lives, you'll understand how good we have it." He twisted his head over his shoulder. "You even have a window. The Danish government has been making a lot of noise about our treatment."

I snorted. "A lot of good they've been," I said. I glanced up at the ceiling. An old leak had stained it.

"It's helped, Rachel," he said.

"Where's your room?" I asked. We had enough space on the floor for another mattress. I didn't like the idea of being separated from Gideon again, even for a minute.

"I was assigned to a room with the Blumes," he said.

Annalise's hand flew to her mouth. "The Blume sisters are here?" she asked. Ruth and Ilse owned the Copenhagen cafe next to the movie theater.

"Afraid so, but I fixed up my own place." He fiddled with a button on his shirt.

"Your own place?" Annalise said. "How did you get that?"

"It's not a room, really. Just an old air shaft in the attic I converted, but I don't have to share."

"You don't have to live in an old, drafty attic now that we're here." I assumed he would want to be with us as much as I wanted to be with him. "You can stay here."

He froze, and his mouth hung open like I'd just pulled a memory from him. "I need...um..." Gideon stood up too quickly and smacked his head on the top bunk. Annalise arched her eyebrow and smirked.

"Wouldn't you rather us all be together?" I asked.

Gideon passed his hand down his cheek. "I can't..."

Annalise stretched out a hand, patting my shoulder. "I think he's trying to say he needs his privacy."

The way Annalise said the word *privacy* made me blush to the roots of my hair.

"Maybe he's met someone special?" Annalise nudged him gently.

No way did Annalise have it right. Not Gideon. But when I looked at him, he was blushing too. He *should* be embarrassed. How could he think about girls in a place like this? He was worse than Annalise.

"C'mon," said Gideon, not denying any of it. "I'll show you around."

Chapter Nine

"THERE WERE THIRTY-FIVE OF us in that church attic," Gideon said as we descended the stairs. "The first group, the one with my parents, all made it to their boats and off to Sweden, but the rest of us were raided right before I was supposed to meet you."

"Did you ever find out who betrayed you?" I asked.

"Peter Jorgensen, if you can believe it."

"Peter?" He was a classmate of ours. We'd played handball with him a million times. He picked me first whenever he was captain. "A Nazi sympathizer?"

"Nothing like that." He clasped his hands under his chin and batted his eyes. "He was in love," he said in a sarcastic falsetto. He rolled his eyes and gritted his teeth. "The fool."

"What does love have to do—"

"He'd been yammering on about Hanka Finegold for months." Gideon pushed his fist into the palm of his other hand, letting off a quiet snap as the knuckle cracked. I glared at him, and he brought his arms to his sides.

"Doesn't sound like an anti-Semite to me," Annalise said.

"He wasn't one," Gideon said. "Not until he found out she was seeing Jacob Levine—you know, that Polish refugee. He didn't like that much." He wrinkled his nose as if he smelled something bad. "Can you guess what happy new couple was hiding in that church with me?"

"Hanka and Jacob?" Annalise asked.

"They're around here somewhere." He pointed around Terezin. "I think Peter may have seriously undermined his chances with her."

"He turned them in because he was...what? Heartbroken?" I rubbed my brow, squinting my eyes shut. "That's crazy."

"Love makes you act crazy," Gideon said. Annalise nodded solemnly. I pursed my lips together. Like either one of them knew the first thing about it.

"Sounds like you forgive the traitor," I said.

"Not really. I just have lower expectations of people than you."

Gideon's tour took us to Dresden, the women's barracks. Danish families got to stay together in West, but men, women, and children of all other nationalities were split up. I imagined Birgitte being forced apart from Mama or my parents being separated from one another, and an ache knotted in my throat.

There were no toilets on this side of the ghetto—only a series of holes under a long plank of wood, with walls on just three sides. The smell of the open latrine made my eyes water.

Although the women's barracks was half the size of West, it held ten times as many people. The bunks were piled three high with an aisle between them only wide enough to squeeze through. There would have been a dozen people in a room the size of ours. The beds were just rough wooden slats.

"People live like this?" I asked, covering my nose with my arm. I shouldn't have complained about my uncomfortable mattress. At least I had one.

"A rabbi holds services here." Gideon pointed to the building behind the laundry. "A service on Friday at sundown and a shorter one on Saturday morning before work."

"They let us worship?"

"No, but people do it anyway." He scanned the area. "There are thousands of us and only about a hundred guards. The German guards are strict, but there are only twenty of them. The rest of the guards are Czech gendarmes. They aren't as bad, with some notable exceptions like your buddy the Cauliflower."

"Oh, we know about the Czechs." Annalise grinned as if we were conspiring over a poorly guarded secret. "Lukas." She sang the name like an angel's call.

"Lukas?" he asked me. Gideon required an interpreter with Annalise sometimes.

I thought about Gideon's little private cubby in the attic and the girl (maybe even *girls*?) he entertained there. "He is awfully cute," I agreed. Gideon rolled his eyes and pointed to a tall, gray building.

"This is where I work. The Electrical Department."

"Naturally," I said. I reached up to touch the scar on the back of his head, but he flinched away.

Gideon's fascination with all things electrical began when a live wire fell on him when he was five. As practical as he was, he never shied away from the thing that could have killed him.

"Every inmate over fourteen has to work. Have you filled out the paper with your skills yet?"

"That's what that was for?" I asked.

Annalise wrote she could play piano and sing. I wrote that I liked to draw. It wasn't like I could mention my ability.

"I doubt there's much work for artists here," I said. What would they make me do instead?

"You're wrong, actually." Gideon pointed down the street. "See the brick building on the right?" It was as large as the Electrical Department. "The bottom floor is the Art Department. They do propaganda work and commission art for offices and homes, but mostly they help the engineers and architects draw up building projects all over the Reich."

"Slave labor, you mean?" I asked, my hands on my hips.

Gideon frowned at me. "You'll get paid, but you're in a ghetto, not a spa. Or did you believe the stories about this place?" He turned to Annalise. "Musicians have day jobs, but at night, during leisure time, they practice and perform." Gideon gestured toward the other side of the ghetto.

"Musicians?"

"We have a lot of concerts here." He ticked off his fingers. "Lectures, plays, and gallery shows too. There's at least one event every night. You're in the only place in the Third Reich where Jews can legally gather in groups, go out at night, and play an instrument in public."

I hadn't imagined having leisure time to enjoy cultural pursuits. "I thought we'd be doing hard labor."

"Not us. I've heard bad rumors from people transported here from the camps in the east, and sometimes they ship some of us out there. The hours are long here, seventy hours a week or so, but it's not too bad, especially for Danes."

"It doesn't make any sense," I said. "Why is it so much better here?"

"It's all part of the propaganda of this place. They take tons of pictures of the events." That explained the photographer and the fancy luncheon. The beef stew roiled in my gut. He lowered his voice and checked to make sure no one was listening.

"And whenever the Nazis come across some high-profile Jewish scholar or musician, they stick them in here. 'See? We're treating the Jews well,' they say. 'Look at Rafael Salzberg. He's fine.'"

Annalise—who had been distracted by the sights of our new home—perked up.

"Rafael Salzberg is here?" Annalise pointed to the ground at her feet. Gideon nodded, but she still looked doubtful. "Here?" She scanned the street as if she expected the man to materialize in front of her.

"He said yes, Annalise." I turned back to Gideon. "So, they're using us to cover up what they're doing in other camps?" I worried I might lose my lunch. Part of me *wanted* to be rid of it.

Gideon gave me a look like I was six years old. "That's true, but it means things are better in here for us," he said.

Annalise bounced on her toes as if warming up before a race, repeating *Rafael Salzberg* over and over again.

"*Pokkers*, Annalise. Who is Rafael Salzberg?"

She gawked at me like when I said I didn't know where Ingrid Bergman was born.

"A famous choral director, Rachel!"

"Yeah, he leads one of the choirs here," Gideon said.

Annalise brought her hands together as if in prayer.

"I'm sure he'd be happy to have you," he said. "Let me show you the library."

Annalise hopped along after us, not caring much about books.

The library carried one-tenth of the books of our school library back home, but I hadn't expected one at all.

Hebrew titles were embossed on the spines of the books in the first section, followed by Czech, Dutch, and Hungarian. I had to explore three aisles to find something in a language I knew.

I selected a German one off the shelf. I doubted I'd have much time for reading but—

Ida Goldstein.

Someone—presumably Ida herself—had carefully written her name on the top right corner of the first page in neat pencil. The book felt heavy in my hands.

Gideon peered at the name over my shoulder. "Probably took it from her at the Sluice."

I replaced the book and chose another one.

There wasn't a name on the inside of this one, but a bookmark slid out when I opened it. The owner had only been about halfway through when it was taken.

"I could be singing with Rafael Salzberg," Annalise said, more to herself than to us. She paced up and down the aisles, barely able to stand still.

"I don't see how you could be excited, Annalise." I banged a shelf with an open palm. "I can't believe that *gonif* Elder Tesler let us write those postcards and took those pictures of us. We have to get word back home about all of this." I tugged on Gideon's sleeve, hoping to enlist his help.

He looked at the man stacking books on a shelf. He had a yellow star on his chest. "Careful, Rachel," Gideon said and directed us to the ghetto store on the other side of the square.

We entered to the familiar sound of a shop bell, but instead of a friendly shopkeeper like my father, a scowling Czech officer stood at the register. Not all the Czechs were as kind as Lukas, it turned out.

There were aisles and aisles of items. Candles—burned down to a stump. Wool socks—a small hole in the toe. A silver compact—a J already engraved on the lid. Annalise twisted up a lipstick to discover the impression of its previous owner's lips.

This was worse than the library.

"So, we can buy things here with the money we make?" Annalise asked. She tested the lipstick on her hand to see if the color suited her.

"Sure," he said. Gideon spoke loud enough for the gendarme to hear, then dropped it to a whisper. "But ghetto money doesn't buy you much."

Gideon led us back to the courtyard where we'd had our fancy lunch. A dozen inmates were taking off the linen tablecloths and collecting the dirty dishes. These people looked more like the one I'd given my package to. Every morsel of food had disappeared.

A single man stood on the platform where the orchestra had been. He looked like he was in charge, but he had a yellow star on his chest like the rest of us. He wore an armband that read *Ghetto Police*.

"Move faster, now," he yelled down to the working inmates from on high. He spoke German with an accent, like Lukas. His eyes caught on us as we passed. "We work while the Danes enjoy their full bellies."

"Do you know him?" I asked Gideon.

"I know of him," Gideon said. "Yakov doesn't like Danes much."

"How does he know we're Danish?" I turned away, afraid he could tell I had a full belly from the look on my face.

"There may only be a few hundred Danes here, but once you see more of the camp, you'll understand. We stick out like sore thumbs."

"It's not our fault we get treated better," I said.

"Of course not, but you can't expect them to like it."

After seeing that the children's and men's barracks were as crowded as the women's, I was grateful to return to West.

Annalise wanted to lie down, which was code for a dose of insulin. I was exhausted too, but Gideon insisted on showing me one more spot.

We weaved through back streets that seemed as familiar to him as Copenhagen's. I couldn't believe he'd only been at the ghetto for a couple of weeks. We ended up back at the gate where we'd arrived just this morning. We climbed the stairs in the ramparts to the top.

Tiny stooped figures dotted a field outside Terezín's walls. A blur of yellow flashed from a patch on a sleeve. "Inmates are harvesting the vegetable gardens," he said. Gideon pointed to the western corner of the field beyond. A smaller version of Terezín, constructed of the same brick, gates painted the same green, sat beneath the setting sun.

"The Little Fortress," he said. An archway in its walls led to a pitch-black corridor, like a gaping mouth. It reminded me of the cattle car that brought us to Terezín. I shuddered at the sight of it. "It's the prison for people who break the rules in here. The people who work those gardens say they can hear the screams of the inmates they torture inside."

I spread my fingers out like a fan across my pounding heart. "Why are you telling me this?"

"You look so tired, Rachel. You can't overexert yourself." It was less of an observation and more of an accusation, like a warning against using my ability, but he couldn't know, could he? He tucked a lock of hair behind my ear. "You're in danger here. More so than Annalise or me."

"Why do you say that?" I asked, mesmerized by the relentlessness of his stare.

"This place is filled with stray cats, Rachel." He skimmed his thumb over the scar the angry swan left on my cheek. Unlike him, I didn't flinch away. "And these bullies don't throw stones."

Chapter Ten

GIDEON WAS RIGHT ABOUT one thing. Danes had it easier in Terezin. The SS gave us a week, then assigned Annalise to one of the ghetto's four hospitals as a nurse's assistant, and they placed me in the Art Department.

Walking to my first day of work, I shielded my mouth and nose with a bent elbow to block the stench of the men's barracks' open latrine. I almost lost my breakfast and couldn't afford to lose the calories. I muttered to myself how unfair it was that they didn't have running water like we did at West.

I should have averted my eyes too. Only a couple of knotty boards separated the latrine from the main thoroughfare of the ghetto, and my eyes met with a man sitting on the plank of wood while he relieved himself. I spun away, and heat rushed into my face for catching him in a moment of such intense intimacy. I considered erasing the assault on his dignity from his memory, but the man didn't react and went about his business. Besides, I didn't want Gideon to be right about me.

He said my lack of impulse control would wear me out. He couldn't have known about my ability, but he did have a point. I'd have to conserve my energy, but people would want to forget their sorrows. I'd pulled memories seven times in Terezin, once for every day since I'd arrived. An old man screaming for his dead wife, and a small child sobbing for the dog she'd left behind. I had been able to sketch them right away, but with my new work schedule, there would be little time to draw.

I heard the woman before I saw her. "I can't put you on a train alone," she said over and over. She bent, sobbing, over a boy of ten or eleven.

"It's all right, Mama," he said. "It won't be so bad." He held a small suitcase in one hand and a slip of paper in the other. Gideon had explained transport slips to me. When an inmate received one, they were to report to the train depot, usually within a couple of hours. From there, they would be sent to the labor camps in the east. When I'd heard about the slips, I hadn't imagined one clutched in a child's hand.

"You'll be alone in the dark!" the mother screamed and dissolved into sobs. The boy's face strained with a brave little effort to hold back his tears before his face crumpled, and he broke down too. Their cries attracted the attention of an SS officer across the street.

"You there!" he yelled at the grieving mother. "Quiet down!" When her weeping didn't abate, his hand touched the gun at his hip. The small crowd gathered around the pair scattered at his approach.

Before I could think about it, I pulled her memory of the train. She still cried, but she quieted enough for the officer. He took his hand off his weapon, looking pleased with himself that he'd frightened her into submission.

I quickened my pace into the wind, gathering my collar up around my cheeks. I missed my wool scarf. I had given it to Annalise since she lost her fox cape at the Sluice. Buildings were rarely warmer inside than out. If they were, it was due to extreme overcrowding, not efficient heat.

Not so with the Art Department. A blast of warm air greeted me when I first entered. I slammed the door behind me in an effort to block out the cold. A girl my age jumped at the noise and knocked over a pot of ink. She placed her hand to her chest and let out a long breath when she saw only me at the door. She leapt to her feet to sop up the seeping ink with a cloth.

"Sorry," I said, moving papers out of the way.

"My fault," she said through clenched teeth. She adjusted her wide black headband. "New girl, huh?" She returned to her work, only pausing to point to herself with her pencil. "Julia."

I introduced myself and shucked off my coat. The bitter smell of Papa's black-market pipe tobacco crept into my nose. I scanned the noisy crowd of men bunched in the back of the office for him, but he wasn't there. Julia jerked her thumb at her fellow artists. "The Hens can't stop clucking over the war." Now that she mentioned it, the men gossiping in a circle did resemble chickens huddled together, pecking in a yard. "They haven't done a lick of work all morning. Rumor says Italy declared war on Germany."

"Really?" I tried to listen in on their conversation, but too many of them were talking at once. Mussolini had been deposed that summer, but I hadn't hoped Italy would turn on their old ally. It could mean the end of the war, but Julia didn't look impressed.

"They haven't stopped talking about it all morning." Julia waved a hand over the pile of unfinished recruitment posters stacked on another nearby desk. They looked naked without their swastikas and angry slogans.

I wriggled out of another layer of clothes.

"Hottest place in Terezin," Julia said without looking up. "The heat is connected to Commandant Becker's office next door, and the thermostat is broken."

The group of men at the back she'd called the Hens burst into a gale of laughter, and Julia fixed a withering stare back at them. She gestured to the empty desk next to hers, and I sat at it. "You can use Adam's paints since he's blabbing with the others."

I had a little time before I would feel the effects of using my ability. I could finish whatever she needed me to do quickly and slip away to sketch the image I'd pulled in the street, the boy in the darkness of the train.

Julia handed me a stack of postcards. Each one featured a familiar bucolic sketch of Terezin. I had sent one to Uncle Stellan. The card with Elder Tesler's lies. Only, these hadn't been colored yet. Julia expected me to help with that. To be her accomplice, more like. My nails dug into my palms as I balled my hands into fists.

"I'm not painting those." I pushed the cards away from me.

Julia still didn't look up. "At least it's warm here. There are worse places to work, my friend." The use of the word *friend* softened the threat. I knew what she meant. On one of our many walks during my first days in Terezin, Gideon had shown me the factory, where people were forced to chip flakes of mica from stone to make airplane parts. The workers developed lung diseases within months. Gideon had used the factory as another cautionary tale—like the Little Fortress—even though no Dane had ever set foot in either place.

Gideon expected me to make trouble. The threat of his "I told you so" urged me to pick up the paintbrush more than the threat of the factory.

The moment I touched the brush to the card, an ache twisted my gut. Now I was complicit in the lie.

For the first time, Julia looked up from her work. "It doesn't make you a Nazi collaborator." When I didn't say anything, she reconsidered her own words. "You get used to it."

She finished her pile faster than me. Her hands flew over the postcards like a machine on an assembly line despite her constant chatter.

Julia's father had owned a successful German factory. He'd showered his multitalented daughter with every type of lesson. When she arrived at Terezin, she'd translated—German, French, and Czech—for the administrators, but she had transferred to the Art Department a year ago. Talented as she was, she had no particular passion for it.

"Daddy knows Elder Wasserman and got me in here," she said.

"So, you're here for the heat, then?" I asked. I flung off another layer of clothes.

"I'm here for him." She jerked a thumb behind her. "Mr. Strauss." Through my experience with Annalise, I expected Mr. Strauss to be a dapper and handsome young man. He was dapper in his three-piece suit, but he was at least fifty. Only a dozen or so scraggly hairs sprouted around the rim of his head. I arched a brow worthy of Annalise at Julia, which made her laugh. "Umm...not like that."

Mr. Strauss had been an art dealer before the war. Julia's father bought paintings from him back when rich Jews could do business together. Now, he was our boss at the Art Department. Rumor had it he'd led the Czech resistance before his internment. Some said they still kept him well informed. If the size of his stomach was any indication, they kept him well fed too.

"He promised Daddy he'd keep me safe." Her eyes darted to the corner of the office away from the men chatting. "And if he can protect Ernst, he can protect anyone."

"Ernst?" I asked.

Julia pointed to a man I hadn't seen before painting alone around a corner. His hair—a mass of soft, black curls—would have made Annalise jealous. He was older than Julia and me, but like us, he wore a yellow star. Something was superimposed over the shape, though. A pink triangle. I puzzled over the symbol. Political prisoners wore red triangles, and criminals, green, but I'd never seen a pink one before.

"Before the war, Daddy wouldn't have let me even get close to one, but everything is different now. All those old rules seem kind of silly, don't they?" Ernst bent over an easel, his canvas a riot of color.

"Oh, c'mon, Julia." I laughed, certain she had to be kidding. "He's not...I mean...he can't really be..."

"A homosexual?" She raised her eyes from her post-card. "Oh, yes." Ernst startled at the word, obviously over-hearing us talk about him. Julia made no attempt to keep her voice down.

"What's he doing here?" I asked. Unlike Julia, I whispered. It wasn't a topic for full volume.

"Mr. Strauss insists he's an important modernist, but he has no skill for engineering, and the Nazis don't like his abstract stuff. Too modern for their tastes, I guess. *Degenerate*, they call it."

"What do the other men think?" I tried to imagine how Papa would react, but he was so far away, and this place was so strange. I couldn't even picture him here.

"Oh, they all just ignore him now," Julia said. She waved her fingers at the group of chattering men at the back. "One of the Hens almost hit him for talking to his lit-tle daughter, but Adam stopped him." She pointed to a young man in the center of the crowd. I couldn't be sure whether he was the outraged father or Adam. His face was clean-shaven but covered in nicks. His razor blade must have been old. He looked too young to have a daughter, and when he noticed us staring, he smiled and waved. Adam. Definitely Adam.

"Mr. Strauss told them a person shouldn't be an artist if they're afraid of homosexuals," Julia said.

Since I still couldn't bring myself to even look at Ernst, maybe I wasn't cut out to be an artist either.

Every day at lunchtime, the soup cart trundled up to the Art Department, and we'd empty into the street to eat our meal in the cold. I gnawed the hunk of black bread we got with our soup. I'd thought the bread at Horserød was bad, but at least it had been made with flour. I tried to pretend we ate Mama's *rugbröd*, filled with cracked whole grains and seeds, not the sawdust they used here.

The food they provided us lacked the nutrients to keep a person active for long. Plus, Annalise's job at the hospital and mine in the Art Department didn't bring in nearly enough money to buy much of anything at the ghetto store. Annalise earned a piece of cheese or bread every time she played piano for a private party. I earned a slice of margarine or half a potato for a portrait of a family member about to be transported away. Lukas stole more for us than Annalise and I earned combined.

My mouth watered when the inmate dipped the ladle deep into the soup pot. I'd learned in my month at Terezin that the farther down the ladle sank into the kettle, the heartier the meal. Broth didn't fill a stomach the way potatoes and meat did. I held up my bowl before any of it spilled back into the pot. I fought the urge to lick my lips, ashamed of my desperate hunger. When he'd emptied every drop into my bowl, I carefully brought it over as I sat on the rock wall beside Julia.

"Look at the *faygele*," said one of the artists Julia referred to as the Hens. Despite Rivka's Yiddish lessons, I didn't recognize the word. From the direction of his sneer, I knew who he was talking about, and that the word wasn't meant to be kind.

Ernst held out his bowl at the front of the soup line, hanging his head as if he already knew what would happen. The inmate stared at the pink triangle on Ernst's chest and skimmed the top of the soup, ladling only thin broth into his bowl.

"It's just wrong," I said.

"You couldn't even ask him to borrow a paintbrush the other day," said Julia.

I'd searched everywhere for the department's best brushes. When I realized Ernst had them, I begged her to intercede for me.

"It doesn't mean I want him to starve to death."

"He's not starving," Julia said. She was right. Ernst was lean but in an athletic way. Like Annalise and me, he must have supplemented his rations with extra work. Still. It wasn't right that the inmate gave him less food because of his pink triangle.

I should have pulled the soup server's memory of it so he would give Ernst some meat for once, but I had to save my energy. I hadn't pulled a memory in weeks. Two bowls of soup and a hunk of bad bread a day were hardly enough to live on, let alone make up for the drain my ability had on my strength.

Ernst brought his bowl—careful not to spill a drop—to the outskirts of our group. From behind me, Adam waved Ernst over to where he sat with the rest of the Hens.

Ernst looked around, certain Adam couldn't be addressing him. He trudged over as if resigned to a kick or an insult. Instead, Adam raised his bowl, nudging a chunk of potato to the rim with a finger. Ernst brought his bowl close, like they were making a toast, and the potato splashed into his broth.

He gave Adam a wordless nod and sat on the cold ground.

"Thank you, Adam," I mouthed. It was the kind of thing I would have liked to have done, though it never occurred to me to share one of my potatoes with anybody.

Julia flinched beside me, which meant the Cauliflower and his lackey, Officer Novak, had arrived for their daily inspection of the soup line. Annalise never saw the Cauliflower at the hospital, but he haunted the Art Department like a ghoul. He paid me no special attention, but I wondered if he somehow remembered me. After that day at the Sluice, I had plucked the memory of my face from his mind, but I still imagined him dragging me to the Little Fortress, my own screams echoing out to the surrounding gardens.

Julia didn't like the Cauliflower either, judging by the hunted look on her face whenever he came by.

Officer Novak passed out postcards to the lunching artists. "Be sure to tell your friends how well you're being treated." His words were more of a threat than a suggestion. He squeezed Julia's shoulder. She somehow looked smaller when he touched her.

I took a card from him. I hadn't sent one since that first day. "Now I'll get a chance to write what's really going on," I said to Julia the minute the guard moved out of earshot. My excitement drained out of me when I was confronted by my own brushstrokes on the front of the card.

Julia leaned against me. "You know Elder Tesler censors them. Tell them you're fine. Which you are. If they get a card covered in black marks—or not at all—they'll fear the worst. At least this way, they'll know you're all right."

But we weren't all right, and my non-Danish friends had it even worse. We ate our meager lunches. The cold bit through my coat. The latrine fouled the air from several blocks away. Annalise could reassure Uncle Stellan. I threw the postcard onto the ground and crushed it into the dirt with my foot, obliterating my handiwork.

Chapter Eleven

A TEAM OF INMATES shoveled a path through the snow down Berggasse. I slogged through the drifts rather than walk alongside their supervising gendarmes yelling orders. Snow collected inside my boots, which meant I'd have to sleep in my wet socks to keep them from freezing solid by morning.

I ran up the West Barracks' stairs, hoping to raise my temperature with a little exercise. What waited in my room, though, undid the effort and made my blood run cold.

The bottom bunk was mine, but Annalise was in it. A familiar sweet smell, coming off her sweaty brow in waves, polluted the room. The constant gnawing hunger disappeared as my stomach twisted into knots.

Rivka sat on the edge of the bed darning one of my sister's socks.

"Leah and I found her sitting on the steps." Rivka didn't look up from her sewing, only coughed into her hand and wiped her palm on her skirt.

Insulin and syringes arrived with regularity from the Danish Red Cross, but that wasn't the problem. My sister required little medication these days, a surprising silver lining of slowly starving to death.

If her shaky hands were any indication, her blood sugar had dropped. We had no access to sugar or juice. Lukas would have already stolen some for us, but she hadn't confessed her condition to him. I hoped she didn't expect me to fake a hypoglycemic attack. She was the performer in the family, not me. I flung open her suitcase to check the lining in case she had squirreled away a bit of sugar. She hadn't.

"Just one of my little fainting spells," Annalise said, her eyelids fluttering open and closed again. "You know how I get, Rachel."

"Fainting spell?" Rivka rolled her eyes. "Such *shtus*." She hooked a thumb at Annalise. "Leah went to get Gideon."

I was glad Rivka wasn't ignoring the diabetic elephant in the room. I didn't want Annalise to waste energy denying what Rivka had known for months. I didn't have to worry about that. Annalise hadn't heard her. She was out cold.

In the month Annalise had worked at the hospital, I'd never visited her there. I'd never smelled the horrid mix of extreme filth and the attempt to disinfect it. I'd never heard the moans of the sick and dying. I don't know how she stood it, but when a nurse recognized her, slung between Leah and me as we brought her in, and cleared a quiet corner for her, I was grateful they'd assigned her there.

"Maybe I can lay my hands on a couple of slices of potato. That might bring her back to us," said the nurse, and she disappeared through a door. Annalise sweated and shook and drained of color.

Without room for a chair beside the bed, I sat at her feet. I rubbed her toes through the blanket, a futile little effort, like a shrug in the dark.

"Gideon knows to tell Lukas she needs sugar?" I asked Leah.

She nodded. "Who else might be able to get some?"

"Mr. Strauss at the Art Department," I said.

"Would he be there this late?"

I nodded. We still had hours to curfew. Leah ran out the door we'd come in and left me alone with the sick.

The woman in the bed inches from my sister's sounded like Rivka when her pneumonia was at its worst. Even so, I preferred her to the girl on her other side who made no noise at all. What was the point of even bringing Annalise here?

I missed my mother. Maybe she could have taken better care of her.

A few minutes later, Julia arrived. Was she holding something? It wouldn't have to be big. A square of chocolate. A sugar cube. She wove through the narrow passages between the beds with empty hands.

"Mr. Strauss is working on it. Maybe by morning."

My heart sank. "That'll be too late." It would have to be Lukas.

Julia smoothed my hair and clasped my hands in hers.

The door opened again. My head shot up, hoping for Lukas. Ernst froze when he saw me.

"What's he doing here?" I asked. I blotted Annalise's damp forehead with a corner of her blanket.

"He was in the room when Leah came in to explain it all to Mr. Strauss," said Julia.

"I don't want him spreading rumors about Annalise."

"Who would he tell?" Julia asked. She curled up at the foot of the bed of the child beside us. The girl didn't stir, and I told myself that she was only sleeping soundly. "No one talks to him."

"Well, I don't like him lurking," I said, but he had already left out the door he came in.

"She's going to be okay," Julia said.

I squeezed Annalise's hands, willing her to squeeze back.

"You don't have to stay," I said.

"I'll stay until curfew." She covered herself with her sweater, using it like a blanket. "I don't sleep well in Dresden anyway."

I wouldn't sleep well in the women's barracks either. All those sounds and smells cramped into one tiny room. In my head, I thanked King Christian again for West Barracks and all of our comparable luxuries.

"I get scared," she said.

Of what? Disease? Hunger? Transport?

"We're all scar—"

"No, Rachel."

Julia closed her eyes, not to sleep but to avoid meeting my gaze. "I'm petrified I'll wake up and find him smiling over me again."

"Who's...What?"

"There's a streetlamp outside my bunkhouse window. When he woke me, there was light enough to see his finger on his lips and his gun pointed at my sister's head."

Every muscle in my body tightened like a coiled spring.

"He climbed on top of me, and I knew what he wanted." She flinched when I gasped. I tried to stay quiet after that.

I remembered how scared she looked every time the Cauliflower inspected the Art Department.

"Oh, Julia. The Cauliflower?"

"No, his shadow. The one who's always with him. Officer Novak."

Her chin trembled. "He never stopped smiling. That's all I see when I close my eyes. Those teeth, washed silver in the streetlight. I'm all right when I see him around the ghetto until he smiles. It undoes me when he smiles."

"What can I do?" I reached across my unconscious sister and rubbed her arm.

"You're doing it." She opened one eye. "Thank you." A few minutes later, she slept, but not peacefully.

She twitched with a nightmare. I couldn't heal my sister or undo what had happened to my friend, but I could spare her that pain. I pictured the image of Officer Novak's silver smile and pulled it from her mind. She stilled and slept like the child beside her after that.

Julia woke when the nurse rushed over. My German couldn't keep up with her excitement. Julia was too groggy to understand either.

"Is the war over?" Julia asked.

The nurse shook her head and held up a tiny bottle.

The amber liquid inside barely looked like enough for three cups of tea, but it would be enough to save my sister. The nurse uncapped the little bottle and took a spoon out of her apron pocket.

"Where did you find *honey*?"

"It wasn't me. I found it at the nurse's station with your name on it." She handed me a little slip of paper. In barely legible writing, it said *Rachel*.

"Who could have left it?" I asked.

"No idea," the nurse said. She dipped the spoon into the tiny jar and brought it to Annalise's mouth, careful not to lose a precious drop. The nurse used a tongue depressor to scrape the excess off the spoon.

It would be the kind of thing Gideon would do, sacrifice so much for us and leave it at the desk like a secret, but my name was hardly legible on the little label. Gideon's handwriting was like a typewriter. Maybe some friend of Annalise's at the hospital? But they would have come in or at least left their name.

It had to be Lukas.

Gideon must have found him, and he'd swiped what she needed. Maybe Gideon warned Lukas not to come in, that Annalise would be horrified if he knew.

I wanted to rush over to the nurse's station to see if I could catch him there, but Annalise groaned and her eyelids fluttered.

I positioned my face so it would be the first thing she saw when she opened her eyes. Would she even recognize me? The last time this happened, Mama had grabbed her a glass of juice within minutes and no damage was done. How long had she been out this time before we'd gotten her the sugar she needed? An hour? Two? Had the honey come too late? I leaned over her, smoothing her hair from her sweaty forehead. I wasn't a religious person, but in that moment, I prayed.

Please let her be all right.

Her eyes opened. Were they hazy with sleep or something more permanent?

"Hi, Kitten."

Chapter Twelve

THE FIRST NIGHT OF Hanukkah was the coldest day we'd had in Terezin yet. Instead of sneaking sips of Mama's warm *glögg* and eating fresh-baked *klejner* beside a cozy fire, Annalise and I both squeezed into my bunk with all of our clothes piled on top of us.

"We could eat the sugar as a treat," Annalise said. Mr. Strauss had come through with a small packet of sugar the morning after Annalise woke from her diabetic coma. The honey had done the trick, but we still appreciated the gift. We kept it hidden in her mattress and hoped we'd never need it.

"Absolutely not," I said, although my mouth watered at the thought of the sweet granules melting on my tongue.

Gideon had insisted that he'd never found Lukas that night. Lukas had been on guard duty and couldn't be reached, but the honey had to be from him. Who else could it have been?

"Do you think Mama will let Anders light the menorah this year?" Annalise asked. My brother pestered our parents every year, promising to even forgo presents if allowed to light the first candle and say the prayer. Mama maintained that the head of the household should always light it, to which Papa would hand her the matches.

I'd sworn to myself I wouldn't cry thinking about my family in Stockholm without us, but once Annalise began, I joined in.

On my way to work the next morning, I stopped at West's washroom to throw some water on my puffy eyes. Only frigid water belched from its sinks, but at least it ran clear and the toilets flushed.

When I opened the door, someone's racking cough resounded through the room, and I wondered if I should go in. Sick people were to be avoided at all costs. The coughs came from the toilet warden in the chair at the end of the row of sinks. She lifted her head, and I forgot all about germs.

"Rivka?" I asked.

"I look that bad, huh?" she asked back. "You don't recognize me?" The truth was, I barely had. Sweat covered her face, and her chest convulsed with each wet, sticky shudder of breath.

"What are you doing here?" I asked. Rivka hadn't been assigned to a job because of her age.

"Old Mrs. Kravitz died on Wednesday." Mrs. Kravitz had been at least ten years younger than Rivka. "I'm filling in." We had our Yiddish lessons on Tuesdays and Thursdays, but it had been too cold this week to get out of bed, so I hadn't heard.

A woman rushed out the washroom stall and to the door. "Hey, you *schlump*!" Rivka yelled at her. "Wash your hands. Do you want to give us all typhus?"

If in the proper state of health, I could imagine no one better suited for the role of toilet warden than Rivka. The Germans realized typhus ignored the SS's strict social stratification. It struck guards and inmates alike. Everywhere posters reminded us to wash our hands. Julia's artwork donned the walls in West's restroom. They installed toilet wardens too, usually the old or disabled, to police proper hygiene.

The woman scurried to the bank of sinks—choosing the one farthest from Rivka—to wash her hands before running out the door. Rivka leaned forward in her chair and coughed, clutching her knees.

I touched my hand to her forehead. "You have a fever, Rivka. You shouldn't be working. You should be in the hospital. Annalise will take care of you."

"Don't be a *schmendrick*," she said.

"So rude." I spread my hand over my heart, pretending to be hurt by the insult. "C'mon, you *alter cocker*."

She smiled at the phrase. "It hardly matters where I die, Rachel."

"You'll die back in Denmark, in your own bed." I smiled back at her, despite the growing tightness in my chest.

I tried to lift her out of the chair. Her skin was as thin as the tracing paper in the Art Department, but her arms felt like bands of steel.

"No."

"At least let me take you back to your room." I grabbed under her arm again, and the muscle loosened.

"I'm coming. You don't have to get rough with the *alter cocker*."

On the third step of West, she collapsed. The Blume sisters were coming out and helped me get her to her room. She'd lost so much weight, though, I was able to carry her myself. They left us to get Leah at the bakery where she worked.

Rivka came to once I got her into bed. She coughed violently, and blood streaked her palm when she lowered it from her mouth.

I broke apart the thin layer of ice in the cracked pitcher on a shelf and filled their single cup. I brought it to her lips. She couldn't lift her head, but she smiled with mischievous nostalgia.

"The pitcher reminds me of that old silver coffeepot of mine." She laughed, bringing about a new bout of coughing and more blood on her palm. "You remember. From the train? How many cups of coffee do you suppose some Nazi has drank out of that *schmutsik* old thing?"

"Please let me get you to a doctor, Rivka." I got her a handkerchief, and she wiped her hand clean.

"I am eighty-three years old. Chances were good I wasn't going to survive the war anyway."

"Mr. Strauss said the Germans are losing in Russia. It all could be over soon. We could go home." The burning in the back of my throat turned my voice into a rasp, making the lie sound even more desperate.

"I'm ready, *bubbeleh*." Her breathing sounded like she was underwater. "One last Yiddish lesson for the road."

"No, Rivka. Save your energy."

"*Mishpachah*." She cradled my cheek in her palm like I had seen her do to Leah. "Family." My tears spilled onto her hand.

"*Mishpachah*," I repeated.

She nodded several times until she fell asleep.

Leah flew into the room minutes after my tears for Rivka dried. The months in Terezin melted away enough of Leah's extra weight so she could slip into the space between Rivka and me. She cupped her mother-in-law's wrinkled hands into her own. Her work in the bakery might have provided her family with a bit more bread, but her hands had paid dearly. Multiple burns ran up to where her sleeves began.

Ragged breaths shook Rivka's frail form. Until they stopped.

I thought I had finished crying.

Leah and I were still bent over Rivka's body when a cheer erupted in the hallway. Their joy hurt my ears. I swung open the door ready to tear into whoever was making such a delighted commotion, but an inmate with a stack of Red Cross parcels greeted me at Leah's threshold.

"Leah and Eli Hecht?"

"I'm Leah," she said behind me. She wiped her face and sniffed. "My boy is at the children's home during the day."

The man ticked a check mark next to their names without batting an eye at her tears. They were a common enough sight in Terezin. He passed two parcels to Leah.

"Rivka Hecht?" he asked. He held up another package. The parcels of the dead were returned to the SS for redistribution. That box contained enough food to dull the ache in my gut.

I put a finger to my lips. "She's sleeping," I whispered. Leah's eyes widened, but she didn't correct me. He glanced over to her body in the bed. Would he notice she wasn't breathing or the blood on her palm?

The inmate handed me her parcel and whispered, "Give it to her when she wakes up."

King of Denmark was stamped in the corner of the box. I mumbled an apology to my king.

I thrust Rivka's package at Leah. I needed to go before I ripped it open and devoured its contents. Besides, I had to get upstairs in case parcels came for Annalise and me.

She held up her hands, refusing to touch it. "Take it," Leah said. "You were always so good to her."

"No, Leah. You should give it to Eli," I said, but couldn't take my eyes off it.

"Please take it." She turned away to face the wall. "I can't bear to look at it."

I was sad—I really was—but I was hungrier. I fled the room, Rivka's parcel under my arm, too ashamed to thank her.

I tore into it like a wild animal. No one noticed. Hundreds of ravenous people devoured the contents of identical boxes all over West that day.

Two additional parcels waited for Annalise and me in our room, and we had an enamored gendarme to steal for us. Leah had a child to feed. No parcels were coming to Julia or the others in the Art Department. None of this stopped me from inhaling chunks of processed cheese and handfuls of raisins.

The Germans may have been losing the war in Russia, but they were winning the war for my soul.

By the time I got to the Art Department, I was two hours late. No one noticed. Everyone had crowded around Mr. Strauss. I slipped into the throng beside Julia.

"The SS raided Elder Cohen's room last night. They found enough contraband to rationalize an arrest for dealing on the black market," Mr. Strauss said.

Like Elder Tesler, Elder Cohen served on the Jewish Council. The SS appointed them to make the transport lists and censor our postcards. They were no better than Nazi pawns.

"They brought him to the Little Fortress this morning," said Mr. Strauss.

I hated Cohen and all the other elders, but no one deserved that. The mere mention of that dark, terrifying place made bile rise to my throat.

Or maybe it was all Rivka's food.

"He'll be transported east and placed on a work crew in a couple of days. A good reminder to keep your quarters clear of anything that could be considered contraband," Mr. Strauss said. At the Sluice, they'd called Annalise's fur coat and Jubilee, the stuffed pony, contraband. There was no way to avoid it. Everyone made their way back to their desks.

"Now maybe we can get an elder on the Council who will do some good," Adam said once we were back in our seats. Julia, Adam, and I had become a tight little trio in the time since Adam had given his potato to Ernst.

"They're in an unwinnable situation," Julia said. She sounded like Gideon. No doubt she was thinking of Elder Wasserman, the family friend who'd gotten her transferred to the Art Department. She picked up a pencil and got back to work. "They have to do what the Nazis want."

"Well, Elder Cohen ended up in the Little Fortress anyway," I said.

"Maybe it'll be better for him in the east," Adam said. He smiled. I almost gave him one of Gideon's cynical snorts, but I stopped myself. How could someone who had been through all he had still have such kind eyes?

They'd shot his father in front of him for stealing food in Neuengamme, the last camp he'd been in. His mother and sisters were transported somewhere in the east, but his talent for engineering earned him a transfer to Terezin. I tried to nod, but fell into my chair and dropped my head into my hands instead.

"What's bothering you?" Julia asked without taking her eyes off the poster she worked on. She added a swastika around the words *Curfew is at* 9:00 PM.

Julia never mentioned her visit to the hospital or what she had revealed to me there, but she never complained of insomnia again after I pulled the memory of her tormentor's smile from her mind.

"A friend died." Death was hardly newsworthy. Still, Adam gave his condolences, and Julia looked up from the poster.

"She was old," I said. That Rivka was old didn't make it all right, but my friends had lost more. Both of them had lost family, bunkmates, and friends already. A pile of postcards waiting to be painted sat on my desk. Adam had sketched them this time. Work might help me forget.

On the postcard, a fertile field of grain surrounded the princess castle of Terezin. I lifted my brush and dipped it into the paint. The lie of the rich golden yellow struck me like a punch.

A fat tear dropped onto the card, making the black ink run. "Oh, Adam. I'm sorry. I've ruined it."

Adam took a cloth and blotted the tear, leaving a huge smudge right at its center. "Are you kidding? You've improved it." He opened the drawer to his desk. A dozen sheets filled it, all drawings of Terezin, but bucolic vistas were nowhere to be seen.

They portrayed a trail of bowed heads in the food line, men stacked like kindling at the men's barracks, and Officer Novak, his wooden baton in midflight. I wanted to look at them more closely, to submerge myself in their horror, but the specter of the Little Fortress lurked. Adam could get transported for those pictures. Hadn't

Mr. Strauss just warned us of the ever-present threat of a raid?

He placed my tear-splattered postcard with the others with care and said, "There's beauty in the ugliest truth."

"You should come," Annalise said when I got back to West that night. She was set to entertain for a birthday party at the women's barracks. Even after long days at the hospital, her vibrant energy kept her in high demand.

"Yeah, c'mon, Rachel," Lukas said. "It'll cheer you up."

I made a face. "I need to draw." I sat down to finish the sketch I'd started.

Adam's pile of pictures of life in Terezin had inspired me. Pulled memories produced my most vivid art, but I always burned those drawings. I hadn't considered what they were.

Proof. Testimony.

I had stopped using my ability to spare myself the exhaustion, but now I pledged to do it every day. Once I'd made the resolution, I raced to Leah's room and pulled the image of Rivka's body from her mind. I appraised the drawing, my arms extended.

I'd drawn Rivka in her bunk. She faced the viewer, her mouth slack in death. The Red Cross parcel sat on her bed at her feet, its brown paper untouched. The caption at the bottom read *Too Late*. Annalise and Lukas peeked at it. They shared a grimace at the morbid drawing.

I had just signed the bottom with a flamboyant flourish when Gideon appeared in our doorframe. He hadn't knocked. He never did.

"Not sure I'm in the mood for a party, but I'll tag along for some of Reiner's wife's turnips," he said in Danish, not having seen Lukas right away.

"When are you ever in the mood for a party?" Annalise asked in German so Lukas could understand.

Gideon narrowed his eyes at the gendarme.

"Parties are overrated," he said, still speaking Danish.

"You can talk in front of him, Gideon," I said in German. "He's a friend."

Maybe it was crazy to trust Lukas. He was one of the guards, after all, but Annalise and I would have suffered more without the food he stole for us. Plus, he made my sister as happy as she could be in this place.

"I don't trust uniforms." He frowned at the arm slung around Annalise's neck. "You shouldn't either."

"You realize *uniform* is the same in Danish and German, right?" Lukas clapped Gideon on the back. Lukas seemed to struggle with the concept that someone genuinely disliked him. As two young men who made girls giggle behind their hands, he would have seen Gideon as a natural ally, but that wasn't enough for Gideon.

I winced when Lukas and Annalise laughed. Even with Rivka's picture in my hand, I had almost forgotten.

Gideon shook his head and threw his chin at me. "What's wrong with you?"

"Rivka died this morning." I swiped eraser crumbs from my sketch. Gideon examined it over my shoulder. He took it from my hands to get a closer look.

"I'm sorry to hear that," he said, but his voice didn't sound sympathetic. "But drawing something like this?" He poked at the corner bearing my name. "Signed? Are you crazy?"

"I'm a witness. I have to sign my name," I said.

"What are you talking about?" he asked.

"Mr. Strauss is smuggling artwork to the Czech resistance so people will know what's going on here."

Gideon's eyes flew to Lukas. "Rachel..."

I waved his concerns about Lukas away. "Adam says my drawings are good enough."

"Adam?" he asked. He shook the sketch as if throttling it. "So, you're just doing this because some boy flattered your work? To impress him?" Without warning, he ripped off the corner bearing my signature, taking some of Rivka's bed with it.

The tear felt like a physical assault. "Don't!" I yelled and reached for the picture before he could do more damage to it. He flung the drawing away from both of us, and it fluttered to the ground.

I scurried to the floor after it. "I needed to draw this," I said. I couldn't tell him about my ability but hoped to convey the urgency. His shoulders slumped, and he spoke under his breath.

"I know," he whispered. "You'll wear yourself out, Rachel." He scrubbed his face with his hand as if he were erasing the conversation. "Drawings like that shouldn't be floating around with your name on it." He headed for the door.

"What about the turnips?" Annalise asked.

Gideon looked over his shoulder at me. "I'm not hungry anymore," he said.

Once Gideon was gone, Annalise turned her attention back to me. "Come to the party, Rachel. Reiner's wife's turnips are really good." I was still full from Rivka's parcel.

"Yeah, Rachel. Come with us," Lukas said. "I'll dance with you since Annalise will be playing. It'll get your mind off it."

"I don't want to get my mind off it." I brushed a finger over Rivka's still form in the drawing. I wanted the opposite, to immerse myself in grief.

"We don't sit around moping in my family when someone dies," Lukas said, swinging a companionable arm around me. His father passed away years ago, leaving him the man of the house when he was still a kid himself, with three younger sisters and a sickly mother. "We celebrate life. Dancing. Food." He gathered Annalise into his other arm, curling her into him. "Love."

There'd be a time when I'd reminisce with Leah and Eli about Rivka's Yiddish curses and her coffeepot. I might celebrate the beauty and laughter of her life someday, but for now, I wanted to document the injustice and ugliness of her death.

Chapter Thirteen

My seventeenth birthday that March should have been like all the others, surrounded by my family and friends in my beloved Copenhagen, not in a freezing Nazi ghetto. Annalise hosted a little party in the music cellar for me. The place was hardly festive with its sweaty walls and a cracked cement floor that reminded me of the shower room. My coworkers from the Art Department did not make up for my family either, but I appreciated the effort.

"It still surprises me they let us have these get-togethers," said one of the Hens. He tapped his feet in time to the music.

"They're too good to us," Leah said. She bit into one of the apples Lukas had stolen for the occasion.

"You sound like Rivka," I said.

"I do?" Leah asked.

I'd congratulated myself for saving her from some of the pain of losing her beloved mother-in-law, but I didn't like the far-off expression that flitted over her face when she tried to picture her.

"Well, it's true," Leah said. "It's hard to feel grateful."

"Careful what you say, Leah," Annalise said. Her fingers didn't stop dancing over the piano keys. "There's a spy in our midst." She winked at Lukas.

Lukas feigned outrage. "I can take these back if I'm not welcome," he said. Our bandit gendarme scooped up the apples.

"Oh, no, Mr. Lukas!" cried one of the Hens' daughters. At four, she didn't recognize the twinkle of sarcasm in Lukas's eyes.

"Well, if *you'd* like me to stay, Sadie..." He tossed her an apple, which she crunched into without pause.

"I hope you're happy, Sadie. Now he'll be watching our every move," Annalise said.

"Just *your* every move, *miláček*," said Lukas, using the Czech endearment he saved for my sister.

Gideon rolled his eyes.

"Stop it, Gideon," I whispered to him. "He saved her life with that honey."

"You don't know that," he said.

"He has the stickiest fingers in the whole ghetto. Plus, he loves her. He'd do anything for her."

"Exactly." He poked a finger into my shoulder. "Love makes you do stupid things. He'd make some big, dramatic show of it." It hurt, for some reason, hearing Gideon disparage people in love. I elbowed him so he wouldn't see how his words affected me and get the wrong idea.

"What a romantic you are. If you ever fell in love with one of those girls you spend time with in that cubby of yours, you'd do anything to protect her."

The muscles around his lips tightened. "You're right. I would."

My chest hurt. Who would she be? Too many to choose from if the rumors were true.

Mr. Strauss stepped forward to address everyone. "The war will be over soon. Once the Americans invade Europe, we'll have a real party." He raised his tin cup of water like a flute of champagne. "But until then..." Mr. Strauss presented me with a gift from his vest pocket. "For the birthday girl."

Back home, the present might have been a gold charm bracelet or a pair of fine kid leather gloves. Here, he had tucked six meal tickets into a small box. I threw my arms around him, all professional propriety forgotten in the extravagance of his present.

Several of the men laughed, including Mr. Strauss himself.

"Now I'm kicking myself for not bringing a gift," said one of the other artists. I covered my face with my hands, my smile showing between my fingers.

"Don't embarrass her," said Adam. He handed over half a sausage wrapped in wax paper. "It's not much." He must have bought it on the black market or another Dane sold it to him from their monthly parcel.

"Thank you." He earned a hug too, although not as exuberant as Mr. Strauss's. It still elicited a rumble of chuckles among the men. I drew myself out of Adam's arms, but not before Gideon's knuckles cracked again.

Julia passed me a small copy of stories by Hans Christian Andersen with a twine bow. "I always found him a little grim—mermaids turning into seafoam and all—but I thought you'd like to have something in your own language."

I flicked through the book, hoping it didn't have a name already inscribed or a bookmark between its pages.

"Don't worry, Rachel. I didn't buy it at the ghetto store," Julia said. I loved that she understood. "I learned Danish with that book."

Another one of the Hens handed me a package wrapped in a discarded curfew poster covered in swastikas. I wouldn't have thought gently used socks could elicit tears of joy, but it turned out they could.

These people should not have gotten me gifts. They weren't Danish. They didn't receive monthly parcels. They were piled on top of one another in disease-ridden barracks, separated from their families. But I was hungry and cold, so I took them.

"Oh, the *faygele* has something too?" one of the artists asked.

Our awkward attention fell on Ernst. He must have realized my sister invited him as a joke. He didn't leave the cellar's shadowy corner, just thrust a rolled-up paper with an outstretched hand. The cylinder had a delicate

yellow ribbon tied in a bow. I slipped it off without unty-
ing it. I'd find another use for it.

Mr. Strauss had said Ernst was a brilliant modernist,
but this painting was as lifelike as a photograph. He'd captured my desperation and Annalise's beauty so exactly, I
might have been jealous, but looking at the painting, so
faithful to that horrible night in the hospital, I only relived
the pain of it.

Hospital beds stretched out to the horizon, each occupied with skeletal shapes. Ernst conveyed movement in
their flailing limbs and their agonized groans with their
O-shaped mouths. Annalise's sleeping form illuminated
the foreground, her vitality in stark contrast to the undulating horde of horrors behind her. The light emanating
from my sister reflected off the tears on my face. It made
me think of what Adam had said about the tear-stained
postcard. *There's beauty in the ugliest truth.*

"What did *he* paint?" Annalise didn't try to hide her disapproval of Ernst. She exchanged a look with Lukas, and
they both giggled. "Nothing dirty, I hope." Ernst withdrew
deeper into the dark corner.

Julia peered over my shoulder at the picture. "It's you
and Rachel." I rolled the picture back up, fumbling with
the ribbon, trying to get it back around the paper. The
piano stopped, and Annalise hopped up, ready to admire
herself.

"I'll show you *later*," I said through my fakest smile to
warn her, but she rushed to see how he'd memorialized
her. She snatched the roll from my hands. The painting
piqued Lukas's interest too, which would only make it
worse.

He'd painted her like a renaissance martyr, not like a
Hollywood starlet. The flash of anger fled in a moment.

"*Skjul det nu*," she said through clenched teeth. I did as
she asked and rolled it back up and stuck it in my skirt
pocket without the yellow ribbon. She hooked Lukas's
arm on her way back to the piano, saying something
about needing him to turn the pages for her.

Either people didn't notice the chill coming off Annalise or had enough tact to ignore it, and the party continued. A minute later, Gideon pointed to Annalise and whispered in my ear, "What was that about?"

I turned my back to the crowd and took the painting out. Annalise would kill me if she caught me showing anyone, but it was too remarkable not to share. Ernst's painting was everything I ever wanted my drawings to be. Even when I sketched people's memories, my work wasn't this alive. When I unrolled it, Gideon swore. I wasn't sure if it was for the beauty of its artistry or the horror of its subject.

"Who gives a picture like this as a birthday gift?" I asked.

"It's not my style," said Gideon, "but you always say art should make you feel something."

"He'll feel a swift kick in the *tuches* when Annalise gets a chance." I dropped my voice to a whisper. "I don't know why she invited him. I've hardly ever spoken to him."

Gideon laughed.

"What's so funny?" I asked.

"You. You're not too afraid of hunger to give your food away. You're not too afraid of death to stand up to the scariest man in the ghetto." He poked me in the shoulder. "But you're afraid of what people will think if you're decent to the homosexual?" Gideon left my side to get one of Lukas's apples. I glanced behind me to Ernst's corner, but it was empty.

I took out the painting, marveling at its movement and emotion, its shadow and light. It broke my heart, but I wanted to look at it forever.

"Whether she likes it or not," Mr. Strauss said, sneaking up behind me, "you should keep that picture." He pointed to Ernst's messy, unreadable swirl of a signature in the bottom corner. "It'll be worth a lot of money after the war."

Lukas, Annalise, and I were cleaning up the cellar after the party when Gideon reappeared with something hidden behind his back and a smile on his face.

"Ooh, another gift!" Annalise screeched. "Promise you'll share, Rachel."

Gideon shook his head. "Sorry, Annalise." Although he directed his words at my sister, he didn't take his eyes off me. "This is all Rachel's. Close your eyes."

He demonstrated, squeezing his eyes shut and opening them again.

I copied him and held out my hands, not sure how big the surprise was. Gideon occasionally brought us extra food or half a candle—albeit with less theatrics than this.

Annalise gasped. "Oh, Gideon! Where did you find it?" she asked. I wiggled my fingers, feeling for a clue.

"Isn't she a little old for that?" Lukas asked.

Gideon shushed them and placed something soft in my hands. It wasn't a loaf of bread or a pat of margarine. A sweater, maybe? I opened my eyes.

Jubilee.

"He was in the ghetto store," Gideon said. I stared up at his delighted face. "I worried someone would buy it or they'd send him back to Germany for some Aryan child before I could save up enough to get it, but I'd done some extra work and..." He trailed off, not wanting to make me feel guilty for the trouble he must have gone to.

"Gideon." Jubilee's mane had gotten matted in the six months since I'd seen him. I combed the hair—the exact shade of Erik's—with my fingers like I'd seen Mama do to my brothers before school. The stuffed animal blurred through my tears.

I threw my arms around Gideon and kissed his cheek. When I let go, Annalise's eyebrow had arched practically to her hairline, and Lukas smirked like he'd gotten away with something very bad. They assumed Gideon's gift had something to do with sex, but everything had to do with sex with those two.

Gideon wriggled out of my arms and craned his neck as far from my face as possible.

"I know how much Jubilee means to Erik," he said.

"Uh-huh," Annalise said, her voice dripping with sarcasm. "We all know how much you love *Erik*."

Chapter Fourteen

THE WINTER'S FREEZING TEMPERATURES slowed the flow of new inmates. It also killed all the lice. When the warm weather returned in spring, so did the overcrowding and my itchy scalp.

New residents came from all over the Third Reich—Hungary, Austria, Germany, and the Netherlands. Some even came from Denmark.

A clerical error had sent a dozen or so Danes to the German camps of Ravensbrück and Oranienburg instead of Terezin back in October. Rumor had it the Danish government had been demanding their transfer for months.

Gideon and I paced outside the train depot with other Danes waiting for their arrival. Would one of the people that got off the train be a classmate? A family friend? What news from home would they bring? There had been bombings in Copenhagen. We'd sent our postcards, but we'd received no word from home. Were there craters in Tivoli Gardens? Was my apartment building still standing?

I didn't recognize anyone on the train, but their own mothers might not have been able to. Any thought of interrogating them disappeared. I only wished I had brought food. No luncheon in the park waited for these Danes.

Their clothes matched their skin—gray and stretched over bones. I could count the strands of sinew that held a woman's head to her body.

We didn't have much hidden away, but the new arrivals were so starved, any crumb would have been a feast. Even non-Danes in Terezin, without the extra parcels and better living conditions, didn't look like the living skeletons that came off that train. I could have picked any of them up and carried them to the showers. Some of them needed exactly that.

Gideon passed around a pitcher of water and a pair of cups. Annalise found the only young male and flirted with him, lighting up his pale, malnourished face. Gideon handed a cup to me, nodding at a woman who had fallen to the ground beside the tracks.

I sprinted over and handed it to her, careful not to spill it. She lifted her hand with great effort to take it.

"You're safe now," I said. Yesterday, I would have considered that a lie. We were hardly safe here, but it was a haven compared to whatever anguish she'd been through. Another woman came and helped her stand. They supported one another and followed the Czech gendarme escorting them to the showers.

The gate beside the train spur stood open even after the new arrivals were gone. Several of the inmates who were harvesting one of the fields came and went from the exit. A girl my age with two long braids shuffled in, her clothes coated with dirt. She ducked into a nearby alley out of the guards' line of vision.

Her pants were billowy and tied off at the cuff, but the legs were somehow misshapen, and she had a limp. I couldn't identify what was wrong with her until a potato fell out at her ankle. She caught me watching and froze. I smiled and lifted a hand to wave. When she bent to pick up the potato, three more dropped out.

Her comedic fumblings over her plunder almost had me chuckling until the Cauliflower emerged at a door between us and saw her struggling to hide what she'd obviously stolen.

He took four long strides toward her, his face glowing red. He ripped his wooden baton from its holster and swung it up to strike her from behind. She didn't see him coming. She had her back to him, stuffing the potatoes back into her lumpy pants.

I could pull the memory from his mind, but she would still be standing there with a dozen stolen potatoes. I had to pull his attention as well as the memory.

"Commander Gruber!" The second the Cauliflower turned to face me, I pulled the image of the girl with potatoes. I was so busy erasing the memory from him, I had no time to think of an excuse for having called out to him with such urgency. I gained a moment when he looked down at the baton in his hand, as if wondering how it had gotten there.

I caught a glimpse of the train, just behind a frozen Annalise and Gideon.

"I think some of those Danes need medical attention, sir," I said. It was the best I could do. His fingers tightened around the baton. I couldn't help but stare at the weapon. Gideon had told me he'd beaten an inmate to death in the last camp he served in. Had he done it with that very baton?

"You're one of them, aren't you?" the Cauliflower asked, and in three long strides, he was in front of me. His nostrils flared like a bull about to charge, and I was the red cape.

Potato Pants scurried to pick up the remaining potatoes.

"You think you're so important." A shower of spit hit me in the face with each word, but I didn't dare wipe at it or move away. "But you'll all learn one of these days."

I dared another glance up to see the girl stagger down the rest of the alley and into the children's home. The kids would have potatoes tonight.

"I'm so sorry, sir." I would scrape and bow if that's what he needed. He twirled a finger around a lock of my hair and yanked down hard. I cried out in pain, not because it hurt but because it would please him. The Cauliflower looked satisfied by my change in attitude and joined a cluster of Czech gendarmes.

Annalise tugged my sleeve and whisked me out of sight. We passed Gideon—as red with anger as the Cauliflower. I fled before he could yell at me too.

That night in the music cellar, Rabbi Hertz married Hanka and Jacob, the couple who had hidden in that church attic with Gideon six months ago back in Rungsted. Jacob had come to Denmark from Poland in 1939, just before the invasion. The Danish government insisted everyone brought to Terezin from Denmark be treated as a citizen, so he lived in West Barracks with the rest of us. He received parcels from the Danish Red Cross, the same seal from our king in the corner.

"Look at the ladies cluck over her," Julia said over the din of the party. The bride cupped her hands over her swollen stomach. A half dozen female inmates chatted excitedly around her. "What a scandal it would've been before the war." She clapped in time with Annalise's piano.

Julia was right. Hanka wasn't even trying to hide her pregnancy from the other inmates. There wasn't any need. We all felt protective of her and her unborn child. It was illegal to have a baby in the ghetto, so it was an act of resistance too, like trading on the black market for the food that made up the wedding feast or smuggling in the contraband hot plate that heated it.

"Just look at my mother." Julia pointed to the woman who had her hand on Hanka's rounded stomach. "She was such a terrible snob before, but none of that matters now."

If my family had been there, Anders and Hans would have chased the other children. Erik would have found a willing ear for one of his stories. I had no idea what

Birgitte would be doing. Guilt tugged at my heart. Her first birthday had come and gone.

Julia patted my shoulder. "You miss your family," she said.

"Of course I do."

"Be thankful, Rachel. Missing them means they aren't here," Julia said. I stared at my feet, not wanting to admit that some days I missed them so much I didn't care.

Annalise and her piano shifted from the exuberant hopsa into a less spirited tune, and the dancers slowed to a sway. Hanka's brother asked Julia to dance. She squeezed my shoulder again before joining him.

With Julia gone and nothing to distract me, my head itched. The lice were even worse than in the fall. I'd just lifted my hand to my head to scratch when Gideon came in.

I'd successfully avoided him for the few hours since my run-in with the Cauliflower at the train depot. I headed toward Annalise at the piano, but he was at my side in a couple of quick steps.

"Where do you think you're going?" His voice practically rumbled.

"I'm going to turn pages for Annalise."

"She doesn't need you to do that."

"No, but I'm sick of lectures from you, and from the look on your face, you weren't coming over here to ask me to dance."

We both started, and his lip quirked into a half smile.

He reached out his hand. "Rachel Abramson, would you dance with me?"

He and I never danced at these things. For me, it was an inappropriate demonstration of joy in such a place, like dancing under the gallows. Gideon just didn't like dancing. Or music. Or people.

I took his hand. His borrowed threadbare vest fit like it was made for him. My hand fit his the same way.

His thumb grazed my knuckles, spreading warmth to each finger and eventually everything else. I almost tore myself out of his arms in surprise at the pleasant feeling, but at the same moment, Gideon drew me closer. He smiled, probably relieved by my sudden quiet. I reminded myself to let him lead.

"You missed the wedding," I said.

"I was busy."

"With what?" I don't know why I pretended not to know. When Gideon hadn't come to the ceremony, Hanka hinted he was spending time with Miriam Levy these days. I bet Miriam didn't have a stubborn case of lice.

"It's better you don't know." His eyebrows drew together like he wanted to take it back, to take back the hurt he could probably read in my eyes. I hated the pity I could see in his. "The postcards looked good this month," he said, changing the subject. "Nice job." They distributed cards I'd colored to the Danish inmates this afternoon.

I shrugged. I still hated being a cog in the Nazi propaganda machine. I also hated that he felt a need to soften the blow regarding his little visitors with compliments of my artwork.

"Thanks. Adam did the sketch, though." Gideon's smile faltered. He still blamed Adam for my secret drawing endeavor. I'd continued to draw the harsh realities of the ghetto, but in deference to Gideon's concerns, I'd stopped signing them before handing them over to Mr. Strauss. Gideon didn't recognize the compromise and resented Adam for encouraging me.

"What did you write on yours?" he asked. Gideon disguised secret messages in his cards home better than I did. Subtlety eluded me. I tried, though. I hoped, this time, my card to Uncle Stellan would make it through the censors without a black line through it.

"I said I missed Mama's smoked herring."

"You would have to be starving to eat those things." He gave me an approving nod. "Everyone knows how much you hate them. Well done."

"See? I can control myself."

Gideon pursed his lips as if he wanted to bring up the Cauliflower and Potato Pants, but didn't. "You are a picture of restraint."

I fought the urge to scratch my scalp. "Annalise bragged to Mrs. Madsen about her choir, so *that'll* get through," I said. "What did you tell Mrs. Johansen?" Since Gideon's family was in Stockholm like mine, he wrote his postcards to his neighbor.

"I sent my regards to Mr. Muller." His grin was loaded with mischief.

"The baker?" I pictured him filling bags with loaves of bread, his apron dusty with flour. It made my stomach growl. I had fond memories of the man and his irresistible chocolate tortes. "God, I miss him too. That's good." Gideon smiled at me, but it evaporated the second Lukas came into the room. He had a small blue bag slung over his shoulder, which he plopped unceremoniously on Annalise's piano. I recognized the bag. How many times had Lukas come to our room with food smuggled inside it this winter?

At the piano, he whispered something in Annalise's ear. The music warbled for a moment as she threw her head back in laughter. She finished the song abruptly, stranding Gideon and me out on the dance floor in each other's arms.

He didn't let go right away. If he hadn't just been spending time with another girl, I would have thought he was about to kiss me. I stepped out of his arms and swallowed hard on the words, "Thanks for the dance."

Gideon pulled me off the dance floor by my sleeve to see what Lukas was giving to the bride and groom.

Lukas stuck his hand into the bag and plucked out a wheel of cheese. He placed it in the bride's hands. "A wedding present," he said. He looked at her stomach. "That's for you, Hanka. Not for the party." Jacob shook his hand, and the bride kissed his cheek.

Lukas leaned into Annalise. "There's another wheel in the bag for you and Rachel," he said, loud enough for me to hear.

"What would you have done if you'd been stopped by the SS?" Gideon asked.

"Oh, but they *did* stop me!" he said, smiling like a devil.

"They didn't want to search your bag?"

"They *did* want to search my bag!"

Annalise gripped his arm, her mouth a horrified circle. "No, Lukas!"

He bobbed his head dramatically. He enjoyed performing as much as Annalise did.

"What did you say?"

"I told him he could."

"What?" I asked. The SS could be fairly loose in Terezin, but stealing this much food would earn him a trip to the Little Fortress.

"But I warned him the bag was filled with um...samples—I guess that's the right word—from the typhus ward of the hospital." He laughed. No greater dread existed in the ghetto than typhus, and doctors tested for it in human waste. Now all of us were laughing with him. Even Gideon. "Funny, he didn't want to search my bag after that."

Annalise returned to her playing, and Lukas rubbed her shoulders.

"See? He's nice," I said to Gideon. "You'd like him if you got to know him." Gideon remained unmoved.

"Love's a dangerous thing in here, Rachel," Gideon said. He pointed to Annalise and Lukas. Her head arched back to lean against his stomach behind her. "Whether it's a romance like with Annalise and Lukas, or even love for your fellow man like that girl with the potatoes today, it can kill you."

"What about your love for me?" *Why did I say that?*
Gideon paled.

"I'm not..." He couldn't get more out.

"I don't mean *that* way." I pushed him in the chest, hard enough to make him stumble. I hadn't meant to hit him so energetically, but thoughts of Miriam in his cubby might have powered the push. "Annalise and me. You love us, right?"

Gideon stared down at the floor.

"That can't be dangerous," I said.

Gideon snorted one of his cynical snorts. "Rachel, you have no idea."

Chapter Fifteen

I WAS GOING TO have to scrape my boots when I got to the Art Department. The early-morning sun hadn't dried the puddles left by the overnight rain yet, leaving thick deposits of mud everywhere.

As I turned onto Langestrasse, I recoiled at the too-familiar sound of fists hitting flesh. I should have known well enough by now to put my head down and look the other way, but I couldn't ignore the grunts of pain.

A man fled down the street, his olive-green coat flapping behind him, leaving a big lump in the middle of the street.

The mess of mud and blood was Ernst.

People dodged around him. A woman pushing a wagon over the muddy ruts passed within inches of him without a second glance. Would no one stop and help him? How many watched while the man was beaten to a pulp?

"Who did this to you?" I asked, since no one else was stopping. I spun around to see if I could get another glimpse of his attacker, but he'd disappeared. Ernst tried to answer with a wet rasp.

"Washroom," he said in a hoarse voice. I sat him up. His eyes darted up and down the road like prey scanning for a predator.

He stood and swung an arm around my back. I clutched at his hand, and we shuffled across the street. We slipped into the washroom tucked in an alcove across from the Art Department. It allowed us a little privacy.

He tried to wrench off his muddy shirt but cringed as he raised his arms.

"Let me get that." I lifted it off him and laid the shirt aside. The bruises already forming on his ribs were neat ovals, perhaps the shape of a fist or the toe of a boot. He hung his head when I winced at the cluster of lice bites commingling with his other wounds. I scratched my head as a sign of solidarity, and a hint of a smile touched his lips. His case was worse than mine, for sure, but everyone had lice in the ghetto.

"Think you've broken anything?" I laid a gentle finger on his side. He sucked in his breath. "Sorry."

"I've had worse." He peeked out the door. "You should get out of here."

Back in Copenhagen, a decent girl would never be caught alone with a half-naked, fully grown man, but we both knew that kind of thing didn't matter in Terezin. He could tell I was ashamed to be seen with *him*. He couldn't very well expect me to approve of whatever he'd done to earn that pink triangle, could he? Then again, the Nazis put it there like the yellow star they put on me.

"I'm not leaving you like this," I said and took out a handkerchief. I ran the water for a few seconds out of habit, knowing it would get no warmer, and wet a corner of the cloth. "Besides, I think my reputation is safe with you." He laughed and winced. I pointed to the toilet. "Sit." He sat, too surprised to question.

I dabbed the sticky trail of blood that had gushed from his nose and the mud caked in his hair.

"So, are you going to tell me what happened?"

"The same thing that always happens. I got beat up." He stretched his torso and grimaced. "This guy was just more thorough than usual."

"You should tell someone." I rinsed out the handkerchief.

The cold water numbed my fingers, but it was good for blood.

"Why? To remind them I'm queer?"

I flinched at the word, not the word itself, but at the casual way he confessed it.

I'd always been too busy avoiding him to ever look at him, but I could see how beautiful he was, especially now with his big brown eyes full of gratitude.

"Why don't you just ask?"

"What do you mean?" I didn't look up from my scrubbing.

"You know what I mean." He smiled like we shared a secret. "That question you've been dying to ask since the moment you saw my pink triangle. He pointed to the shirt puddled on the floor beside me.

I'd never imagined it showed in my face, but Gideon always said I didn't excel at keeping my feelings to myself.

"Really?"

"You've done more for me than most people would have. Go ahead. Ask." He used his hands to wipe the worst of the mud from his pants. I was grateful he didn't take those off.

"Why didn't you keep quiet?" I asked.

His head rocked back with laughter, and despite the blood and bruises and mud, he took my breath away.

"Right to the point. Good girl." He pointed a finger at me. "I grew up in Berlin. You're too young to remember, but Berlin was once the best place to live for people like me. There were nightclubs and theaters for us, not like other cities where we couldn't live out in the open. I grew up in that Berlin. It's been a struggle ever since to remember it's gone."

I couldn't imagine whole nightclubs filled with men dancing with each other in Denmark, never mind Nazi Germany. I guess my parents had kept that from us, like so many other realities. Maybe Annalise knew. I'd have to ask her. "I thought Hitler hated..." I picked up his shirt to rinse it out and cover up the fact I couldn't say the word *homosexuals* out loud.

"For a couple of years, his right-hand man was a Commander Röhm." Ernst took the handkerchief again and kept working on his pants. "I knew him. From the clubs. Very public about who he was."

I stared at him. "Hitler allowed that?"

"For a time. But then he didn't, and he had Röhm shot."

"Hitler's never been loyal to his friends."

"Some thought they were more than friends."

"You mean, people think Hitler's a—a—"

"A *ho-mo-sex-u-al*." He laughed again, and I couldn't help but join in, though the joke was directed at me. "There are ridiculous rumors, but mostly because it's the worst thing anyone can think to call him."

"I can think of worse things."

He put his hand to his chest. "I'm touched," he said. "The clubs closed, and if you were smart, you went underground before the arrests started."

"You aren't smart?" I asked with a smile.

"I wasn't going to let the Nazis change me." I froze. His words so completely echoed the ones I'd said to Gideon months ago back in Copenhagen, but I didn't have to wear a pink triangle. I hadn't even had to wear a yellow star then.

"You're very brave," I said.

"Plenty of people would call it stupid." He was right. Gideon had. Annalise and Lukas too.

"How did you end up here?"

"They brought me to Dachau in Germany first." He shuddered.

"Everyone keeps saying Terezin is better than the others," I said, thinking about the skeletons that had gotten off the train from Ravensbrück and Oranienburg.

"They're right. In Dachau, there's even less food, crueler guards, and harder labor, not the stuff you and I do here. I moved rocks for twelve hours every day from one end of a field to another and back."

"What for?"

"To kill us slowly? To make us crazy? Who knows why." He shook his head. "I was only there for a few months.

Someone helped me—an old friend." He took over rinsing his shirt and avoided my eyes. "He got me a transfer here."

I was about to say, "That was kind of him," but he hung his head again like he had when I saw his lice bites. What had he done for his life-saving transfer? I tugged on my ears, sure they'd gone red.

Ernst assessed the damage to his shirt. We'd gotten most of the blood out, but not all the mud.

"I'll have to run back to my room and get another." He wrung out as much of the excess water as possible. It was still soaking wet when he put it back on, and it clung to his chest. "I'll be late. Apologize to Mr. Strauss for me."

Mr. Strauss.

Everyone knew my boss defended Ernst. Mr. Strauss enjoyed a great deal of power for an inmate, but enough to get Ernst transported to Terezin from Dachau? I considered asking, but the shame I had seen on his face stopped me.

"Are you sure you're all right?" I asked. We emerged from the washroom back into the street. I didn't care if someone saw us together anymore, but I should have been looking out.

In the spot where I'd found Ernst, the Cauliflower chatted with a pair of SS officers. His attention jerked to us, and he sneered. Ernst handed me my handkerchief and hid his face behind his collar without answering. I wondered if that olive coat could have been the green of a Czech gendarme uniform.

Ernst didn't come back to the Art Department that day.

When I got back to my room after work that night, I admired Ernst's birthday present for the hundredth time.

I should have gotten rid of it with all the other pictures I'd given to Mr. Strauss, but I couldn't part with it. I cherished it, despite the painful night it portrayed.

How the light radiated from Annalise's pores. How I could practically feel the coarseness of the hospital sheets.

I stretched my arm to secure it back under the mattress where I kept it hidden, revealing blood on my sleeve. Somehow, I'd worked all day and not seen it. I changed my blouse and was rinsing the stain in the washbowl when Annalise and Lukas came in like a flood of champagne bubbles. They both stopped short when they saw the pink-stained water in the bowl.

"Is that blood?" Annalise examined me from top to bottom, her effervescence suddenly flat.

"It's not mine," I said. Gideon arrived behind them. "It's Ernst's."

"Get the sissy's blood off quick, Rachel." Lukas laughed. "Maybe he's contagious, and Julia will start to look good."

"That's ridiculous, Lukas," said Gideon without taking his eyes off me. "What happened?"

I told them how I found Ernst in the street. About the olive coat, the blood and mud on his face, and neat oval bruises along his ribs. After Lukas's stupid joke, I didn't want to tell them about Berlin's nightclubs and Ernst's benefactor.

"Well, what does he expect?" Lukas asked.

He sat on my bed, and I spotted the corner of Ernst's painting sticking out from under the mattress. Lukas leaned back on his hand, and his fingertips grazed a corner. He must have known about Annalise's condition because he had given her the honey, but I didn't want him to see the painting. My sister would be horrified.

"He should've married a woman and had a boyfriend on the side if he had to," Lukas said. "I have a queer for an uncle. That's what he did." I thought about Mr. Strauss again. He was married. Is that what he'd done?

"You know. Like the Blumes, Rachel," Annalise said.

"What about the Blumes?" I asked, wondering what the cafe owners could have in common with Ernst.

"They pretend to be sisters, and no one bothers them," Annalise said.

"They aren't sisters? They're together?" I'd known the Blumes all my life.

Gideon creased his eyebrows at me. "They don't look anything alike, Rachel."

Ilse was tall and blonde and Ruth was short and dark, but I knew all too well that sisters could look very different from one another. "Why don't they have to wear a pink triangle?"

"The Nazis don't persecute women the same way they persecute men," Lukas said. "The Blumes are only here because they're Jewish."

"So, they have to live a lie? Forever?" I asked.

"C'mon, Rachel," Annalise said. "You can't think Ernst should be open about it?"

I wasn't going to let the Nazis change me.

"Why does Ernst have to change?"

Annalise and Lukas looked at each other and shook their heads at me.

Gideon palmed his face. "You should stay away from him," he said.

"I didn't think you cared about that."

"I don't care whom he chooses to sleep with." He scowled at Lukas. "The Cauliflower is always taunting him, and being his friend will only draw his attention."

"What should I have done? Let him bleed in the street, alone?"

Gideon threw his hands up. "Do what you want," he said and mumbled something about *another damn stray* under his breath.

When Ernst returned to work the next day with a cracked lip, a bruised cheek, and a black eye, the Hens giggled like schoolgirls at recess. I liked to think they wouldn't have laughed so much if they'd seen all his other wounds, but they might have laughed even harder. People liked feeling superior to someone in Terezin. Ernst's pink triangle gave them the opportunity.

"Why don't you sit with us?" I asked Ernst as he passed on his way to his usual lunch spot. I patted a space next to me on the rock wall where Adam, Julia, and I sat. Julia scooted over to make room for him without looking up from a book she was reading.

"Are you sure?" Ernst asked.

Adam shifted at my other side, and his eyes darted behind him. I assumed he was checking for the Hens' reaction, who had finally stopped their clucking, but his eyes passed the cluster of artists to the Cauliflower and Officer Novak coming out of the commandant's office. Officer Novak's eyes dragged at Julia's back.

I may have removed the man's smirk, but I hadn't been able to remove the memory of what happened to her. It wasn't something she had just seen. She'd experienced it in every corner of her soul. At least she wouldn't have to imagine his smug smile, though.

Julia looked up as he passed, and his face twisted into that familiar leer. She didn't respond, just returned to her book. I grinned, celebrating the fact my ability had given her the strength to face him.

Officer Novak stopped in his tracks. His smirk evaporated along with my satisfaction. He took a huge step toward her, his face twisted into a snarl. His hand swung back. My muscles tensed, and I squinted my eyes, waiting for him to strike my friend.

The blow never came.

When I looked up, Ernst was standing between Officer Novak and Julia.

"Oh, excuse me, sir," he said.

The gendarme turned his snarl on Ernst, but the Cauliflower made a clicking sound several paces ahead as if commanding a roaming dog. Officer Novak trotted ahead obediently to catch up.

Ernst winked at me, but Julia, so engrossed in her book, hadn't seen any of it. Adam moved so Ernst could sit. I squeezed his hand and mouthed, "Thank you."

The inmate with the soup kettle rattled up with his cart. The one who never gave Ernst anything but broth.

"Put on your jacket," I said to Ernst and thrust the coat he had in his lap around his shoulders.

"Why?" he asked. He scratched the bites at his sides. His long-sleeved shirt provided enough warmth against the chill of early spring in the air, but the pink triangle had fallen off the lapel.

I shoved his arms into the sleeves. I buttoned it to cover the patch on his chest.

"Rachel, he's seen me before."

"Maybe he's forgotten." Or maybe I'd pulled Ernst's face from his memory.

His soup had plenty of potatoes that day.

Chapter Sixteen

"LET'S GO THROUGH WHAT you're going to tell Lukas again."
Annalise patted the back of her newly cropped hair.

"That Mr. Strauss told us this is the style in Paris this year." The idea that my boss would waste valuable intelligence from the outside world on Parisian hairstyles insulted not only the man but the entire Czech resistance. Besides, people might believe Annalise would bob her hair—she looked like Claudette Colbert. Meanwhile, I looked like Harpo Marx. No one could believe I chose this look for any but the most pragmatic reasons.

The Germans feared typhus enough to delouse our rooms, but every new transport introduced a new batch of lice to the ghetto. The only treatment left had been the scissors.

Annalise didn't want anyone to know, especially Lukas. I didn't want it shouted from the rooftops either, but it was nothing to be ashamed of. It happened to everyone. Our mattresses crawled with bedbugs, our food was infested with mites, and our clothes heaved with fleas. Everything pulsed with vermin. Our hair was no exception. Hundreds of Terezin women were sporting "Parisian" hairstyles this May.

Lukas wouldn't be fooled. He probably had them himself.

Annalise picked her fingers through her cropped hair and moaned.

"It'll grow back, Annalise. There are worse things here."

"I know that." She placed her hands on her hips. "It's why I've decided to do the *Requiem*," she said.

"Really?" I had been so excited Rafael Salzberg chose to perform Verdi's *Requiem* with the choir. Some of the singers had refused to participate because the lyrics were too defiant, but it would be wonderful for morale. Besides, I doubted the Nazis even understood the Latin. "That's great, Annalise."

She swatted at me. "Don't act so surprised, Rachel Abramson. You're not the only one who wants to make a difference here. You know that sign by the gate?"

I did. The one that said *Work will make you free.* Another Nazi lie. We'd all been working seventy-hour weeks for months. We were no closer to being free.

"Director Salzberg says it isn't work that makes us free. It's music."

"That's beautiful, Annalise." Maybe art would make me free. There were rumors the Red Cross was coming to check on our well-being. Mr. Strauss was sure the drawings we got to the resistance had done it. Maybe art could make us all free. "I'm really proud of you," I said, trying to keep the surprise out of my voice this time.

"It'll serve them right for doing this to me," she said, jabbing at her hair.

Ah. That was more like it.

"It won't make any difference." Gideon slapped another coat of whitewash onto the outside facade of the children's home in the heat of the afternoon sun.

"Of course, it will. Things are changing here already," I said. Lukas had confirmed the rumors that the Red Cross would visit Terezin. The SS suspended all our usual work to prepare the ghetto for the visit. "Now the Germans know they're being watched, it'll have to get better."

"Watched by whom? The Swiss Red Cross?" Gideon asked with a bitter laugh. "You know who the president is? Max Keller." When this failed to get a response from me, he continued. "Max Keller is a multimillionaire with factories all over Germany. Who do you think works in them?" I had a guess but refused to give him the satisfaction of answering. "Jewish slave labor. No, I doubt he'll jump at the chance to help us."

"But the Danish Red Cross is coming too," I said defensively. "*Denmark* will do something."

Gideon shrugged as if it didn't make a difference.

"The cost of all this could have gone to actually improving conditions here, not just the appearance of it," he said. He gestured to the dozens of inmates whitewashing every building on the street. Across the way, more people were building raised flower beds.

"You're right about one thing." I surveyed the wall we just painted. The whitewash had already seeped into a deep crack on its facade.

"Just one?" Gideon asked.

"These changes are skin deep." I had painted signs that morning for the "cafe" and the "playground." Terezin had neither. Who would believe such a pack of lies? "The Red Cross isn't going to be fooled, and the Germans will have to change things." I dipped my finger in the paint and dotted his nose with the excess. "Maybe even get us out of here."

Gideon didn't move to wipe it off. A train whistle blared.

"Don't forget the thousands of people they're transporting to make the place look less crowded," he said.

"You're so negative." I splattered paint at him.

He held up his hands. "Stop!" He stretched his shirt out to scrutinize the damage I'd done to his already tattered clothes. "You'll mess up my outfit." He gave me a rare smile, the kind he saved for when he was being unbearable.

"Everyone else is hopeful, even Annalise, who's performing the *Requiem* for the visit." I didn't mention she was doing it as revenge for her hair.

"She shouldn't. It's too dangerous." He looked ridiculous debating me with paint smeared on his nose.

"You sound like Lukas," I said.

"No one has ever said that before."

To be fair, Lukas disapproved of Annalise's involvement in the *Requiem* because it was a "depressing old slog you couldn't even dance to," which wasn't really Gideon's point.

"Things are going to get better. You'll see."

"I wish I could think like you," Gideon said.

I wrinkled my nose. "No, you don't."

He kept smiling and took a step toward me. "Yes, I really do."

The intensity of his gaze froze me in place, but a second later, he took two steps back and cracked his knuckles.

"Ugh! Don't do that!" I grabbed both his hands. They stiffened under mine. Heat flooded up my arm like when we'd danced at Hanka's wedding. He took another two steps back, and my hands slipped from his.

"I don't care what you say. It's giving people hope," I said, pretending I hadn't felt anything. "Hope is a powerful thing."

"It's not worth dying for," he said.

"Without it, we're already dead."

Gideon made a quick excuse about having to get back to his cubby. I lied through the pain in my chest and told him I had plans with Adam. He wiped the paint from his nose and left me with all the dirty brushes.

Thankfully, Ernst, Julia, and Adam were washing out theirs at the spigot in the square. I dumped the brushes into the metal bucket Ernst was filling. The clang echoed louder than I'd intended.

Ernst dodged the splash I made. "You all right?"

"It feels like that boy spends all his time up in that cubby of his." I had to stop thinking about it. It wasn't any of my business. That made the pain in my chest worse.

"I heard Esther Halpert visited yesterday," said Julia as she shook two brushes out.

"That church mouse?" asked Ernst. He stepped aside and let me use the spigot. "No way."

"Why not?" asked Julia. Yes, why not? Her head didn't look like a ball of steel wool. She was sweeter too.

"Not his type." Ernst hooked a thumb at me. "He likes them fiery."

I banged my shoulder into his arm.

"See? Fiery," Ernst said. He retied the twine holding his right shoe together.

"All right. These are done," said Adam, holding up the clean brushes. "I'll bring them back to the Art Department. Believe it or not, I have no interest in gossiping about Gideon's love life."

"Agreed," I said to Adam as he walked away. I squeezed water through my brush until my hands cramped. "That he has such a robust one in a place like this is just in bad taste."

"Is it possible you're upset because you wish he brought you up there?" Ernst scratched at his ribs. The bruises must have all healed, but the lice bites continued to torment him.

"I don't want to go up to that dirty, mouse-infested cubby of his." The water from the brushes ran clear, but I still wrung the bristles.

"So, it's not the company or the activity you object to, just the location?" asked Julia.

"I'm not in love with Gideon."

Ernst laughed one of those breathtaking laughs of his. Julia patted me on the arm as if I had just received terrible news.

"I'm not! One day, he's my best friend, and the next, he acts like I'm nothing to him." I didn't mention the heat that flooded up my arm when I'd grabbed his hands.

"Sounds like love to me," said Ernst.

"You've been in love?" I asked. "With a man?"

"No, Rachel, with a coat rack," he said. This made Julia giggle. He smacked my shoulder with the back of his hand. "Of course with a man." Julia continued to smile, but Ernst's evaporated, and he stared at the ground. "Marek." It must not have ended well.

I shouldn't have been surprised that, at nearly thirty, Ernst had experienced heartbreak. I'd never thought about two men in love before, but then again, I hadn't thought much about homosexuality at all. I found my friendship with Ernst very thought-provoking.

Ernst and Julia brought the rest of the supplies back to the Art Department for me, but I headed over to the children's home for a visit. As I approached, wheels creaked over the cobblestones behind me.

There was something that wouldn't make the Red Cross tour.

In a better world, the cart would have been loaded with apples and cabbages in a town square. It rumbled to a stop so the man pushing it could chat with a friend.

A hand—a woman's, from the delicate fingers—flopped lifelessly out of the black fabric shrouding the cart. It made the image of fresh produce harder to maintain.

A row of children filed down the street, returning from playtime in Stadt Park. The sight of the death wagon disgusted me, but the sight of children meandering past it without noticing made it much worse.

Their young caregiver tucked the woman's hand back under the fabric. She wiped her hand on her apron and waved when she saw me.

Hadas and I became friends after I saved her from the Cauliflower with her pants full of stolen potatoes. She was in charge of the four- and five-year-old boys in the children's home despite being only Annalise's age. The braids she always wore and the smattering of freckles across her nose made her look even younger.

"Children have sleep now. Come. We make talk."

One of her children tugged on her shirt. "*Baba*, Zoltan called me a baby."

The offending Zoltan must have been Hungarian because Hadas rattled off words at a speed I'd never heard her speak before. Her German came at a much slower rate.

Zoltan defended himself in Hungarian and pointed to the stuffed bear the other boy clutched. He said a single word in German. "Baby."

Hadas lectured the boy with a pointed finger until Zoltan hung his head. "I'm sorry, Isador."

When we reached their bunkroom, the children scurried through their bedtime routine. One child in a corner ignored all of Hadas's instructions. Eli. He spent his days at the children's home while his mother worked, but he was assigned down the hall with the older boys. He didn't belong here.

"How are you, Eli?" He looked up at me, and his shoulders sagged even more. My muscles tensed, as I thought of Leah, but I'd seen her a couple of days ago. True, she was exhausted and hungry like the rest of us, but I hadn't been worried for her.

"Eli's mother—she's all right?" I asked Hadas.

"She work late," Hadas said, looking up from Isador's bed. She smiled at Eli but had no enthusiasm for it.

Eli stared at the floor again. "I miss Elias and Isaac." Before I could ask what he meant, Hadas waved me over to the other side of the room.

"His room have transport yesterday," she whispered. "Each and all them. To make less crowded for visit."

I was sorry to hear that, but I also knew the visit was our only chance to tell the world what was happening. I looked back at Eli. "He's the only one left?"

Hadas nodded.

"So, they aren't transporting any Danes," I said. Over the last eight months, thousands of men, women, and children had gotten those thin strips of paper telling them to report to the railroad spur by the gate. Germans, Dutch, Hungarians, and Czechs. None of them were Danish. Not one.

"You hear Benedek die?" she asked. Of course I had heard. Everyone had.

"No one knows why the Cauliflower did it," I said. "He just walked up to him and beat him to death." Annalise was working at the hospital the day they brought him in. He'd held on for months and finally succumbed to his injuries the day before. "The Cauliflower's a monster."

"Do not to feel sorry for Benedek," she said. Hadas knew him from her village in Hungary. "He is...how you say"—Hadas bit her lip, searching for the right word—"a kicker of puppies?"

"A bully?" I said.

"Benedek brag he beat up the *faygele*. Your friend."

"Ernst?" I hadn't heard that. Had it been Benedek who'd beaten up Ernst the day I helped him?

"How do you know I'm friends with Ernst?"

"Everyone know you friends with the *faygele*."

"Don't call him that, Hadas."

She clasped her hands together as if in prayer. "I'm sorry. Is that not right word?"

"He'd prefer *homosexual*, I think," I said.

Benedek had hurt my friend, but it hardly made the Cauliflower a hero. I played it safe and hated them both.

Chapter Seventeen

THE MOMENT THE RED Cross's limousine pulled into Terezin, the curtain rose on our little performance. We waited in our assigned places for our cue. Adam and I played the role of coffee shop patrons, which meant cups of real coffee—well, real ersatz coffee—on a patio by the square.

I would have spotted the delegation when they entered Marktplatz even if they hadn't been escorted by Commandant Becker. They could spruce up the ghetto along the route, but they couldn't fill the hollow cheeks of its inmates. They couldn't give all of us fresh clothes. Well fed and well dressed, the delegates were as conspicuous as blood on snow.

Despite the intricately dressed windows, only one storefront housed an actual place of business. I couldn't even be sure which one until Commandant Becker ushered the delegation inside.

Among the bustling shoppers, something familiar caught my eye. "That inmate is wearing Annalise's fox cape," I told Adam, watching her caress the soft fur. I wanted to rip it off her. My sister had gone all winter without a coat.

Adam tugged at the brim of my hat. It wasn't mine either. The SS had handed out some items from the Sluice. We'd have to return it all by curfew tonight.

Just as the delegates emerged from the shop, a cheer erupted at the *fodbold* field across the square. A boy kicked the ball, charging for the goal, his pursuers hot

on his heels. As the delegation passed the field, the
ball soared into the net. The small crowd of spectators
cheered. The rest of the passersby acted as if the game
were an everyday occurrence, as if the square hadn't
been fenced off until the day before.

"They can't honestly believe this *schmegegge* story," I
said.

"I don't know," Adam said. The *fodbold* star threw his
fists into the sky. "I think David has a future in the theater.
He's quite believable."

Two of the delegates thought so too, based on their
cheers. The third took notes in a little leather journal.
He must be the Dane. He lagged behind in the square as
the delegation moved on, but he didn't give the shoppers,
their bags stuffed with purchases, a second look.

"C'mon, ask to see what they've bought," I said aloud.
Ruth and Ilse Blume had filled their bags with old rags
when they left West this morning.

The *fodbold* players scampered off the field and surrounded Commandant Becker as if a celebrity had arrived. He passed out tins of sardines to the children.

"More sardines? No chocolates this time?" asked one of
the children. Not to be outdone by David, he delivered a
disappointed scowl. The sardines would feed him for an
entire day. "Well, thanks anyway, Uncle Becker."

My laugh was as bitter as the ersatz coffee. "Oh, come
on," I said.

We drained our cups and left them on the table. As
soon as the delegates were out of sight, an inmate would
deliver the pretty china by back streets to the brand-new
restaurant where the delegation would have lunch. Adam
stood and held out a hand for me. No one had ordered us
to hold hands, but a couple out strolling together might
do that, so I took it. It was more like when I held Erik's
hand to cross the street, not at all like when Gideon had
cradled my hand in his.

We watched Uncle Becker identify different notewor-
thy features of the town. He gestured to the school,

gleaming in its obvious newness. They passed the *Closed for Vacation* sign on the door and the newspaper-covered windows without comment. If I could make a memory stronger instead of erasing it, I'd burn the images on the Danish delegate's brain, but my ability didn't work that way.

"See through this!" I hissed at him under my breath. A tingle of energy trickled up my spine, indignation revitalizing my depleted spirit.

The Dane halted as if he'd somehow heard me from across the square. I hoped he'd cup his hand to his eyes over the windows or ask the commandant to let them see inside the school—which was actually a delousing station. Instead, he jotted a note in his little leather journal.

The commandant shouted something in a friendly tone to the Dane, and the delegate slipped his book into his pocket. He gave the school/delousing station a backward glance before joining the other men at the new bakery.

Adam nudged me and threw his chin at the fake bank. A man stood in front, posing as its proprietor. He had a fat brown cigar in his mouth and a handful more waiting for the delegation.

"They have Rudolph Cooperman passing out cigars?" I asked.

"Uh-huh."

"He spent three months in the Little Fortress."

"Uh-huh." Adam tried not to laugh.

"For trading cigarettes."

"What can I say? The Nazis have a sick sense of humor."

Mr. Strauss emerged from an empty storefront next to us. It used to be where they kept the death wagon.

"Well, don't you make a fine-looking couple, out courting," Mr. Strauss said. "That's the part you're playing, isn't it? I'm playing a contented shopper in search of a little something for my sweet tooth." He lifted his bag, and I peeked inside. He'd stuffed it with old scrap paper from the Art Department. He looked around. "Isn't it all so festive?"

"Rachel and I were saying the delegation can't possibly believe any of this."

"The Swiss?" He snorted. "They're no friends to the Jews."

"But there's a Dane over there too," I said, bristling.

"A representative from a small occupied country is not a powerful ally, Miss Abramson." He sounded like Gideon, but I would never roll my eyes at him. He looked at the delegates and dropped his voice. "It will be up to us to get the word out to the world." He never explained to us how he did it, but he continued to smuggle our pictures out of the ghetto to the Czech resistance. "Besides, with the Americans in France now, it's just a matter of time before they're knocking on Hitler's door." Mr. Strauss had been glowing since the news reached us about the American invasion of Normandy, certain it meant the beginning of the end for the Germans.

"I sure hope you're right, Mr. Strauss," I said. It would be nice to be home before another winter.

"Just a matter of time. Now, if you'll excuse me, I have to go to the bakery for some of those delicious fresh-baked *croissants*," he said with an exaggerated French accent. He winked dramatically and sauntered in the direction of the delegation.

We followed them, too, and sat on the corner of a raised flower bed filled with red roses when they stopped. I hadn't seen the new outdoor music pavilion yet. Like everything else along the visit route, it was too new, too pretty.

"You realize that's where the women's latrine used to be."

Adam laughed. "There's an awful poetry to that."

As soon as all of us were in position, the orchestra struck up a lively tune. I caught sight of a uniform near the back. The Cauliflower played a violin.

"He's actually good," Adam said. I couldn't disagree. The Cauliflower's features relaxed when he played. I'd never have guessed he'd beaten at least two men to death.

"I miss the latrine. At least it was real."

We rounded a corner toward West. Our part in the play was over. We stopped to observe the rest of the show from the space where the set ended and reality began. Crumbling walls replaced the whitewashed ones, and raked gravel made way for rutted dirt streets. We watched the delegates leave the bakery, munching their croissants.

"Is there *anything* here that's real?"

"Of course there is," Adam said. "The beauty of the music is real. The laughter of those boys playing football was real." He raised our hands, the fingers entwined. He squeezed.

"This is real," Adam said.

Gideon was leaning on my door when I got back to West.

"You need to be careful about what you say," he said.

"Well, hello to you too, Gideon," I said back.

He ignored me. "The Danish Red Cross can do more good for us here if they're on friendly terms with the Germans," he said.

"We've been through this, Gideon," I said.

"Do you want them to stop giving us parcels?"

"Give me a little credit. Annalise depends on those packages."

He followed me into my room. It smelled of fresh paint.

"New curtains?" Gideon asked, pointing to the blue panels hanging at our window.

"I guess so. Must have put them up while I was out." Just in time too. The delegation was on its way.

"Just don't do anything stupid."

The folded square of paper in my skirt pocket was small enough to fit in my palm, but it weighed on me like an anvil.

"I would never—"

"You would. Always. Until today." He fluffed the thin pillow on my bed, another recent addition. "Not today, Rachel." He straightened my flimsy blanket.

"I'm not going to let them scare me into—"

He spun on me and grabbed both my shoulders.

"Listen to me for once," he said in a fierce whisper, and I stiffened at his intensity. He let out a deep breath and leaned his forehead against mine, sending pointless goose bumps from where our skin met down to my toes. "Please." He swept his finger over the scar on my cheek.

When the delegation knocked on the door, we sprang apart. The Dane entered first, followed by the two Swiss men. An SS officer I didn't recognize joined us and glowered at me as if I'd already misspoken. I reached for the note in my pocket to be sure it hadn't fallen out.

The Dane handed me a large box. "From our king, Miss Abramson. For your sister." Glass syringes clanked inside.

The SS officer shooed Gideon out. As I lost sight of him behind the closing door, his eyes fixed on me. *Be careful*, they seemed to say. I gave a tiny nod and smiled at my guests.

"Please, come sit," I said and gestured the men into our new seating area. Our neighbors had been evicted and crammed into another room. The SS knocked down a wall so we could have space to entertain our guests.

"One, two, three, four." The Danish delegate counted the chairs. "Funny, you happen to have just the right number." We grinned at each other like we shared a joke. I *told* Gideon they wouldn't fall for any of this. "You were sixteen when you arrived."

I nodded and played with my hair, hoping they'd notice how crudely it had been cut. Lice had continued to be a problem into the summer. Why else would I have cut it like this?

"And you never attended school here."

So he *had* noticed the closed sign and papered windows as if he'd heard me in the street earlier.

"No, sir. Never." I lowered my head, trying to infuse as much disappointment in the answer as possible.

The Swiss delegate interrupted the Dane's line of questioning. "You work in the Art Department, I understand. Do you like your work?"

"Very much, sir." I looked at the SS officer looming in the corner.

"What sort of work do you do there?"

I draw sketches of food lines and old women on their deathbeds and sneak them out to the Czech resistance.

"I create decorative pictures, portraiture, that kind of thing."

The Swiss man looked pleased with this answer. "Sounds like pleasant work for wartime."

"What a charming animal!" the other Swiss delegate said. He had Jubilee in his hands.

"It's my brother's." I tore it from the man's grip, and the SS officer in the corner took a step away from the wall.

The Swiss delegate dismissed the SS officer back into his corner with a wave. The Nazi scowled but didn't come closer.

"This is a cheerful color yellow, Miss Abramson," the Danish delegate said, gesturing to the walls of my room. "It smells fresh. When did you have it painted?"

"Yesterday." My eyes darted to the SS officer. He had withdrawn back into his corner. I folded my hands over Jubilee in my lap. "I like the color very much." The Dane wrote something in his journal.

"Your community is far from the front lines of war," said a Swiss delegate. "You must feel safe here." The SS officer leaned forward as if he could hear the thumping of my heart.

Safe? The looming menace of Little Fortress. The gnawing hunger. The sweeping spread of disease. The constant threat of transport to the hard labor camps in the east. I tried to relax my fingers, clutched in Jubilee's mane. "Yes, I feel safe here. Very safe." My voice shook, and the SS officer furrowed his brow.

"We came from the hospital," the Danish representative said, his tone turning somber. The Swiss delegates never stopped their smiling. "I noticed there wasn't a maternity ward. A place with"—he shuffled to a previous page in his journal—"six thousand residents should have a maternity ward."

Six thousand? Was that what the Nazis told them? Even with all the transports this spring, it was three times that. And *a maternity ward*? I tried to unclench my jaw. Having babies was illegal. Hanka's baby died a week after he was born. He might have survived if his parents could have brought him to the hospital.

"We have four hospitals, sir." It wasn't a lie, but it wasn't the truth either. All patients had been crammed into the other three hospitals. Two of the Hens, along with a hundred or so other completely healthy inmates, played the role of the mildly sick in the hospital the delegation visited.

There were a few more nonsense questions from the Swiss men until the SS officer took a step forward. "We really have to be moving on," he said. The folded paper in my pocket scratched against my leg. This was my only chance. My heart rate lurched to a gallop.

The SS officer opened the door, Gideon slipped in, and the men said their goodbyes. The Dane, the closest to the door, left first before I could get the note from my pocket, but I was able to slide it into my palm as the second Swiss delegate reached the door.

"Thank you so much for coming, sir," I said and stuck out the hand to shake his. "And thank the Red Cross for my sister's medication."

When he felt the note secreted there, he yanked away as if my hand were the clammy one.

"You're most welcome, Miss Abramson," he said in a friendly tone that didn't match his expression. "I am glad to find you so well."

So *well*?

Gideon waited politely until the men filed out and the door was closed behind them. He stuck his hand out, palm up.

"All right. Hand it over."

I held it out to him. "Did you see how he refused to take it?" I pointed to the hallway.

He snatched it from me, unfolded the paper, and read it. *What you see isn't real. Please help us.*

"Are you crazy, Rachel?" He tore the note into small, unreadable pieces.

"They're supposed to *want* to help us!"

"They want to stay neutral more."

I had hoped my note would reach the king of Denmark, or even just to the west like Mr. Strauss's artwork, but the Swiss wouldn't even take it.

"Who cares about Swiss neutrality?"

"I bet the thousands of Swiss Jews care about it a great deal."

Inmates and guards packed the men's barracks' cellar to watch the choir perform the *Requiem*. I had to stand at the back where Gideon had saved me a space.

The delegation sat in the front. The SS leadership from the ghetto and Prague took up the rest of the section. One of the Swiss delegates laughed at something Uncle Becker said. The elders sat behind them, fidgeting like their seats were made of pine cones. They had tried to cancel the *Requiem*, but the commandant knew such a difficult piece would impress the guests and insisted the performance go on. I was relieved. The delegation would have to acknowledge our suffering after hearing it.

The choir filed in. It was smaller than it had been this spring. It had shrunk over the last couple of months in preparation for the Red Cross visit. Annalise may have gotten the solo because so many had been transported east. There used to be two hundred, but only sixty stood waiting for Rafael Salzberg to begin.

When he swung his baton, it wasn't just his arms that moved. He conducted with his entire body, his passion for the music writhing through him like a fever. His singers didn't share his fervor. They stared woodenly at the uniformed SS officers in the crowd as they sang. My shoulders slumped. The piece was being beautifully executed but had none of the emotional range it needed to get the message across.

That all changed when Annalise took three steps forward for her solo. She raised a fist into the air and placed her other hand over her heart, obscuring her yellow star. Her voice rang through the cellar with ferocity. Her words spit out like a curse. The Nazis didn't need to understand Latin to know this death hymn was sung for them.

How great will be their terror,
when the Judge comes,
who will smash everything completely!

By the time Annalise's solo was finished, the choir had been infected with their director's and Annalise's fever. Their hands covered their yellow stars. The music had made them free.

The elders stopped fidgeting in their seats. The muscles in the commandant's neck strained, and his face went scarlet. Several of the SS officers sat with their arms crossed over their chests, their faces as hard as stone.

I forgot about the inspiring music. I forgot about heightened morale. I didn't even care about sending a message to the delegation anymore. All I could think of was the Nazis' rage directed at my sister.

As the final crescendo crashed through the room, the screech of Lukas's chair shook me out of my terror. Our only protector sprinted from the cellar. The music ended. Elder Tesler bowed his head.

Gideon grabbed both my hands to stop me from clapping, not realizing I—like everyone else in the room—was much too frightened to applaud.

I ran to the Sluice and thrust my borrowed hat and gloves at a gendarme stationed there. He threw them into the pushcarts all around him. I gave him my name and bounced on my feet while I waited for him to cross my name off the list. I had to get back to Annalise. As soon as he put a check next to my name, I turned to run out of the building and barreled into Ernst, who was returning a gold watch to another gendarme.

I patted his chest where I'd smacked into him. "I'm sorry, Ernst. I have to go. I'm worried sick about Annalise."

He nodded. He'd seen it too. He'd been sitting near the front at the *Requiem* performance.

"I'll walk you back," he said.

On our way to West, we passed the new garden plots they'd planted this spring. We would get to keep them and the fresh food they'd bring to the ghetto this summer, but we wouldn't get to keep much else. The goods that had been displayed in the shop windows now filled pushcarts along the visit route. An SS officer yelled at a group of kids to get off the new playground across the street. A gendarme was already taking it apart.

I didn't pay much attention to the dismantling of the facade we'd created. I was practically running back to West. Ernst's long strides kept up, and the shine on his shoes caught my eye. No twine held them together. "Don't you need to return those?" The Germans made it very clear the items we'd borrowed were only for the day.

He reddened as words failed him, and he didn't meet my gaze. "The person that saved me from Dachau? He got me the shoes." He scowled at them.

"You don't have to explain anything to me," I said. "I'm glad he got you new shoes. You could barely walk in the old ones." Ernst looked away and ran a hand over the back of his neck.

"I don't just get things for me, you know. I got sulfon-amide pills for Sadie Haas when she had pneumonia last year." He finally looked at me. "And the honey for your sister."

"That was you?" I had been so sure it was Lukas.

His brow furrowed, and his face reddened again. "I didn't want to talk about..." He was looking at his new shoes again.

"We all do things we're not proud of in here, Ernst."

"Not you."

I'd taken Rivka's parcel and colored all those postcards. "Yes, me. At least you saved my sister. Thank you," I said and kissed his cheek.

He startled at the gesture, and his eyes darted around us.

I said goodbye to Ernst at a full run as soon as West came into view. Raised voices echoed down the stairwell as I climbed. Lukas and Annalise didn't stop arguing when I raced in.

"Is everything all right?" I asked.

Lukas rolled his eyes, but Annalise said, "Everything is fine."

"Everything is not fine! You can't defy them like that!" His volume even seemed to startle himself, and he dropped his voice. "Steal. Sabotage. That's the kind of resistance I can get behind. What did you accomplish with that little stunt today?"

"You can't tell me what to do, Lukas."

He dropped his arms to his sides. "I have a family to protect. Some of the gendarmes know you're my girl. You put us all in danger."

Annalise's pacing stopped, and she spun to face him, hope lighting her face. "Your girl?"

"Of course, *miláček*," he said. He held out his arms, and she fell into them.

I made a gagging sound. "That's all he has to say to make you give in? Of course it was dangerous," I said, "and I'm scared too, but it might be worth it if the delegates see—"

"They don't want to see," he said, stroking Annalise's back. "They told the Cauliflower they were *impressed*." My sister stepped out of his arms.

I shook my head. It couldn't all be for nothing. "Not the Danish delegate," I said. He had noticed the fresh paint and the paper on the windows of the school.

"Not him. Just the Swiss," said Lukas. I let out a breath. "But the Dane said it was acceptable."

Acceptable?

Hope must have been holding me up, because I crumpled onto my bed.

Someone had taken away all the chairs.

Chapter Eighteen

"SO, THIS IS WHY Rachel never invites us to her bunkroom,"
Julia said to Ernst as we entered West Barracks. I regret-
ted coming back to get a sweater, but it was a chilly night
for August, and if I planned to sit through a two-hour play
in the women's barracks' cellar, I'd need it. Julia was right.
I'd never brought any non-Dane to West, too ashamed of
its comparative opulence.

"Look at how wide these hallways are." She craned her
neck to peek into a room with its door ajar on the first
floor. She clutched Ernst's arm. "There are only *four* beds
in that room. There would be a dozen of us in a room that
size in Dresden."

I bit my lip. What would they think when they saw my
room? There were only two beds, and it was twice the
size.

"Do they all have doors?" Julia asked, scanning the
hallway.

"Why don't you guys wait here," I suggested for the
third time. "No reason for you to climb all the stairs."

Julia's eyes widened in mock horror, and she brought
her hand to her heart. "Stairs? You mean to tell me you
don't have an elevator?"

"We'll get through this hardship together," said Ernst to
Julia, the traitor.

As we climbed, she pretended to mop her brow with the back of her hand, and Ernst used his handkerchief to blot her forehead. I bumped my shoulder into him.

Julia hooked her arm through his. "You may have to carry me, Ernst." When Ernst swung her in his arms, I could see spatters of fresh blood on his shirt at his sides. Perhaps an old wound opened up or he'd scratched too much at his lice bites.

He'd only carried her for three steps before we heard voices on the floor above us. It might have been my hallmates milling about during their leisure time, but I doubted it.

Army boots on the floorboards of West had a distinctive sound.

Ernst and I froze and stared up at the ceiling. He put Julia down.

I stopped. "I don't really need the sweater."

"There's nothing to worry about, Rachel," Julia said. She locked her arm in mine. "We have hours to curfew. We're not breaking any rules." There were no more jokes as we ascended the last flight of stairs.

The Cauliflower was at the edge of the next landing with several members of the Ghetto Police and Officer Novak. I expected Julia to freeze when she saw her attacker, but it was Ernst who went no further. He pulled his jacket over his pink triangle.

"I can't. I'm sorry," he said as he fled down the stairs.

I turned to Julia. "You too," I said. I shooed her like a stray cat down the hallway. "Go wait outside."

"Don't be silly," she said. "The Cauliflower has no reason to trouble us."

"But Officer Novak—"

Julia's eyes darted down the hallway right past him. "He's here?" Her voice was quiet and small.

All those times he'd come to the Art Department, she hadn't reacted. I thought it was because forgetting his smile made her brave enough to face him, but when I'd taken his smile, I'd taken the rest of his face with it. She didn't recognize him.

"Never mind. It wasn't him," I said, and she relaxed. We bowed our heads and approached the crowd of guards. Officer Novak waved us by like a chivalrous knight. His hand covered the place where his heart should be. That nightmarish smirk curled his lips. Julia had to brush up against him to get past, despite our wide hallways in West. He watched her like a dog watches a bone, hungry for her terror. He waited, so sure it would manifest itself. When she denied him the satisfaction, he grabbed her by the arm and yanked her into his side. "It's a pleasure to see you again."

She wrinkled her eyebrows at him. Maybe she was trying to place his voice, or maybe she was wondering why this complete stranger was speaking to her. "I'm sorry, do I know you, sir?"

Julia was being polite, but she couldn't have said anything more offensive to him.

Red fury bled into his expression. I pulled Julia through the crowd to my end of the hall. I let out a breath, grateful he was too surprised to follow us. My relief didn't last. The Ghetto Police were tearing apart my room.

It was a raid.

They had overturned our suitcases first. Two men with yellow stars stitched to their shirts squatted at the pile. They handled each item and flung it away. Two others checked the floorboards and undersides of furniture.

"What are they looking for?" Julia asked, clinging to my arm.

"No idea," I said.

Annalise appeared beside me at the door out of breath.

"How did you hear?" I asked.

"Lukas," she said.

The Cauliflower and Officer Novak stepped around us in the threshold and walked into the chaos. The Cauliflower leaned against a wall and glared at me.

"I'm sorry, Annalise," I whispered. "I don't know why he hates me so much." I had enraged the Cauliflower at the Sluice and again at the train depot with Hadas, but it couldn't have been that. I'd erased those images from his memory as soon as I had the chance. Unless it hadn't worked on him? Or maybe the drawings I gave to Mr. Strauss had been traced back to me.

"This time it's my fault, Kitten." She patted my shoulder. "They raided Rafael Salzberg and most of the choir too. Turns out the SS aren't music lovers."

"That was two months ago," I said.

Annalise shrugged. "Are they going to find anything?" she asked. If it had been Gideon who had asked, there might have been judgment in the words, but Annalise only wanted to know what to expect. I didn't know how to answer.

I had just dropped off a bunch of new drawings to Mr. Strauss, but Ernst's painting of Annalise and me at the hospital was still under my mattress. Ernst had signed it. What would happen to him? What would happen to us for having it? I took a step forward, hoping to get to it first and crumple it into my pocket, but one of the Ghetto Police held up a hand and let me go no further. Another tossed my mattress onto the ground with enough force to pop the seam and send wood chips across the room, but no paper fluttered into view. The pallet beneath was bare too. The painting wasn't there.

A third Ghetto policeman picked up Jubilee from the little shelf with the water pitcher. He squeezed it, searching for contraband hidden inside. I recognized him from our first day, yelling at the crew cleaning up our luncheon. Yakov, Gideon had called him, and he hated Danes. He caught me staring and tugged at the seams of Jubilee's back. He smiled with little cheer but plenty of teeth. I remembered what happened the last time I'd tried to protect Jubilee. This time, I just dug my fingernails into my palms.

Elder Tesler had handpicked this man for the Ghetto Police. He might have picked someone fair like Gideon or kind like Adam, but he picked this man who could smile while he destroyed something I cherished.

"Where did you get this?" asked Officer Novak. I half expected the painting to have appeared in his hands.

It was worse.

He lifted the white canvas bag. The one with Annalise's insulin and syringes. The one that held Annalise's life.

Our parcels had arrived two days ago. She wouldn't get more supplies for another month.

"Where did you get this?" he repeated and shook the bag. He'd break the bottles if he kept it up. The insulin would seep through the canvas and onto my overturned mattress.

"They're Danish. They get packages," Julia said. Mentioning our Danish status did two things. It provided us with an excuse for having such a luxury and served as a gentle reminder they were trashing the room of someone with prominent status. Officer Novak looked to the Cauliflower for how to proceed. He gave a curt nod.

Officer Novak crossed the room in two long strides and held up the white bag. Julia lowered her head. "This is black-market contraband," he said. He jerked up Julia's chin so their faces were an inch apart. "Do you wish to contradict me again?"

She stayed silent.

He stormed out. Annalise's medicine went with him.

At least the sugar Mr. Strauss had given Annalise was still inside the mattress. It wasn't much of a comfort. Julia went to find Lukas to see what he could do.

My sister gathered the wood chips from the mattress in silence. I considered erasing this horrible reality from her mind, but I would need my ability tonight, and not to use on my sister.

"Lukas was right. I shouldn't have done it." Her head fell into her hands.

"I'll fix it, Annalise," I said. "Your insulin, I mean," I added, in case she thought I meant the popped seams of our mattresses. "Where does the hospital keep confiscated medicine?" I asked.

"Don't, Rachel," Annalise said, snapping out of her stupor. "Mrs. Mendelson will have extra." Mrs. Mendelson had lost so much weight, she didn't need her insulin anymore, but she wouldn't give it to us for free. Annalise could tell what I was thinking. "Lukas will get us food to trade."

I shook my head. Even if he could steal enough, Annalise needed her medicine today.

"It's summer," she said, trying to soften me. "There's so much more food for Lukas to steal now." I stood up and brushed wood chips off me. I yanked on the sweater I'd come for, Ernst's play tickets forgotten.

She held me back by the skirt. "Where are you going?" she asked.

"I'll be right back," I said.

Her eyes widened. The pull at my skirt grew more taut. "It's impossible, Kitten."

I bent to pry her hands from my clothes. It would be easier for her to just come along, rather than pulling at my skirts all the way. "Let me show you," I said and offered her a hand up. She followed me out of West, talking the entire time.

"The medicine is locked up in an office. There's a gendarme stationed there at all times—not one of the nice ones either. He's never so much as cracked a smile at me." Annalise expected smiles, at least. "Nurses have to get a doctor's prescription or a requisition form from another hospital. If you think I'll ask my friends to risk their lives to get one for me, you have another think coming. They aren't Danish, Rachel. I can't protect them."

"I can," I said.

She shook her head. "How?"

"How many guards are there?" We were outside the hospital doors.

She didn't answer. "This is crazy."

"Just promise to go along with what I say and not ask any questions until we're out of there."

"Why don't you explain your plan to me now?" Annalise asked. *Because you won't believe me*, I thought.

"You'll have to trust me. Now, about those guards?"

"Two by the front door, one in the back of Ward Three by the supply closet."

The pair of guards at the front tipped their caps to Annalise, and we were inside.

"Where are the requisition forms?" I asked.

Annalise got me one and watched while I wrote up a request to transfer the insulin in a white canvas bag to Hanover hospital in the care of Rachel Abramson.

"Give me a name of a doctor on the ward."

"We'll only get into more trouble for forging a doctor's requisition." Her eyes darted from one end of the room to the other. "There's no point to any of this."

"Annalise, you agreed to do what I asked."

She let out a breath and stared at me, her mouth a hard line. "Dr. Golding. He's nice, Rachel. Don't get him into any..." I scribbled the name at the bottom of the form. "His signature doesn't even look like that!" Annalise said. She didn't understand it didn't matter.

Luckily, the unsmiling gendarme was unfamiliar with the doctor's signature too. He stabbed the requisition form onto a small spike on his desk for safekeeping and retrieved the medicine in the back office.

"Please don't do this. We can still get out of here." Her eyes darted around as though an attack could come from any angle.

"Shush..." I said when the gendarme returned with the white bag.

He checked the paper again before he handed it over. I unzipped the bag to be sure it was Annalise's and tucked it out of sight in my coat. The gendarme dismissed us with a nod. I turned as if to leave, but at the last second, I snatched the requisition form from the spike. Annalise—who had already started to go—made a little squeal.

The officer lunged forward and grabbed my arm, thinking I'd try to get away. He let go the moment I pulled his memory of us and the little white canvas bag from his mind.

"Good evening, sir," I said when his jaw and the hand on my arm slackened. I averted my gaze as they liked us to do. Annalise stared at me like I'd grown a second head.

He shook off the stupor that still clouded his eyes. "Yes?"

"Our room was raided by mistake, sir. We would never use the black market. My sister received that medicine in her Red Cross parcel, sir."

"What are you doing?" Annalise whispered in my ear. This must have looked insane to her, beginning a polite conversation smack dab in the middle of a disastrous one. Of course she didn't understand that our first encounter didn't exist for the officer anymore.

The soldier laughed. "Sure, you never use the black market." He crossed his arms over his chest like a spoiled child. "I'm not helping you, Jew."

I sniffled, pretending to be close to tears. I yanked Annalise out of there before she demanded to know what the hell was going on right in front of him.

"Look like you're crying as we leave," I whispered. "The men at the front desk need to see we're leaving without what we want."

"But that man back there..." She turned to the guard at the supply closet. "He's the one who *gave* us the med—"

"No questions, remember?"

Reminded of her promise, she threw herself into the role, bursting into actual tears as we passed by the guards at the front.

"We should really keep these somewhere safe." I hugged the canvas bag inside of my coat as we crossed the street. "Maybe Gideon will hide it in his cubby...if it won't infringe on his sacred privacy too much."

"Don't change the subject, Rachel Abramson." Her hands flew to her hips like a scolding schoolteacher. "What the hell happened in there? Why did they let us go?"

"Not in the street, Annalise."

I waited until we were just inside the door of our room. I let out a deep breath while Annalise tapped her foot. I took out some scrap paper and a pencil.

"Rachel! You are not going to doodle now!" She went to snatch my pencil, but I pulled it out of her reach. "How did we get out of there?"

"He forgot we were there." I drew the gendarme's desk.

"In the two seconds we were standing there?" Her hands were on her hips again.

"I can make people forget things." Annalise snorted, but I ignored her. "I pulled the memory of us getting the medicine from that guard." I tapped my drawing with my pencil. "I need to sketch the images I pull soon after or I get really tired." I sketched a disembodied hand snatching the top paper from the spike on the gendarme's desk.

"Okay, very funny. So, you're some kind of psychic now? This isn't a game, Rachel. We're going to get into serious trouble." Annalise peeked out the door, expecting the SS to come charging down the hall any minute.

"I knew you wouldn't believe me." I continued to draw, sketching out Annalise beside the gendarme's desk. I drew her face distorted in confusion and sporting a large wart on her chin.

She took in a little outraged gasp. "Rachel, erase that right now!" I laughed but did what she asked. Once she was satisfied with the likeness, she continued. "So, you're telling me he won't remember us getting the medicine or you stealing the requisition form back." She ran her finger down the length of her wartless nose.

"That's right."

"Because you pulled the image from his brain."

"That's right."

She rolled her eyes. "The only thing you're pulling is my leg!"

"How else could I have gotten him to let us go with the medicine?"

"Who knows? Maybe you're in cahoots?"

"Cahoots?"

"Well, I don't know, Rachel. It makes more sense than you having magic powers."

"Remember the time I spilled grape juice on your pink silk blouse?"

"No!" Her eyes widened as if I'd threatened a beloved pet. She'd loved that blouse.

"That's right. You don't remember. I made sure of that." My smile was smug, but it had a touch of remorse in it. It had been her favorite.

"I lost that blouse."

"No. I threw it away."

Annalise's hand flew to her chest. "You didn't!"

"And that time I promised to do the dishes for you and forgot? And you got into trouble with Mama?"

Annalise gasped and smacked my leg. "Rachel!"

My remorse was gone. I wiggled my eyebrows at her for a change. She'd missed a date that night because Mama was so angry.

She tilted her head and pursed her lips into a fine line. "Okay, then. How does it work?" The question was more a test than curiosity.

"Not sure." I sketched my own image, my expression probably braver than it had been in reality, and my hair was all wrong. "The first time was right after Ezra died, and I just wanted Gideon to be happy again. It took me a while to even figure out what I had done." There was a long pause.

"Fafa?" Annalise asked.

I didn't answer. I focused on my drawing. I hated sketching myself.

"I always thought I forgot her too quickly." She stared at the wall as if trying to picture our grandmother but twisted back to clutch my arm. "You won't take this memory, will you?"

I had never considered that. I could have confided in my sister a hundred times and erased the confession the next minute. Annalise could see me think about it. "Promise me you won't, Rachel." I promised, but she peered at me from the corner of her eye.

"She had it too," I said.

"Had what?"

"My ability. Fafa could do it too."

Her body stiffened. "What makes you say that?"

"Remember how she had each of us come into her room just before she died to say goodbye?"

"She gave me her pearl brooch," Annalise said. I'd been so jealous when Annalise got that brooch. Fafa had worn it everywhere. Thank goodness Mama brought it to Sweden with her; otherwise, some Nazi hag would be wearing it right now.

I had gone in after Annalise. Fafa's room was dark, lit only by a small lamp at her bedside, her silver hair pooled around her shoulders. I'd never seen it down and averted my eyes, like I'd caught her coming out of the bath. A smell, like fruit gone soft, combined with a generous spray of her favorite perfume, had made me gag.

"She said she wasn't going to give me a gift. That she'd given me one already." She'd also said it was much better than any old pearl brooch, but I didn't say that to Annalise. "Fafa told me she'd been able to do it since she was a girl too."

"Did she explain how it works?"

"She was too sick." She died that night. I was lucky to get that much out of her.

"I never knew her to draw," Annalise said.

"Maybe she didn't need to." Maybe her power was stronger than mine.

Annalise considered the drawing. I had gotten the guard's expression exactly right, just at the moment when confusion twisted into rage.

"That's really good," she said.

"My drawing is always better when it's a pulled memory."

"Huh. I wonder…"

"What?" I asked.

"It's just…Fafa's music." She stared off as though she could hear my grandmother's piano. "She played with so much more emotion than Mama or me. "Maybe she didn't need to draw. Maybe she played the memories instead."

A knock interrupted the silence that followed Annalise's thought. Annalise and I clutched each other. Maybe my ability had failed me, and the SS had come for me. But it was only Julia in the doorframe, her large eyes wide, a stack of drawings under her arm and a thin strip of paper in her hand.

A transport slip.

"I couldn't find Lukas," she said. Red splotches covered her face as if she'd been crying but had waited until she stopped before she came to see me.

"Oh—Julia," I stammered. "That doesn't matter now." An hour ago, it had. Now, that little slip of paper was the only thing I could see.

"Get these drawings to Mr. Strauss for me." She shoved a stack of papers into my hands. "They won't raid your room twice in one day. I have to get to my family. I don't even know if they're going too."

I cradled the drawings like a baby. This was happening too fast. If I hadn't just used my ability, maybe I could have stopped it.

"I'll see you when you get back," I said.

"My friend." Julia's look was a rebuke. We both knew no one ever came back from the labor camps. She hugged me anyway.

"After the war. I'll find you," I said into her hair.

I considered what Ernst had experienced at Dachau. The dogs, the barbed wire, the pointless moving of rocks back and forth. I prayed she wasn't going there. "I'm sure it won't be bad."

She didn't seem to mind the lie this time.

Chapter Nineteen

"WHERE IS EVERYONE?" I asked Adam from the doorway. The Art Department had dwindled down to eight inmates in the two months since Julia was transported, but Adam was the only one in the room to answer. I fell into my chair. "Was there another train last night?"

"I don't think so," he said, "but Ernst isn't coming in today." Adam lived in the bunk room next door, and they walked to work together every morning.

"Did someone hurt him?" Someone was always hurting him.

"Not exactly." Adam winced. "He was ordered to latrine duty again." It was nasty work, mucking out the men's latrine. Ernst seemed to get picked for it more than anyone I knew. Mr. Strauss could usually get him out of it, but he wasn't in today either.

The raid on my room had spooked Ernst. The next day at work, he'd told me it wasn't safe for us to be seen together. He didn't speak to me after that, and never acknowledged me outside the Art Department. He got into so much trouble in this place already. I didn't blame him for not wanting to attract more by having me for a friend.

"Maybe the others had a party last night, and we weren't invited," Adam said.

"Well, they left us with all the work," I said. I held up a corner of one of the sketches.

"We'll get it done," he said. "Besides, we can be social rejects together." He laid his hand on top of mine. It felt nice enough but still lacked the fire of Gideon's touch when we'd danced at Hanka's wedding.

The door to the Art Department swung open and slammed shut in an instant. As if the memory had summoned him, Gideon stood just inside the doorway, panting as if he'd run the length of the camp. It reminded me of when Uncle Stellan had appeared at our door when we found out about the roundup, and a chill ran down my spine.

"Those pictures you gave Strauss, any of them signed?" His neck strained into cords.

"Pictures?" I asked. I withdrew my hand from Adam's. Gideon hadn't even noticed I was holding it.

He crossed the room and banged his palms on my desk. "Were they signed?" Gideon asked.

"What happened?" Adam's voice sounded like a summer breeze over Gideon's raging storm.

Gideon didn't look at Adam. He reserved his glare for me. At least he lowered his voice.

"Drawings of Terezin made their way to a Swiss newspaper. The SS raided Mr. Strauss's bunk an hour ago. They confiscated a dozen pictures. He's been taken into custody."

"Not Mr. Strauss," I said. He'd always seemed too well connected to be caught unawares.

"The Hens too."

"Ernst?" I asked. Had they taken him from latrine duty? The thought of him at the Little Fortress made me sick.

"I don't know."

Adam swore under his breath.

"Lieutenant Colonel Eichmann is interrogating them himself," Gideon said.

"Eichmann is here?" I asked.

The lieutenant colonel was the Nazi in charge of all the deported Jews in the Reich. No one that high up had ever been to Terezin.

"So, I'll ask you again, Rachel. Were they signed?"

The truth was, I didn't know. Mr. Strauss had taken several of my drawings, and yes, some of them were signed. I didn't know which ones he'd sold on the black market and which ones he'd smuggled out to the Czech resistance, though, and I couldn't think straight while the specter of the Little Fortress loomed.

"I..."

Gideon took my hesitation for a confession.

"Damn it, Rachel!" He pounded my desk with his fist. "How could you be so stupid?"

Adam put a protective arm around me. "I don't think it's necessary—"

Gideon looked at him for the first time. "You got her involved in this, Kaplan."

Adam stood. "You should go, Gideon. You're upsetting her."

Gideon stalked to the door to storm out, but Officer Novak swung it open instead. Gideon's shoulders slumped, all his anger gone. He drooped against the wall behind him.

"Rachel Abramson?" The gendarme scanned the room as if it were crammed with possible Rachel Abramsons. His eyes landed on me, pale and trembling, surrounded by the empty desks of my friends. He smiled—that same one I'd pulled from Julia's memory—and my knees buckled like a crushed can.

At least I wasn't brought to Lieutenant Colonel Eichmann. The blessing was of the disguised variety, though, because Officer Novak brought me straight to the Cauliflower.

"Get the pictures from the lieutenant colonel," the Cauliflower said to Officer Novak.

Once alone, he directed me to sit in the low chair opposite his desk in SS headquarters. He towered over me in his higher one. His office decor consisted of the usual Nazi decor, a portrait of the Führer, landscapes of farms, and military men on horseback, so the single modernist painting caught my eye. It was good, and I wondered who he'd stolen it from.

Officer Novak came back with a pile of papers stiff with dried ink and paint. My eyes followed the stack like a pointed gun. The drawings could be just as deadly. Did they contain enough evidence to kill me?

"There's no cause for alarm, miss. It's just one simple question." He handed a pack of pictures over his desk to me.

One depicted a horde of emaciated inmates scrounging for the last scraps from a soup kettle. The next was a sketch of the mica factory. Tiny particles floated through the air, while several workers choked or covered their mouths. The third showed the gendarmes whipping a construction crew with the new music pavilion half complete in the background.

"Who drew these?"

All of them were clearly signed by one of the Hens. I identified them without hesitation. I couldn't save them.

The Cauliflower nodded, never changing his expression. "They've all been arrested already," he said, picking up the next bundle of pictures. "But you knew that, didn't you?"

The next set of drawings had no signatures. The top one had been in the pile Julia gave me the night she'd been transported. It depicted uniformed soldiers loading men, women, and children into cattle cars stretching out into an infinite horizon.

"Who drew this?"

Julia was far from the Cauliflower's rage at a camp in the east. Maybe I could keep her safe.

I shook my head.

I had never seen the next drawing, but I recognized the bold brushstrokes. It depicted a bunk, a hundred beds high, reaching heaven, each with an emaciated form. At the top, an angel extended her arms toward the occupant. She had golden wings and my face.

It was Adam's.

"Who drew this?"

It didn't have a signature. If it had, he would have been arrested too.

"I don't know, sir."

The next drawing had a torn corner.

I'd been so angry when Gideon had ripped off my signature, but if I ever got out of SS headquarters, I would thank him.

"There's no signature," I said, hoping it sounded like confusion rather than relief.

He came around his large desk to hover behind me.

"The artist has real talent," he said. He pointed to the blanket covering Rivka's body. "See how she uses shadow to build the layers of the fabric?"

The chill sent down my spine by the word *she* straightened my back like an arrow. I was the only female in the Art Department since Julia was transported.

"Any idea whose it is?" he asked.

"I don't recognize it." I clamped my hands together in my lap to stop them from trembling.

"You must be familiar with your fellow artists' styles." His voice lilted into a question.

"We don't do pictures like this in the Art Department, sir," I said. Gideon would have been proud of that response, but I wasn't sure they'd let me live long enough to tell him about it.

"That's true. It's the most despicable horror propaganda." He paced behind me. I had to fight the urge to turn around to keep an eye on him. "This is just the kind of thing the Allies have been accusing us of for years." He came back around to face me. "You can understand why we want it to stop."

"Of course, sir." I opened my eyes as wide as possible, a trick Annalise had taught me. She'd meant for it to be used when I'd forgotten homework or gotten into trouble with Mama, but it definitely applied in these circumstances too. "Anything I can do." The Cauliflower nodded as if he appreciated the offer.

Officer Novak came in with that smile and a rolled-up piece of paper tied up with ribbon. "That boy brought this one in, sir."

Officer Novak unfurled the picture at the doorway to look at it before he handed it over. The ribbon floated to the ground.

It was yellow.

The painting was on thin paper, so the bold outline of the two girls showed through. All the other times I'd marveled at it, I'd relived the terrible moment or been awed by Ernst's talent. This time, I only worried about what it meant for my friend and how I might save him.

"She hasn't put it together yet," said Officer Novak, who still held Ernst's painting.

"She's too busy trying to get out of the trouble she's in," the Cauliflower said. "She hasn't asked herself how we got it." The moment I considered the question, the answer came right behind it.

Lukas.

"Now she gets it," the Cauliflower said when he saw my face fall.

I had asked Lukas if he took the picture from under my mattress after the raid. He had denied it, but I'd suspected he lied. He must have taken it to protect us at first, knowing the raid was coming. Whatever his reason, he'd given it to Officer Novak now, knowing it might kill me.

Officer Novak passed the painting to his commander. The Cauliflower's eyes widened at the sight of it, probably surprised by the mastery of the work. "This isn't yours." He laid the painting on the desk. He held it open with two hands on either side and stared, probably searching for clues as to who painted it. Ernst's handwriting was messy, but with a little research, the Cauliflower could figure it out.

"You have untrustworthy friends, Miss Abramson." Did he mean Ernst? Or Lukas? He stepped back from his desk, and the painting rolled up on its own. He snapped at Officer Novak to hand him the yellow ribbon on the floor.

"All right, then," the Cauliflower said as he tied it back around Ernst's painting. Hope flared when he pointed to the door, but Officer Novak stood between me and freedom. "Maybe a change in scenery will jog your memory," the Cauliflower said.

Officer Novak escorted me down the hallway to a truck outside. The engine was already running. Another gendarme opened a gate, revealing where they were taking me. I drew back, my heels digging into the gravel of the road.

It took both guards to drag me to the back of the truck. Officer Novak threw it open, exposing the Hens and Mr. Strauss cowering in the sudden bright light. Mr. Strauss had a split lip, and one of the others, a bloody nose. Would my blood spatter my clothes soon too?

I was pushed in, and like the tunnel at the end of the road ahead that led to the Little Fortress, the dark swallowed us whole.

Chapter Twenty

WHEN THE TRUCK OPENED, the daylight was as disorienting as the dark had been. They yanked me out, and the stench of acrid smoke bit into my lungs. I gagged and stared at the smokestack rising to the sky before me. From Terezín, it could be mistaken as part of a factory, but here at the mouth of the Little Fortress, it was unmistakable for what it was.

The Germans couldn't be bothered to bury the thousands of people who died of disease and malnutrition in the ghetto. The crematorium was beside the Little Fortress.

I wasn't given time to gape at it. We were herded inside and down a concrete hallway. A guard pushed the Hens into a room already filled with people. Another tried to shove Mr. Strauss in too. I seized his sleeve, still certain my mentor could save me. Officer Novak held the back of my shirt, preventing me from rushing into the room with them.

"Rachel." The stony tone of Mr. Strauss's voice stopped my lunging. He patted my hand once and pried my fingers from him. He glanced down at his blood-splattered shirt. "You don't want to go where we're going, child," he said.

That got me pulling on his sleeve, hoping I might be able to protect him for once, but Officer Novak yanked my hands from him much less gently. The Hens and Mr. Strauss disappeared behind the door before I could say goodbye.

The gendarme pushed me into a room more like an office than a cell. It had a thick wooden floor and paneled walls but no furniture.

At the sight of the window, I dashed over to get a glimpse of the world outside Terezin for the first time in a year. At one end of a long wall, a scaffolding of gallows loomed, its wood weathered to a smoky gray. Bullet holes flecked with blood scarred the other end. I scrambled as far from the window as I could after that.

While I waited, I considered ways to use my ability to get out of there, but I'd have to get by too many people, and even if I did, where could I go?

Someone down the hall screamed, sending gooseflesh down my arms. Which of the Hens was it? Was it Kurt, who never cleaned the ink from beneath his fingernails? Or Martin, who had shown me how to center my lettering? I winced with each scream, but they kept coming.

Officer Novak appeared in the threshold during the third bout of screams. With the thick door open, the cries were even louder. He didn't move to close it. He wanted me to hear.

The Cauliflower came in with the stack of pictures a second later. He tossed them to where I sat on the floor. "Whoever the artist is, I hope she won't mind that I added a little touch of my own." My drawing of Rivka was on top, her face splattered with fresh blood like Mr. Strauss's shirt.

"Who drew these?" the Cauliflower asked.

"I don't know," I said, unable to take my eyes from the blood. Whose was it?

"How do you get them out of Terezin?"

"I've never seen them before," I said.

He kicked the pile into my lap, smearing blood on my dress.

Ernst's painting was not among the others. Did the Cauliflower keep it in order to mete out some special punishment for him? Were those his screams echoing down the hallway? Maybe the Cauliflower had stolen it because he knew it would fetch a good price. It wouldn't be the first time a Nazi stole something from us.

Footfalls echoed down the hallway toward me. Had the Cauliflower called in reinforcements to torture me so my screams would join the others? Instead of a guard with giant fists and thick boots, it was only little Sadie Haas, one of the Hens' daughters. She skipped by, a flash of light-blue cotton and black curls, just like she'd skipped through the Art Department a million times.

All of the women and children that followed were too aware of the trouble they were in to skip.

"Oh, yes"—the Cauliflower gestured to the hall-way—"we have some other new guests with us." I froze, listening for any slowing approach at my own door. I'd take the arrival of fists and boots over Annalise or Gideon.

"Is there someone I should send for?" he asked as if offering me tea and biscuits. "Someone to keep you company?" I shook my head. His pretense of hospitality vanished. The Cauliflower crouched down into a squat beside me. "I'll find everyone out there you love and bring them here if you won't tell me who drew this." He stroked the blood splatters, still wet, blotting out Rivka's face.

A confession meant not only my own death but the death of my loved ones too. The artists down the hall were caught. It was too late for their families. One more drawing wouldn't make a difference. I took a deep breath and silently apologized to my mentor for my lie.

"It was Mr. Strauss."

Officer Novak hit me with a closed fist in the eye. Pain exploded across my face. My neck snapped back and my head struck the wall behind me. Everything went black for a moment, but my vision cleared.

The Cauliflower laid a hand on his arm. "Eichmann ordered us not to touch her. She's Danish," he said and

bent back to my ear. "Think about my question." Their
boots clicked on the floor to the door. As he closed it, the
Cauliflower said, "I don't care what Eichmann says. If she
doesn't cooperate, I'll kill her myself."

They threw me into the truck and brought me back to
Terezin at dawn the following morning. I stumbled to
my room to find Annalise on my bed with Jubilee in her
hands, Adam on the floor, and Gideon in a corner tinkering with a ball of wire.

Annalise's squeal of happiness died in her throat once
she got a good look at me. My eye had swollen shut. Blood
crusted my cheek where Officer Novak's ring had torn my
skin.

Annalise lifted my arms and spun around me. "Are you
hurt anywhere else?" She yelped when she saw the blood
from Rivka's drawing on my dress.

"I'm fine, Annalise." I brushed past her to Adam. "Has
Ernst been arrested?"

"No, he—"

"We have to warn him. They have his painting. It's
signed."

"He already knows," Adam said. "I went to tell him you
were arrested, but he already knew." He knew I'd been
brought to the Little Fortress and he didn't come here to
check on me?

"I guess he's right to stay away." I shook off the ache in
my chest. I had to warn Adam too. "They have a drawing
of yours too."

Adam paled. "The angel?"

My eye contact broke when I remembered she had my
face. "It was a good thing you didn't sign it."

"Did they have any of yours?" Annalise asked.

"Yes."

Annalise's eyes widened. She mouthed the words so Adam and Gideon couldn't hear. "Did you have to pull?"

I shook my head. "They couldn't be sure I'd drawn it. Being Danish didn't hurt." Gideon had continued to fiddle with the ball of wire without saying a word the whole time. "Thank you, Gideon. You saved my life when you tore off that signature." I reached out for him. I don't know if I hoped he would embrace me or at least take my hand, but he pushed off the wall with his back and marched out.

"He was here all night." Annalise stroked my hair. "He was worried sick too."

I didn't want to tell her about Lukas—not in front of Adam—but I didn't need to. She already knew.

"Rachel...Lukas...He..." Annalise said, blinking back tears.

"I know." I wrapped my arms around her. "It doesn't matter."

"One good bit of news," Annalise said. "Julia's dad came by after work last night. He got a postcard from her yesterday." It was about time we'd heard from her. She'd been gone for two months.

"What did she say?"

"All the usual you expect from one of those postcards. Plenty of food. Conditions aren't bad." The same lies we told in ours.

"Is she in Dachau? Ravensbrück?"

"No," Annalise said. Some of the tension in my neck relaxed. That was a good bit of news.

"Where is she?" I asked. When the war ended, I wanted to know where to look.

"Some camp in Poland...Auschwitz."

"What a relief."

Chapter Twenty-one

THE ONLY SIGN OF the Hens in the Art Department was the smell of their pipe tobacco. The SS had cleaned out all their desks.

"It's too quiet," I said. No one responded. Adam was dropping off plans to SS headquarters, and Ernst was still not speaking to me, even with no one else in the room. He shifted in his chair, his eyes darting to me from the enlistment poster he was drawing.

"It's okay," I said. "You don't have to talk to me. I understand."

"I don't think you do," he said under his breath. They were the first words he'd said to me in months. He dropped his head in his hands, holding it at the temples.

A child's laugh chimed from the street. I sat up, hoping to see little Sadie Haas skip by. Instead, a crowd of children and their caregivers marched past our windows like tiny soldiers. Eli stood out, so much taller than the others. He was still the only ten-year-old in Hadas's room. She passed the Art Department in a daze, wringing her hands, followed by the rest of her boys. Isador and Zoltan must have made up, because they swung their clasped hands. A trio of SS officers escorted them at the back of the line.

They usually played in Stadt Park on the other side of the ghetto. They had no reason to be over here, and they were never guarded by SS officers on their outings.

"Where are they taking the children?" I asked, but the sight of SS officers must have reminded Ernst to keep his distance from me, and he didn't answer.

I slipped out once they'd passed and followed until they reached the open green gate. The parade of children followed the path out of the camp and toward the Little Fortress. Toward the gallows and the wall scarred with bullet holes. Toward the screams of my friends. An SS officer swung the gate closed behind them. I didn't hear a gendarme approach over the sound of my heart pounding in my ears.

"Why aren't you at work?"

I found myself looking for Lukas to save me before I remembered what he had done. I apologized to the guard and scurried away, pretending to obey, but instead, I climbed up the rampart where I'd first seen the Little Fortress with Gideon.

He was waiting for me there but didn't bother to say hello.

"They aren't hurting them," Gideon said.

"How can you be sure?" I shielded my eyes with my hand from the late-afternoon sun. Sure enough, the children headed to the smaller building beside the Little Fortress.

I rushed to the wall to grip its edge, and the rough concrete scratched my palms. "What are they doing at the crematorium?" I asked. The taste of the acrid smoke filled my mouth like it had the day I had gotten close to that smokestack.

"Don't worry about it." He stood and tried to turn my shoulders in the direction of the stairs. "We should both get back to work." The children and caregivers formed a line extending out of the building to a truck parked just outside.

I jerked his hands off me. "No, Gideon. Tell me. What are they doing?"

He looked like he might tell me to keep my head down or something equally impossible, but his gaze caught on my still swollen eye, and he softened.

"It looks like it hurts," he said. He passed a gentle thumb over my bruised eyelid. "I'm really glad you're okay." He took one of my hands and cradled it to his chest.

"Nice try." I tore my hand away. "That kind of thing may work on that boy-crazy Lena Waal, but it doesn't work on me."

Every muscle in Gideon's face tensed. Mine did too. I hated to think my words against Lena struck a nerve.

"Hadas and Eli are down there," I said. From this distance, I couldn't make out which was Eli or Hadas. I squinted at them. "What are they doing?" They were passing dark cubes from the building to the waiting truck like a strange game of hot potato. The blocks were pitched into the bed of the truck by the last person in line. They blew apart into dusty clouds on impact.

"What are those things?" I asked. A sick gnawing in my gut whispered the answer, but I needed to be sure. "Please, Gideon?"

The *please* melted the stiffness in his jaw. "They're destroying the urns. They'll take them to the river and dump them when they're finished." Gideon wasn't watching the line.

I thought of Rivka. No Kaddish prayer had been said for her. Her family hadn't been allowed to sit shiva. Now they were dumping her ashes into a truck. They were destroying her all over again. I should have been angry, but I was too hungry and tired. And afraid.

"Why are they doing this?" I couldn't look back at him. If he saw my fear, he would lie.

"They're losing the war. They're erasing the evidence."

"But that doesn't matter. We've all seen what they've done," I said. "We're witnesses."

"That's what I'm afraid of," he said.

My eyes darted to his for only a second before a woman in the line screamed.

She fell to her knees, clutching a box to her chest. Her hair was too dark to be Hadas, but her grief still tore through me.

"The urns must have names on them," he said. My aching chest made it hard to breathe. "It must be someone she knew."

An SS officer grabbed the box from the woman, but she wouldn't let it go. After a struggle, a puff of dust rose from it. It had fallen apart in her hands, emptying the ashes in the dirt and all over her dress. Her cries turned to wails.

I couldn't bear it. Without thinking, I pulled the memory of the name on the urn from her. After a moment, she stood and brushed the ashes of a person she loved from her knees.

"You just took it, didn't you?" Gideon asked.

Every muscle stiffened. "Took what?" I asked, peeking at him from the corner of my eye.

"Her memory or her sadness." He crossed his arms over his chest. "I'm not sure how it works," he said.

"What?" I laughed, loud enough to make some of the fieldworkers below turn to look up at us. "That's crazy." I pointed to the stairs. "You're right. We should get back to work."

He blocked my path. "Don't lie to me, Rachel. I've been watching you do it since we were kids." I stopped midstride. He knew? The whole time? "Your mouth hangs open, and you look like you're about to drool."

My hands flew to my hips. "I do not!"

"So, you don't deny it?" He sounded like a detective in a movie. "And it is what you look like." He let his jaw go slack, and his eyes glazed over as if in a trance. He groaned, and his tongue lolled out of his mouth.

Did I? Heat flooded to the tips of my ears. "I do not!" I repeated.

"Yes, you really do." His glee dried up, and he laid a hand on my shoulder. "Does it hurt?"

I paused. Now that Annalise knew, it didn't seem so strange to talk about it with Gideon. I dropped my hands to my sides. "It makes me tired."

He nodded as if he already knew that. "You need your strength in here."

"I only took the memory to help her bear it." I took a step toward the edge. The woman was standing again, passing the urns down the line. The SS officer had moved on. "That guard might have hurt her."

Gideon shook his head. "You're doing the same thing the Nazis are doing down there."

My hands shot back to my hips. "What the hell does that mean?" I didn't wait for an answer and started down the stairs. Gideon followed.

"Erasing the evidence, Rachel. Why did you give Mr. Strauss your drawings if you didn't want everyone to know what happened here? We would be better off if you could make people remember forever. We already forget too easily."

"That's ridiculous, Gideon." We were down by the closed gate again. "Who would want—"

"I did."

His confession knocked the breath out of me like I'd been dunked in a cold pond. As much as I'd botched it, I didn't think Gideon ever knew what I'd done to him.

"One minute, I was crying, and the next, my brother's face was gone," he said. "I couldn't picture Ezra for a year." He took off his cap and slapped his thigh with it. "A year, Rachel." He looked at me. "You *stole* that from me."

Stole?

"I couldn't stand to see you in pain."

"So, you didn't do it to spare me. You did it to spare yourself." He held up a hand when I opened my mouth to argue. "I get why you did it. You just didn't have the right."

It was my turn to follow him. "Gideon—"

"Hey!" a voice called out, and a gendarme appeared in the threshold of an alley. I thought it was the one who had stopped me at the gate earlier, but it wasn't.

I hadn't seen Lukas since before I'd been taken to the Little Fortress. Dark circles stained underneath his eyes, and his uniform—usually an outlet of vanity for him—was rumpled and ill-fitting as if he'd recently lost some weight. If I hadn't gone to sleep to the sound of Annalise crying every night since he'd turned me in, I might have felt a little sorry for him. As it was, I took a perverse pleasure in the change.

"I need to speak to you," he said. He didn't look at either of us, so I wasn't sure which of us he meant.

"C'mon, Rachel." Gideon tugged on my arm without stopping. I had frozen in the middle of the street at the sight of him. "We don't need anything from him."

"You need to know this." Lukas reached out with some urgency but didn't leave the alley.

"I don't want your sorry excuses, Lukas." I took a step toward him as I said the lie. I *did* want his excuses. I wanted there to be a reason for what he'd done to me. What he'd done to Annalise.

"I'm not here to talk about that." He scanned the street and turned to be sure no one was behind him.

Gideon tugged me, and I got moving again. "I know where the transports go," Lukas said. That froze both of us. "A couple of months ago, a Czech named Teodus Godocik was transported."

"Thousands of Czechs have been transported," Gideon said, but he didn't move.

"He came back last night," Lukas said. Gideon's tugging on my arm stopped. No one ever returned to Terezin after being transported east. "The SS caught him sneaking in. They brought him to the Little Fortress."

I shuddered. Did he stay in the room where my friends had been beaten?

"Why would anyone come back here?" Gideon asked.

"To warn you."

"Warn us of what?" I asked.

"The camp he was sent to..." Lukas dropped his chin to his chest, unable to look at us again. "The camp where we've been sending the transports...It's not a labor camp."

This didn't surprise me. From what I'd heard about Dachau from Ernst, some of the camps were just to torture us.

"It's a death camp, Rachel," Lukas said to the ground.

"What?" I'd never heard the term, but ice still wound through my bloodstream at the word.

"They keep the strongest to maintain it, but kill everyone else," Lukas said.

"Thousands are getting transported," said Gideon. "How could they kill so many at a time?" Leave it to Gideon to ask such a horridly practical question.

"They're gassed," Lukas said.

"Gassed?" I asked.

"They use Zyklon B."

"The pesticide?" asked Gideon.

"We use it to clear out the mice and bugs." Lukas's nose wrinkled in disgust. "But they put it through the showerheads." His voice cracked. "People don't even know it's coming."

"And they don't have to even look us in the eye," said Gideon.

"It can't be true," I said. I looked up at Gideon. My only hope was that he'd poke a hole in Lukas's story, but he was quiet. "How did this man get back here?"

"Godocik confessed the Czech resistance helped him get back, but he got caught before he could warn anyone."

What had the SS done to the poor man to get him to betray the partisans? I winced, remembering the sounds of the artists' screams echoing in the Little Fortress. I don't know when Gideon's hand slipped into mine, but he squeezed it.

"While Godocik was with the resistance, he heard stories from the British press on their radio. Someone in this camp smuggled a camera out. The pictures were released a couple of days ago in the London papers. The Germans are calling it more *horror propaganda*, of course."

"Not all the camps in the east," I managed hopefully. Too many people had been transported. Thousands—tens of thousands—would be dead.

"Which one was he sent to?" Gideon asked.

Lukas took a deep breath, and his eyes finally landed squarely on mine.

"Auschwitz."

I shuffled backward, trying to escape the truth of it. "That can't be right." I looked between Gideon and Lukas. I gripped Gideon's arm and shook it. "Julia's family got a postcard saying she was fine. That the work wasn't hard, that there was enough food." But I already knew her postcard didn't mean anything. How many had we all sent full of lies?

"Julia," I said. Somehow I had ended up on the ground.

"Rachel," Lukas said. I couldn't look at him. I focused on a crack in the wall behind his head instead. The crack was hard to see. Someone had crammed a paintbrush full of whitewash into it to hide the crumbling brick from the Red Cross delegation this summer.

Maybe it had been me.

"I'm so sorry, Rachel." Lukas's voice sounded like a child's. "For everything."

Gideon's hand left mine, and the next thing I knew, Lukas was pinned up against the alley wall.

"Did you see Rachel's eye? Did you see what that monster did to her because of you?" Gideon stuck his finger into Lukas's chest. "You don't get to apologize to her."

I reached up to clutch the hem of Gideon's shirt. "Don't," I said. Gideon fell to the ground beside me and wrapped an arm around my waist while I gulped through the spasmed hitching of my chest.

I remembered my first shower. How cold, vulnerable, and scared I'd felt. Had Julia died feeling that way?

"I always thought this place was hell," Gideon said as he led me away. "But it's just the waiting room."

Chapter Twenty-two

THE NEWS ABOUT AUSCHWITZ spread through Terezin even faster than the lice. That Friday night, Rabbi Hertz led a Kaddish prayer for all who were lost. I tried not to think of Julia when the prayer for the dead was said. I clung to the chance she was still alive, but each line conjured her face.

"May there be an abundant peace from Heaven and life, upon us and upon all Israel. And let us say..." Rabbi Hertz held out his hands to signal the congregation's response.

"Amen," we said. Our voices didn't echo much with the low vaulted ceiling and the large crowd crammed into the small space, not like at our temple back home.

When Rabbi Hertz had arrived in Terezin two years before, he discovered an abandoned storage room behind the laundry and transformed it into a synagogue. I admired the straight lines of the Stars of David and the precision of the Hebrew prayers painted on the walls. He could have had a job in the Art Department if he wanted one. There were plenty of empty desks these days.

I thought because my family hadn't been active members in Copenhagen, there would be nothing for me in the little hidden temple behind the laundry, but that may have been the wrong way to think about it. Attending Shabbat services was an act of defiance, like my drawings and Annalise's *Requiem*.

"He who creates peace in His celestial heights, may He create peace for us and for all Israel." Rabbi Hertz again held out his arms to elicit the choral reply.

"Amen." The salt from my tears burned my ravaged eye.

The rabbi didn't let the quiet settle. He clapped his hands and rubbed them together as if he was warming them by a fire. "And now for some joyful news. A wedding," he said. His transformation from solemnity to happiness felt like slamming a door closed with Julia on the wrong side. The rabbi called Ruben Hirsch and Mila Wolff up to the front.

"One of Otto's boys?" I whispered to Annalise, dabbing my eye. Otto lived on the floor below us in West with his seven handsome sons. One for each day of the week, Annalise had joked.

Annalise nodded and watched as Ruben and Mila made their way through the tightly packed crowd. "He's Tuesday," she sighed. "They got engaged only a week ago."

"Who's the girl?" I asked.

"Mila? She's German. My guess is she works in the factory." My sister wrinkled her nose at the girl's wedding dress. It was caked in gray mica dust. The stuff was impossible to get out.

There would be no *chuppah*, the canopy couples stood beneath during a wedding ceremony, and no breaking of the glass at the end. Ruben had made a ring, though, an old iron nail bent into a circle.

"Since you're a Dane now, Mila," Rabbi Hertz said after the short ceremony, "I don't see why you can't move into West Barracks with your husband. You should be eligible for a job reassignment too." Rabbi Hertz said this to the bride but spoke loudly enough for the entire congregation to hear. "If any other Danes are considering marrying one of the less fortunate, it's important you know, they won't let me issue an official *ketubah* here." He smiled broadly, hoping we were getting the hint. "Which means it won't be legally binding."

I could tell from the way Ruben kissed Mila's hair and the way she curled her head into the space beneath his chin that they would marry officially the second the war was over. They hadn't done this just to improve her living conditions.

It must have been hard for Annalise to watch such a sweet couple with Lukas's betrayal so fresh, but she didn't show it. She knew my loss had been worse.

I didn't look up when Adam came into work the next day.

"Ernst isn't coming in," he said.

"Latrine duty again?" I asked, still focused on the plans we were working on.

"No."

When he didn't explain, I looked up.

"He's sick." Ernst had a nasty cough for the last couple weeks, but nearly everyone had a nasty cough in Terezin. Would the hospital take him? I'd have to make sure Annalise would care for him if he came in.

"Your eye is much better," Adam said as he sat.

I could almost see out of it again. All the crying these last couple of days hadn't helped. "I wish everything healed up as fast." I scanned the empty desks of the Art Department and stopped at Julia's.

"You don't know she's gone. They keep some of them alive," Adam said. His optimism never wavered. Maybe because accepting Julia's death meant he had to accept his own family's possible fate. I couldn't disillusion him, so I just nodded.

The door swung open. Adam and I spun in our chairs. Commandant Becker and the Cauliflower entered the room. A couple of SS officers I had never seen before followed them in. From the insignia on their lapels, they were a higher rank than the commandant, probably from nearby Prague. I gripped the edges of my desk as they approached us. The commandant eyed the blueprints from over Adam's shoulder.

"We expected these plans weeks ago," he said.

I let out a breath. They weren't coming to take us away.

"I know, sir. I'm sorry." Adam lowered his head, his eyes to the floor. "We'll have them done this week." I almost scoffed out loud. The two of us would never finish the plans that quickly. Adam was the only one with any architectural training, and with Ernst sick, we would need more time.

"Your delays cost the Reich," the Cauliflower said. "Are you a saboteur or just an idiot?" The SS officers smiled.

Adam stuttered he was neither.

"Maybe some time in the Little Fortress will motivate you to move faster." The Cauliflower lifted Adam out of his seat by the collar of his shirt.

I grabbed Adam's arm. "He's the only one who can finish the work, sir."

It had been a good save, but the Cauliflower had been looking for an excuse. He jerked the wooden baton from its holster at his hip. I raised my arms to guard my face. My pulse hammered in my bruised eye.

The commandant called out, "Commander Gruber," in a disinterested way, then turned to the SS officers. "She's a Dane. They think they're above the rules." The SS officers murmured their sympathy.

"This week," the commandant said, and the SS officers followed him out the door. I peeked out from behind my arms like a mouse coming out of a hole. The Cauliflower had stayed behind. His bald head was flushed red. His baton was still in his hand.

"Afraid of another one of your friends going to the Little Fortress, are you?" he asked. "Your last friend we had as a guest did not fare well. You're right to be afraid." He bent to my ear, and his whisper felt wet and hot. "Strauss confessed *he* painted the unsigned pictures, but I know some of them were yours." He raised his baton and brushed my cheek with it. "We killed him anyway."

A low, pained moan escaped my lips. I hated myself for the sound, both for the weakness it showed and the pleasure it gave him.

He slipped the baton back into his belt. "If I ever get you back there, I'll crush your pretty little head." He put his hands at my temples. "Did you hear what happened to the others?" he asked. From the smile on his face, I already knew what happened to the Hens, their wives, their children. "They went to Auschwitz. You know what that means now, don't you?" His smile widened when another sob sputtered out of me. "There's another transport leaving this afternoon."

"You can't transport her," Adam said at his desk.

Quiet, Adam. I can't lose you too, I thought.

"No, no." The Cauliflower had another torture in mind. "I can't send you out on the train, but I can make you load it," he said.

When he was gone, Adam rushed to my side, but I couldn't hear what he said to calm me.

"They're dead," I said, my hands gesturing around the empty room. "All of them." Adam embraced me, but my arms were limp at my sides.

"Not all of us," Adam said in my hair as I cried.

"Mr. Strauss..." He'd died for me. "I killed him."

"You were beaten and scared. You could've given up Ernst and me, but you didn't. They could have killed you."

I looked up at Adam's face. "The war isn't over yet. They still might."

The trains looked like the ones that brought Annalise and me to Terezin, with their slats chalked with yellow stars. The same smell of hay filled the air. This time, though, there wasn't room for anyone to sit for the long trip. No fancy luncheon or photographers waited for them on the other side.

Several other inmates collected slips and helped the old and sick up the ramp. No one fought back. They all seemed to understand. That only made it worse.

I wished I could have relied on ignorance and hoped they would be all right like when Julia was sent away. I knew too much for such blissful luxury now.

At the fifth car, I helped an old man limp into the train. His artificial foot clunked against the ramp. Many veterans of the Great War had such limbs, but they were supposed to have prominent status. The same prominent status that had protected Danes from transport all this time. I tried not to think about my own long-term safety. People were marching off to their deaths. Tonight.

An SS officer pointed to the veteran. "I believe that gentleman has something of ours." The foot was not much more than a wooden block, but at least it would keep him upright. He nudged one of the other gendarmes, and they laughed. It solidified my resolve.

"We all know where this train is going," I said. I lowered my eyes and told myself I was only pretending to be frightened. "Please let him die on his own two feet."

"One of those feet is ours." He pointed to a cart another inmate pushed up and down the tracks. I didn't dare peer in to examine what he had collected so far. "Take it from him. Now."

The wooden block clanged when it went into the cart. One of the other inmates helped him into the cattle car before the doors shut.

I confiscated more prostheses at the eleventh, sixteenth, and nineteenth cars.

The sound of singing rose up from car thirty-two. Gooseflesh crawled down my arms when I recognized the song.

The *Requiem*. I broke into a run.

Rafael Salzberg and his choir sang as they lined up, the first few already handing over their transport slips. I rushed down the tracks, listening out for a certain powerful soprano. Had Annalise received a last-minute slip during my absence?

I stopped at the end of the car, gasping, my hands on my knees. Annalise wasn't there.

As I caught my breath, the choir started my sister's solo.

How great will be their terror,
when the Judge comes,
who will smash everything completely!

The "Judge" hadn't come in time for them. Their defiant performance would only get them killed. Why had I celebrated their bravery? What good had it done?

I collected the transport slips from Annalise's friends. I wanted to thank Rafael Salzberg for everything he'd done for my sister, but by the time I reached him, my throat burned too much to speak.

There were no war veterans or defiant singers at boxcar forty-eight.

Just a long line of children.

My dinner rose in my throat when Hadas's little Isador waved at me. "We're going on a train ride," he said. He clutched his grubby stuffed bear. He and his toy could have been Erik and Jubilee. I'd missed my brother's fifth birthday. I had drawn Isador a picture of his bear for his.

Four more of Hadas's boys waited to be loaded into the train car behind Isador.

"Is it okay, Miss Rachel?" asked Zoltan. He drew his sleeve over his sniffling nose.

"It's fine, children," said a voice behind me. Officer Novak laid a hand on my shoulder. "Tell them, Miss Rachel."

Zoltan looked from Officer Novak to me, but I couldn't move.

"Is there a problem?" the gendarme asked.

"I won't help you murder children," I whispered.

"Then you'll die with them," he said.

"You can't transport me," I said. But was that true anymore? I had just loaded war veterans onto the train.

"Plenty of people die right here."

"I don't care." That was a lie. Gideon sometimes joked I had a death wish, but it wasn't true. I didn't want to die, but how could I live with myself if I did it? "I won't."

His smile evaporated at that. He pursed his lips, the evil wheels of his mind turning.

"You might be right, Miss Abramson. You and your sister will be here a long time. My friends and I will be sure to keep you both company." His smile resurfaced—the one that haunted Julia. Now it would haunt me.

I lined them up—all fifty-three children—and loaded them onto that train.

I wanted to get back to West before I cried. I'd choke to death on the burning lump in my throat before I gave Officer Novak the satisfaction of seeing what he'd done to me.

Gideon paced along the courtyard that led back into the ghetto just outside the train depot. When he saw me, the hand raked in his hair fell to his side.

The second he wrapped his arms around me, my resolve broke, unleashing racking sobs that shook my entire body, I no longer cared what Officer Novak saw. Gideon clawed frantic fingers into my hair as if he thought I might be swept away in the flood of my overwhelming grief.

"He only had to threaten me, Gideon." I couldn't look him in the face when I told him about the children.

"It wouldn't have changed anything for those children if you hadn't, and they would have hurt Annalise too. You know they use our loved ones against us." He held my gaze unblinkingly.

I wanted to drink in all of that intensity, but I kept having to look away. "They're winning, Gideon. I'm as good as theirs."

"No." He wiped the tears from my face. "Not you. You'll always be your own." His hand smoothed my hair. "Maybe a little bit mine." He rested his forehead to mine and pressed his lips to the top of my head. Gideon didn't have an ability like me, but that kiss pushed a whole series of images into my mind. That I was good. That I had tried. Maybe that he could love me.

I clung to him, wanting to believe it all, but I broke away when he kissed my head again. My grief still had unfinished business with me. He took me back to the barracks where I curled up in my bed and let it do its work.

Chapter Twenty-three

THERE IS A LINE *of children disappearing into the train. Isador is first. He clutches his grubby stuffed bear. Zoltan is there too. He's scared. He trusts me. He raises his eyebrows to ask me if it's all right to go into the dark opening of this terrible train.*

I murder him with a nod and a smile.

My sister nudged me, thinking I was asleep. I hadn't slept at all. Neither had she. Concern showed through her own red and puffy eyes. I'd killed her friends too.

"C'mon, Rachel. You'll miss work."

"I can't, Annalise."

"You'll get in trouble."

Trouble? I let out a laugh, although it must not have sounded much like one, from Annalise's grimace.

"They made me a coward." My swollen eye burned from a fresh round of tears.

"You were trying to keep us safe. You couldn't have done anything differently." She tucked my blanket under my chin and buttoned her coat without taking her eyes from me. "I'll tell Adam you'll be late. He'll make your excuses."

I let out a strangled laugh again. No one remained to make excuses to. Ernst was still sick, and everyone else had been transported east.

Just like the line of children disappearing into the train.

"You should pull it," Annalise said at the doorway. It took a minute for me to figure out what she meant. She tapped her temple. "Whatever is doing this to you, Kitten. Pull it out." The door clicked shut, and her footsteps receded down the hallway.

There is a line of children disappearing into the train. Isador is first. He clutches his grubby stuffed bear. Zoltan is there too.

A knock disrupted the memory, but Isador and Zoltan didn't disappear. The door creaked only partway open as if the person knew the visit would be unwelcome. There were no locks in West. With another wave of grief, I remembered how jealous Julia had been of our doors.

Lukas's appearance in our room startled me, like finding a penguin in the desert. We'd joked and shared food, even danced here. Annalise and I tried to teach him the horah before a wedding once.

"What do you want?" I didn't bother to get out of bed. Maybe he'd come to take me in for being late to work. It would have been just like the Cauliflower to send Lukas to arrest me. "Annalise isn't here."

"I waited until she left." He came in but left the door behind him open. He had his familiar blue bag over his shoulder. My stomach was empty but spun at the thought of food.

"Take whatever is in there and get out, Lukas. We don't want anything from you." The truth was, I feared the brave front my sister crafted this past week would crumble with one look from him. I was grateful he had been too ashamed to show his face while she was here.

"I had no intention of giving them that painting. I took it to protect you when I found out about the raid. I kept it because I wanted it. She looked so beautiful, but they threatened my family, Rachel. My mother and three sisters. They were in the Little Fortress with you that night."

He took a hunk of cheese and a fat loaf of bread out of the bag and laid them on Annalise's bunk under her blanket.

"I'm sorry," he said when I stayed silent. "I'll have to live with it forever, but I'd do it again to keep my family safe." He probably thought I'd closed my eyes to shut him out, but I was letting his crime blend with my own.

There is a line of children disappearing into the train.

Maybe Annalise was right. I could pull the image out of my own head. I had never done that before.

Isador is first. He clutches his grubby stuffed bear.

Even if the image vanished from my mind, would the pain go with it? My grief felt like a part of me. I couldn't imagine its absence, like waking up without a foot.

Zoltan is there too. He's scared. He trusts me.

I didn't think about how if I pulled the image, I wouldn't remember to sketch it, that I'd be exhausted and wouldn't know why.

He raises his eyebrows to ask me if it's all right...

I didn't think how confused everyone would be. How I could give away my secret.

...to go into the dark opening of this terrible train...

I didn't think about Hadas. That she deserved to know I was there.

I murder him with a nod and a smile.

I don't think. I don't think. I don't think.

Chapter
Twenty-four

THERE WAS A COMIC irony to Hadas giving language lessons.

"You must use ear, Walter." Hadas tickled the boy's earlobe. A riot of giggles filled the room. "Now, to repeat. *Délet*. Door." She pointed to where I stood at the threshold, her eyes still on Walter.

She couldn't use paper. She couldn't leave any evidence of her Hebrew lessons.

She clapped when Walter made a better attempt, and his classmates joined in. I cheered too, and Hadas spun to shield the children with outstretched arms.

Once she recognized me, she clutched her chest to catch her breath.

Why was she so on edge?

One of the boys poked her and said, "Boo!" to which Hadas feigned terror. They continued the fun until she pretended to faint. They fell on her in attempts to wake her. I had to step over some of the children in order to give her a hand up.

"I've brought you a present, children," I said as I set my bag on the floor and took out a series of thick boards. I had worked on them for days.

There were four, and they were thick enough to withstand their rough little hands. I hadn't had a real one to copy, just my faded memories.

"Monopoly boards?" one of the children exclaimed happily when they recognized the telltale color-coded rectangles and train engines.

"Not quite," I said, holding up one of the boards so they could take a better look. I stifled a yawn. I was so tired for some reason.

"That's Dresden Barracks. My mom lives there."

"Stadt Park is where Marvin Gardens is supposed to be," said another.

They'd have to share the single pair of dice, but I'd made plenty of tokens. There weren't as many boys as I thought. I could have sworn there were eighteen. Where were the others? My stomach began to churn. The boys set about looking for scraps of paper to serve as money and property deeds.

"Where is everyone?" I asked. Hadas turned her back so the children couldn't see her face crumble into restrained tears.

She managed to get out one word. "Transport."

"What? Last night?" A fresh pain tore into my chest. "The Cauliflower made me work that transport. I didn't see them." I looked around the room.

"Isador? Zoltan?"

Hadas clamped a hand over her mouth to smother a sob. I tried to pull the memory of her little lost boys. My knees buckled beneath me, but tears continued to stream down her face. Why hadn't it worked? Maybe I was too tired. I'd get a good night's sleep tonight and try again in the morning.

Annalise's choir and the man with the prosthetic foot had been bad enough, but an entire car full of children? I said a quiet prayer of thanks that I hadn't been asked to put children on a transport train.

I couldn't even imagine.

Adam was surprised when I got to work only a few minutes late. He didn't ask me about the night before and even let me nap with my head on my desk all afternoon, even though we had so much to do. It didn't do me any good. I was still tired.

On my way back to West at the end of the day, I passed Gideon sitting on the stoop of the Electrical Department. I could still feel his warm lips on my forehead.

"I thought you didn't go to work today," he said. He tinkered with a ball of wire like he had while he was waiting for me the night I was in the Little Fortress.

"I felt better once I got up." I was about to tell him about the children, but he changed the subject.

"They let Mila move into West this morning. She was reassigned to kitchen duty," Gideon said. "No factory work for us Danes."

I thought of Mila's wedding dress coated in dust and smiled. "So, the SS gave her prominent status because she married one of us?"

He nodded. "Rabbi Hertz wants to marry us all off now. He performed five weddings today. The Blumes married the Ornstein brothers."

"Those boys are a bit young for them, aren't they?" Moshe and Victor were a better age for Annalise and me than the middle-aged Blumes.

Gideon shook his head. "We'll see if the SS comes for them. It's a risk. One I'm not ready to take yet."

"No? Not even Esther or Lena?" I asked, even though I didn't really want to talk about Gideon marrying someone else after last night's kiss. It had only been on my forehead, so maybe he hadn't meant anything by it.

He rolled his eyes and let out a little laugh. "You shouldn't listen to gossip, Rachel," he said. His smile dried up. "I suppose you'll marry Adam."

I loved the jealous little edge in his voice, so I nodded, although my first thought had been Ernst.

A small group of children ran past us, giggling. They weren't Hadas's boys.

Gideon's smile disappeared. "Are you okay?"

"Not really," I said, watching the children pass. "I brought those Monopoly boards to Hadas and the boys."

He ran a hand down my arm, and a trail of warmth followed. "You didn't have to do that today after last night."

How had Gideon known what happened to them? "You heard?"

He cocked his head and narrowed his eyes at me. "You're the one who told me."

I shook my head. He had it mixed up somehow. "I only found out this morning," I said.

He tore his hand off me as if I had typhus. "You took it."

"Took what?"

"Your memory of last night."

"I haven't pulled any memories today." I'd tried to take Hadas's. It hadn't worked, but I was only tired...

My stomach twisted. "I don't want to talk about this, Gideon." Something hideous scratched below the surface of my mind, like a monster just beneath a layer of ice on a lake. I couldn't put my finger on it, and I didn't want to.

"How could you?" Gideon asked. The muscles in his jaw tightened.

I took a step back. "I didn't do anything!"

"What happened last night was terrible, but you had to do it—to protect yourself, and to protect Annalise and me—but you didn't *have* to erase that memory. You did *that* to save yourself the burden. You betrayed all our dead friends when you pulled that weight off your shoulders." He tossed the ball of wire into the street. "It's the only cowardly thing you've ever done."

I let him walk away. My memory of the night before was completely and terribly clear. The man with the wooden foot. Annalise's choir. I hadn't seen the children. I hadn't erased anything.

I *hadn't*.

Gideon wouldn't be happy until everyone was as miserable as him. I raced back to the Art Department and asked Adam to marry me.

Chapter Twenty-five

I WASN'T THE KIND of girl who pictured her wedding much. That was more Annalise's kind of thing.

She'd cut out pictures of dresses from her favorite magazines and practiced doing her hair in different styles. She knew what music would be played and the flowers she would carry. Her husband would have the charm and approximate features of Cary Grant.

I had imagined a pretty dress. Mama would cook my favorite foods, and Papa would drink too much akvavit. I would love my husband very much. That was all I needed.

My sky-blue wedding gown had been hemmed three times, and worn by more women than I could count. A faded yellow star was stitched over my heart where my corsage should be. There wasn't any food or akvavit in the damp and cold music cellar, only mice skittering around in the dark corners. My family was a thousand miles away, and the boy I loved may as well have been.

Rabbi Hertz had been marrying off Danes all week. He filed the papers at SS headquarters for the religious ceremonies, and the Germans, Czechs, and Hungarians became prominent Danish inmates.

"You've done a *mitzvah*, Rachel," Rabbi Hertz said after the short ceremony. I didn't answer. No need to tell him I'd partially done my good deed to hurt Gideon.

Across the room, my new husband grinned like a genuine bridegroom. I told myself he was happy because I had saved him from transport, but when our eyes met, he blushed, and I remembered that the angel he'd drawn had my face.

"Maybe you'll want to make it official when you get home?" Rabbi Hertz asked.

I shook my head a little too emphatically, and he regarded me over his spectacles.

"My father would never approve of me getting married so young," I said, trying to cover my panicked expression. Explaining to Adam the strict parameters of our arrangement had been awkward enough. I wasn't about to repeat the experience with a rabbi.

"Well, he'll be proud when he hears what you've done." His smile crinkled the corners of his eyes. "You have saved a life." That made me happy. Maybe not wedding-day happy, but happy.

The rabbi took his leave when Adam approached us. Someone must have lent him a newer razor for the wedding. None of the usual nicks covered his face.

"I'll help them clean up and meet you back at home." *Home.* He had only moved his few belongings into our room this morning, but he called it home already. His mattress lay as far from my bed as possible. He could take full advantage of his new status as a Danish citizen, but he wouldn't be taking full advantage of his status as my husband.

He took my hand and kissed it, looking down at the ring he'd surprised me with during the ceremony. Old braided copper and steel wire twisted to form the band.

"Gideon guessed your size perfectly."

"Gideon?" When word of my sudden engagement spread, I thought Gideon might barge into my room to tell me how ill-advised it was. That it would raise the Cauliflower's attention. I had hoped it would force Gideon's hand to declare himself in some way, but he didn't even have the decency to show up vaguely tortured to crack his damned knuckles. Instead, he made the ring another boy would slip on my finger.

"Do you like it?" Adam asked.

"It's beautiful." It was beautiful. And heartbreaking.

"I can't believe you got married before me," Annalise said once we were back at West.

"You can get married too, you know," I said.

"I will, I will, but I can't just choose anyone, Kitten." She kicked at Adam's mattress. "We'll have to live with this person."

"Adam will be easy to live with," I said. "He's a sweetheart."

"Oh, yeah? I can sleep at the hospital tonight if you and your husband would like some time alone." My sister nudged me in the side.

"Shut up." I wiggled out of the blue dress and left it in a puddle on the floor. I leaned on the door so it wouldn't open while I was in my underwear. I hadn't thought about the complex logistics of sharing a room with Adam. I'd have to get up early every morning to get dressed before he woke up. Maybe we could rig up some kind of partition like the cubbies in the attic. For sort of the opposite purpose. I yanked off my camisole. "It's not like that with Adam."

"The way you're throwing your clothes off..." Annalise nudged me again. She was a real nudger.

I grabbed my nightgown from a hook on the wall and shimmied into it without leaving my position in front of the door. "Only because I want to be dressed when he comes back."

Annalise had been more subdued since Lukas had disappeared from our lives, but you'd never know it from the way her eyebrows wiggled now. They flapped so wildly—like a fish fighting to escape a hook—I half expected them to fly off her face and hit me in the head.

"Disappointing. How are you going to give me a little niece or nephew with your nightgown on?"

I wrinkled my nose and chucked Jubilee at her, laughing. "That's disgusting, Annalise!" I sat on my bunk to roll up my longest socks so only the skin on my face and hands showed. "I made it very clear to him I don't see him that way." He had taken it well, like he already knew.

"Okay, this has gone on long enough," Annalise said. She sat on the bed next to me. Thankfully, without elbowing me again. "What did you two fight about?"

I squinted at her. "Nothing. Adam and I never fight."

"Not Adam, silly. Gideon."

I thought I had kept it from her. It wasn't like Gideon and I had spent every waking moment together before we'd fought, but we never went this long without speaking. I guess she'd noticed.

"He thinks I erased the memory of something I did. Something terrible." I kept my eyes down, my hands in my lap. That monster was tapping on the frozen lake again.

"You told him about your magic powers?" She clapped her hands together. "I knew you two were involved somehow."

"I didn't tell him, Annalise. He figured it out. Something about my mouth hanging open every time I do it." I fiddled with the sleeve of my nightgown. "Believe me, nothing romantic about it."

"And how did he notice that?" She poked me in the ribs. "Because he doesn't take his eyes off you whenever you're in the room?"

Really? I wanted to believe that was true, but the hiding monster wouldn't let me enjoy it.

I took in a long breath and looked up at her. "What did I do, Annalise?"

Her shoulders slumped and her smile disappeared. "Do you really want to know, Kitten?" So, Gideon had been right. I squeezed my eyes closed. She put an arm around my shoulder.

"It's okay to just let it go, you know," Annalise said.

I shook my head without opening my eyes. "Tell me quickly."

She held both my hands between us. "The transport...Hadas's boys..."

"Oh." I didn't feel anything right away. It was just like when I had sliced my finger open while cutting onions with Mama. I watched my skin split and blood bead, but felt nothing. I had enough time to know just how much it would hurt before I felt the sting. This time, when the pain caught up, it slammed into my chest and took my breath away. Annalise held me while I cried.

"How could Gideon think people want this?" I sniffed and wiped my nose with my sleeve. "What possible good does it do?"

Annalise took a couple of seconds to find a handkerchief for me. "Well, it's kind of like when my sugar crashes. It hurts, but if it didn't, I wouldn't know, and I'd die. Sometimes pain has a purpose."

"I can't stand to watch people suffer." Well, this time, I couldn't stand to suffer myself.

"Of course!" Annalise said, squeezing my hands together. "Listen, I don't know who's right, Kitten." She wrapped an arm around me. "But I know you'd never hurt anyone on purpose."

"But you're not mad I pulled your memory of Fafa, are you?"

"Not mad, no." She shook her head. She considered her shoes and asked much more quietly, "Do you think I could have it back?"

I wrinkled my nose at her. "I'm not sure it works that way." I'd never tried.

"Can you try?"

I blinked at her. "That memory..." I thought of my own puffy eyes and aching chest. "It will hurt."

She didn't hesitate. "I know."

I pictured my grandmother, and instead of pulling the image toward me and away from her, I pushed it at my sister. A little spark shot up my spine, straightening my back like a ruler. I looked at Annalise, but her expectant expression hadn't changed. Maybe I needed to connect the memory I'd taken with ones she still had of Fafa.

"What's your strongest memory of her?" I asked.

"At the piano in her apartment." That was easy for me to picture. Fafa playing. She turned to look at us. When I could see her face, I pushed the image toward Annalise.

A jolt of energy surged from my stomach to the tips of my fingers and toes. My shoulders slammed back, knocking my chest out and stiffening my neck. My blood strummed with strength as if electricity had been zapped through me. I doubted I'd have to sketch this memory. In fact, I doubted I would be able to sleep tonight.

Annalise's mouth clamped shut until a sob tore it open. Her posture matched mine. I wouldn't be alone with my insomnia.

"Oh, Rachel. Thank you!" A strange mix of happy and sad tears streamed down her face.

"You can remember?" I didn't need to ask.

"What does it mean?" Annalise asked, wiping her cheeks. I shook my head. I wished Fafa were here to explain it to us. I needed to figure out this new facet of my ability, but Adam might come in at any moment.

We still had an hour until curfew, but Annalise and I slinked through the streets like we had something to hide. No one in their right mind would be out in the cold if they didn't have to be, but the Art Department wasn't far, and it was always warm.

I gestured for her to sit in Adam's chair. I cleared away the blueprints for the new vegetable storage unit we were working on and grabbed one of the postcards of Terezin I'd finished yesterday. I held it out for Annalise to see.

"I want you to memorize this picture."

She looked from the postcard to me and back. "You're going to pull it?" She gripped the edges of Adam's desk with both hands.

"I'll give it right back."

"You'd better." She didn't look back up at me.

"How many trees in front?"

"Six."

"Who signed it?"

She squinted to make out the signature. "Adam Kaplan."

"What season is it in the picture?" Bright-green buds bloomed from the six trees.

"Spring."

"All right." I flipped the postcard facedown. My sister's fingers tightened on the desk, and she squeezed her eyes closed. "It doesn't hurt, Annalise."

"Just do it already."

I pulled the town, the budding trees, and Adam's signature from her mind. The familiar drain sank into my bones. I hoped I wouldn't have to draw the image, that I'd get another shot of energy in a minute when I pushed the memory back to her.

"Tell me about the postcard."

"What postcard?" Her hands flew from the edge of Adam's desk to her face, and she gasped. "I know I'm supposed to know, but I don't. Oh, Rachel, I don't like this one bit." Her voice was strained as if she might start to cry.

"Don't worry. I'll bring it right back." Her distress was natural. It wasn't like I usually told people before I took their memories. Of course it would be distressing to know someone was rummaging around in your mind. It didn't mean Gideon was right.

I pushed the memory back to relieve her, but the image wouldn't budge. The base of my spine tingled, but Annalise's expression told me it hadn't worked.

With Fafa, it had helped to picture not just her face but the setting around her as well. This time, when I imagined the postcard, I also called to mind the Art Department around us and my own hand holding it up for her.

It was no mere tickle this time. My back shot straight, and Annalise mirrored my posture.

"Trees?"

"Six." Annalise gasped for breath too.

"Signed?"

"Adam Kaplan."

"Season?"

"Spring." Annalise let go of Adam's desk and grabbed my hands. "That was supremely strange, Kitten. Never do that to me again."

We laughed until the door swung open and freezing air blew into the Art Department. It was Adam.

"One of the nurses came to find you at West, Rachel. It's Ernst. He's..." Adam looked down at the ground. "He's asking for you."

Chapter Twenty-six

Typhus.

The disease the Nazis feared more than any other.

They'd secluded Ernst in his own room at the hospital in the hopes of quarantining him. Annalise didn't want me to get close to him, but the nurse said his delirium meant he had very little time, so there was no keeping me out.

He was asleep. Sweat soaked his hair and clothes. His white shirt clung to his body. Unlike most places in the hospital, this room had enough space for a chair beside his bed. I sat in it, trying not to disturb him. I could feel the heat of his fever coming off him without even touching him.

He shook with a hoarse cough, his chest spasming with shallow little gulps to catch his breath. His head whipped back and forth, making it impossible to tell if he were nodding or shaking his head. "No, no," he said with a rasp. Tears streamed down his face, leaving trails through the sweat.

I considered pulling whatever image plagued him. I had plenty of energy after my experiments with Annalise. Gideon may have thought it was wrong, but it couldn't hurt to soothe Ernst in his final moments. I had no idea what was upsetting him, though, and his delusions made it impossible to pluck anything from the chaos.

When Fafa lay dying, Mama spoke to her about my grandfather. It had given her peace. I wanted to do the same for Ernst, but I didn't know much about Marek.

Weeks before, I had found a drawing he had hidden in his desk when I was looking for one of the good brushes—Ernst was always hogging them. The sketch depicted two men, their backs to the viewer, ambling hand in hand through a city. They were probably in his beloved Berlin, from the German on a nearby theater marquee. Ernst's head—I recognized his mass of black curls—leaned on the other man's shoulder.

I wasn't sure how their story ended, but the drawing depicted a light and happy moment.

I pushed the image, and a new flood of power hammered through my entire body. Some strength must have flowed into Ernst too. His chest puffed up with a deep breath. When he let it out, a word escaped his mouth.

"Marek."

He opened his eyes and smiled at me with warm recognition. I smiled back, relieved he wasn't upset I was here.

"Mama," he said. Though it pained me, the thought of his mother seemed to comfort him, so I didn't correct him.

A smile split his disease-ravaged face, and he swayed his head as if to music.

"He plays like an angel," he said. His voice was a gravelly rasp. "I paint better when he's playing." He was no longer in 1944. The image had transported him to a place before the arrests and pink triangles. "He says my laugh takes his breath away."

"I've thought that too." I wanted to hold his hand, but typhus was so contagious. I laid my hand on his shoulder instead. "You have a beautiful laugh."

"You'll like him too, Mama, even though he isn't Jewish."

"You can't have everything," I said.

"I think I'll just stay in," Adam said.

He was supposed to go to a lecture on Roman architecture during leisure time tonight, but Annalise was late coming home from work. After Ernst died, my sister and Adam must have made a pact to never leave me alone with my thoughts for too long. They were right to keep an eye on me. I'd had some dark days in the last month when the only reason I got up was their worried faces.

"You don't have to babysit me, Adam."

He froze. "Oh, I know." He bounced on his toes. If he didn't leave soon, he'd be late. "You should come with me."

I scoffed. "It's twenty degrees out there."

Adam shivered. "It's twenty-three degrees in here."

"Not under my pile of clothes, it isn't." I gestured to the mound of fabric on my bed. I pushed him out the door, and once he was gone, I snuggled down in my bunk. It was freezing in here. How was Gideon staying warm in that air shaft of his in the attic? We hadn't spoken since our fight. I understood his point better now, but I couldn't believe he was still ignoring me over it.

When Annalise finally blew in, a cold gust of air came in with her. She didn't strip off any of her clothes.

"Where were you?" I asked from under the pile.

When she turned to face me, she was wringing her mittened hands. She refused to look at me.

"What?" I asked.

She still didn't meet my eyes. "You need to know, but I'm not sure I should tell," she said. "It will hurt, Kitten."

They were the exact words I'd used to warn her when she wanted me to return her memory of Fafa. Like my sister, I found I was willing to take the risk.

"What, Annalise?" I peeked my face out from behind my clothes.

"Greta came to the hospital right after work to ask me something about Julia."

"Why would Julia's sister come to you and not me?" I asked with an edge to my voice. She had been my friend, not my sister's.

"It was about the raid," Annalise said. "She knew I was there."

"Oh," I said, my tone softening. That made sense. Everyone knew the raid on our rooms had been punishment for Annalise's participation in the *Requiem*.

"Officer Novak did an inspection in the kitchens where Greta works today—"

I propped myself up on my elbow. "Did he hurt her?" Julia always worried he'd turn his sick sights on her younger sister. Annalise sat on my bunk.

"I don't think so. She wanted to know what Julia had done that day."

"Why?" I asked.

"I don't know how to..." She stared at the ceiling as if the right words might be scrawled up there.

"Annalise, please," I said, but maybe she was right. Maybe I didn't want to know.

She squinted her eyes as if bracing herself, but she was really bracing me. "He told her Julia was transported because she'd been impertinent that day."

That didn't make sense. She had hardly spoken at the raid. She had been nothing but polite to him.

"Julia was never impertinent," I said. She had only upset him when she didn't recognize him. Annalise bit her lip and smoothed my hair.

My sister was the only person I'd told about what he'd done to Julia. The only one I'd told about how I'd saved her from the memory of Officer Novak's evil smirk.

"Oh, Kitten," Annalise said. "I think he put her on the transport list because—"

"I made her forget to fear him." I couldn't breathe. My lungs felt full of concrete.

I had tried to spare her, but I'd killed her instead.

"You sure you want to do this?" Annalise asked.

I really wasn't.

We were standing in the stairwell of the children's home.

"Just let me know if someone comes," I said. Annalise looked up and down the stairs while I gave myself a second to hope it wouldn't work. That I wouldn't be able to return the memory of the terrible night of the train. But only a second.

I imagined the smell of hay, the sound of the cart of artificial limbs trundling over the tracks, and Annalise's choir singing. The silver glint of Officer Novak's smile in moonlight. I pictured a line of children at the train's opening and pushed. The details of the train car returned first with its chalk Stars of David. The specific faces of the children followed, filing into the car's dark interior. Zoltan's wave goodbye came into focus last. Despite the steady current of energy, pain rolled over me in waves. I let each one swell and crash.

Annalise grabbed my hands, powerless to do anything but gently coo over me as I cried. My tears weren't even dry when I left her to find Hadas.

I found her sorting dozens of Red Cross packages on the floor of the boys' rooms alone. The children must have been out with their parents for leisure time.

"Need some help?" I asked and sat beside her. Hadas's face lit up when she saw me. She was too distracted by the plenty to notice my tears.

"Look to what Elder Tesler bring!" she said. Happy to delay what I had come to confess, I took a parcel from the pile and began sorting. A box of powdered milk for the infants' home. A bottle of sulfonamide pills for the children's hospital. I unwrapped a bundle of wax paper and nearly dropped the cheese it contained. It wasn't unusual to see food infested with mites or covered in mold, but this had both. I set it aside to be thrown away.

Hadas tutted at me and picked it back up. She cut off the end undulating with vermin and wrapped back up the piece covered in blue fuzz. She added it to a box of food going to the older boys down the hall. "They always hungry."

"You should complain."

"Who wants to know? No one care what I say." I hated when Hadas said things like that. Not because it wasn't true—sadly, it was—but because it made me feel worse than I already did. Why didn't her countrymen fight for her, like mine fought for me?

"We get new curtains while you're expected to eat moldy cheese. It's so unfair." I hung my head. I thought of Yakov, the Ghetto policeman who hated Danes. "I can't blame people for resenting us."

Hadas grabbed a piece of the brown paper that had wrapped one of the packages. She pointed to the stamp in the corner. *From King Christian of Denmark.* "These from you." She pointed to the parcels spread out on the ground. "*Grateful*, never angry. Guardian angels, you are."

Some guardian angel.

I couldn't accept her gratitude. "I lied about the transports, Hadas." Technically, I hadn't lied, but I couldn't explain it all to her. "I was too ashamed." That part was true enough. "I saw the children. I didn't stop it."

She covered my hand with hers. "I don't stop it either, Rachel. A guard came and shout names. They have slips." She beat her chest with an open palm. "I know where they take boys. I hand them over anyway."

Then, she surprised me with perfect German. "Did Isador have his bear?"

The image of the boy disappearing into the train clutching his bear was seared into my mind forever. I was so glad I could answer her. "He did."

Her face cracked open and tears flowed out.

This was usually the moment I would pull the memory and relieve the person I loved of their pain. Instead, I just said, "I'm so sorry, Hadas," and let her cry.

I'd never been to the attic at West before. Piles of mouse poop littered the corner, and spiderwebs covered the ceiling. Multiple makeshift doors each led to individual cubbies. One had a piece of fabric that didn't quite reach the floor. Candlelight filtered through the thin curtain, and two bodies moved inside. Moans echoed off the nooks and crannies of the attic, making it impossible to tell which cubby they came from. My face flushed red at the thought of what was going on behind at least one of the doors.

I had wanted to tell Gideon I returned my memory of what I had done the night of the transports. I'd tell him I was sorry.

I'd tell him I loved him.

Gideon's was the fourth on the left, and I knocked on his—thankfully solid—door. While I waited for him to answer, I adjusted a bobby pin in my hair and straightened the seams of my skirt.

"Who is it?" he asked.

"Rachel," I said.

"Okay, hold on." A girl giggled and someone shushed her, but like the moans, I wasn't sure where the sound came from.

It took him too long to answer. Was he putting his clothes on?

I shouldn't have come.

Gideon finally came to the door just as I made a move to escape down the stairs. His hair looked mussed, like I'd woken him or gotten him out of bed.

He stepped out into the attic and closed his door behind him.

He glanced back at the closed door, obviously impatient to go inside. "What do you want, Rachel?"

To confess my undying love for him? In this place? With another girl possibly behind the door? No, thank you.

"Julia was all my fault." I couldn't explain because the sob I'd been stifling escaped with the words. I gulped trying to contain it. Softness flashed in his eyes for a second, but he crossed his arms over his chest and didn't move from his leaning position on the door. The night of the transport, he'd been unable to see me distressed without moving to comfort me. What had I done to push him so far away?

"And Ernst died." I was piling it on, hoping he would feel badly enough for me to move an inch closer, but he didn't. He stiffened, no doubt surprised by my humiliating display.

"I was sorry to hear."

"You heard?"

"Your husband came here looking for you when Ernst asked for you."

Adam thought I'd go running to Gideon's cubby an hour after our wedding? I stared at my shuffling feet. Gideon's shuffled too. He wanted me gone.

"I guess you think I'm pretty silly to be upset when Ernst and I weren't friends anymore." He still didn't say anything. "Pretty silly wanting to talk to you about it when we aren't friends anymore either." He didn't correct me.

"I don't blame him," I said. "Or you." I turned to go.

"It wasn't you," Gideon said.

I stopped at the top stair and turned, surprised by the tenderness in his voice. His arms were still crossed over his chest, but something in his eyes had changed.

"Ernst, I mean. He didn't stop caring about you just because it was too dangerous to be friends. It probably hurt like hell to keep away."

I took a step forward, thinking that soft tone meant it could be all right between us. A giggle came from one of the other cubbies. She sounded like she was right next to me. Was she laughing at me? "Maybe we could take a walk?" I asked.

He looked back at the closed door to his room and shook his head. When he looked at me again, his eyes had hardened into two little stones. "I'm busy."

"With what?"

"Surely, a married woman can understand, Mrs. Kaplan." He slipped back into his room, preventing me from seeing who was inside.

Chapter Twenty-seven

THE THIRD REICH WASN'T building much by early spring of 1945. They were too busy losing the war. Even so, with only Adam and me left in the Art Department, we stayed busy.

"The plans for the poultry farm and vegetable storage area are back from Prague," Adam said. He unrolled the blueprints on his desk.

"That was fast. They really are in a rush." I bent over the plans to see what changes we would have to make and pulled my hair back with a ribbon to keep it out of my face. I'd let my hair grow when the lice died over the winter.

We were under pressure from the SS in Prague to get the projects started. We also hoped the new facilities might improve conditions at the camp. Then again, maybe it wouldn't matter. On quiet nights, the Soviet army's artillery sounded like far-off thunder. They were so close. We just had to hang on a little while longer.

"Huh," I said to Adam, looking over the changes the SS had made. "Why do they need such high walls?"

Adam bowed his head to get a closer look. He calculated the numbers in his head. "Eighteen feet on a poultry farm wall? What are they afraid of? Flying chicken poachers?"

"Duck saboteurs?" We laughed in the easy way of good friends until I caught him glancing down at my wedding ring and remembered I had married him. I forgot sometimes. My laughter dried up. I never wanted him to get the wrong idea. Adam had spent our entire marriage on the mattress on the floor.

He pointed out another change on the plans. There were large X's through two of the three entrances we'd placed in the wall surrounding the poultry farm.

"The workers will have to trudge all the way around." I traced the route on the plans with my pencil.

"Seems like a waste of time."

"And they usually love their efficiency."

Adam laughed. *Inefficient* was always the number-one criticism of Adam's plans. He scanned the cost analysis. "Gates are more expensive than walls," he said. "Makes the area easier to guard too, so it's more efficient in that way, I guess."

"Maybe. But to have only one exit for this huge area..." I gestured to the acres of land the poultry farm would entail. "I mean, the whole ghetto could fit in here." The words clicked in my brain, and my limbs went numb.

The whole ghetto...in one place.

"Let me see the vegetable storage building." I shuffled through the blueprints spread out on our desks. I found it near the bottom and laid it on top.

"What, Rachel?" he asked when my shoulders slumped.

I pointed to the two notes scribbled on the plans. The first directed us to replace the wooden door with a thick metal one. A second—written in the same handwriting—said that the single window needed to be sealed. The old vegetable storage unit on the other side of the ghetto had a wooden door and two poorly insulated windows. Why was this one different?

"Why did they change the ventilation system?" Adam pointed to the red X's on the roof. The X's were made by the same red pencil as the ones on the gates of the poultry farm. They'd moved it from the roof to the side wall. "Ventilation systems work better through a roof, not out the side. It makes no sense."

But it did make sense. Horrible, terrible sense. I'd heard enough rumors about Auschwitz by now to know exactly what I was looking at. I pointed at the X's with a shaking finger. "Because it's not a ventilation system." I checked several views of the project. My insides felt hollow, like the echoing black tunnel to the Little Fortress. "It's for the plumbing."

"Vegetable storage doesn't need—"

"Oh, Adam. It's not a vegetable storage area." I lifted my eyes up from the blueprints to Adam's nicked face, but all I could see was Julia. "It's a gas chamber."

I pored over the blueprints, looking for the perfect spot for sabotage. Adam had left me alone with my thoughts of death camps and Julia to "ask someone something." I was too busy to ask for details. Planning a suicide mission can be very distracting.

When Adam returned, I didn't waste any time.

"We have to blow up the site," I said. He froze with just his shoulders out of his coat, probably expecting me to say I was kidding or something. He didn't know me very well.

Adam blinked a couple of times and said, "That's exactly what he said you'd say."

"Who?"

"Hello, Mrs. Kaplan." Gideon stood in the doorway.

"What are you doing here?" I asked.

"Your husband is under the misguided impression that I can make you see reason." He didn't come in, just hovered in the doorway.

I rounded on Adam. "You brought him here?"

He looked sheepish, at least, as if he realized how awkward it was to involve Gideon—of all people—in our first disagreement.

"I thought we needed another mind at work here," Adam said.

"What did I miss?" Gideon came in and shuffled through the blueprints on my desk. "Did she suggest we blow it up yet?"

"How did you—" Adam asked. His coat was still hanging below his shoulders.

Gideon plucked the pencil from behind my ear and wrote some dimensions on a scrap of paper. "Because it's impulsive and insane."

"I agree with you," said Adam.

"First time for everything," Gideon said.

"Why is that, when we have so much in common?" Adam said to Gideon, then looked at me.

"It's not insane," I said, ignoring the two of them. "They're going to turn Terezin into a death camp."

Adam paced across the Art Department. "It's dangerous," he said.

"They'll kill us all anyway. It's worth the risk," I said.

Adam jerked to a halt as if on a taut leash. He took my hand and rubbed my wedding ring with his thumb. "I'm finding it difficult to accept any reason good enough to lose you." They were lovely words. If only the right boy had said them.

The right boy only cracked his knuckles. "You can't go off half-cocked and start blowing things up," Gideon said.

"You did," I said, reminding him he'd been part of the Danish resistance. "You blew up that Nazi factory in Copenhagen."

"That wasn't me. I was a messenger boy. Besides, we don't know if your theory is true or not yet."

I jabbed a finger at the walls for the poultry farm on the plans. "There's a note here to line the walls with crushed glass, Gideon. Do they want to stop the ducks from climbing the walls...or someone else?" They both paled. Gideon bent over the plans to read the note himself. We shared a wall with Commandant Becker's office, so I lowered my voice. "They'll put us all in a field as some kind of holding area while they kill us in the gas chambers."

"If we blow the site now, they'll know we did it," Gideon said. At least he was saying *us*. "We're the only people in the ghetto who've seen the plans."

He had a point. "Then we'll have to go to the workers and make sure we're right," I said. "If we are, they can slow the work until the war ends." The Soviets would arrive soon. If we delayed long enough, we could save everyone.

"The workers will go to the SS," said Gideon.

"We'll have to trust they won't."

Gideon let out a joyless squawk of a laugh. "You can't trust anyone in here, Rachel."

"The Nazis are losing," I said. "You're the one who said they would erase the proof of their crimes. We're the witnesses." I twirled my finger at the three of us. "They want to erase us, but the Soviet army is standing between us and Auschwitz." The name of that place stuck in my throat.

"We're Danish, and thanks to you, your husband here is safe," Gideon said. "If we just keep our heads down—"

"What about Hadas?"

"I'll marry her," Gideon said without hesitation.

"The children, Gideon. I can't let more of them die."

"You're really not going to stop, are you?"

"How long have you known me?" I asked.

"Yeah, I know." He nodded and stared out the window. He let out a breath in the long second of silence that followed. "I know what I have to do," he said and started to head out without another word.

What the hell did that mean? "Gideon?" I reached out to him. It didn't break his stride toward the door. Where was he going? SS headquarters? To blow up the work site himself? He'd get himself killed. "Gideon!"

The sound of me shrieking his name made him pause as he passed through the threshold, but he didn't turn to face me. "I know I can't stop you, so be careful," he said and shut the door behind him.

I fell back into my chair.

"So, where do we start?" Adam asked.

Chapter Twenty-eight

ADAM AND I WENT to the work site to talk to the crew. I considered stopping at to the hospital to warn Annalise when we passed, but kept going. I could fill her in later. Gideon was right about one thing. We had to find out if my theory was true before we did anything about it. He was wrong about everything else.

Certainly, we could trust the Austrian foreman Reiner Kirsh, who'd spent two months in the Little Fortress rather than report someone who had stolen tools from a work site. He had returned with a missing pointer finger "since he wasn't using it to accuse people," a joke of Commandant Becker's.

Reiner shot up from the bench when we told him about the changes to the plans. "I should have known when the SS from Prague came *twice* to inspect the site." He gestured wildly with his hands as he fidgeted. I couldn't help staring at the place where his missing finger had been.

"They don't usually come out during new building projects?" Adam asked.

"Not even during the beautification before the Red Cross visit." The only time they'd visited the Art Department was when they put the rush on the plans.

Two separate visits to Terezin from Prague for a duck pond and a glorified root cellar. Not even the beautification, with all its international diplomatic importance, had warranted a single trip. The secret murder of thousands of men, women, and children, however, would require oversight from Prague.

"Do you know where we might find the lead carpenter?" Adam asked. "We need to find out if these changes to the window and door would make this airtight."

Reiner stopped his frantic fidgeting. "Airtight?"

"In order for the gas chamber to work, the room has to be fairly airtight," Adam said. "That might be why they want to block up the window and install a thick metal door."

Reiner's hand ran down his face. "The masons were ordered to seal up all the old cracks last week."

The little hairs on the back of my neck stood up like the hackles on a petrified cat. "Who ordered that?" I asked.

"The SS officers from Prague. I thought it was a waste of our time just to make it look better, but I don't ask a lot of questions anymore." He wiggled his four remaining fingers.

Leon Krause, a carpenter, detailed how he'd shown the commandant, the Cauliflower, and the two Prague SS officers around on their second visit a couple of weeks ago.

"Did they do or say anything strange?"

"Other than show up at all?" He'd also made it clear the SS didn't concern themselves with the building activities at Terezin. His eyebrow crinkled. "What's going on?" We explained our suspicions about the poultry farm and vegetable storage area.

"Becker." He said the commandant's name like a swear. He pointed up to the ramparts. "They asked to see the site from above. They marched straight to that end of the roof. Ordered me not to follow. The commandant swept his hand across the field like this." Leon stretched out his arm and swung it in an arc in front of him, like a boy playing soldier with a pretend gun. "He said something that didn't make much sense when it was supposed to be just chickens, but now..."

"What did he say?"

"We can cover the whole area with just one pass.'"

I wasn't sure we'd learned enough to convince Gideon of the Germans' plan, but both Reiner and Leon agreed to slow progress on the site to a crawl. We would need to keep it quiet until we had a plan.

Adam and I rounded a corner as we left the site and disturbed a knot of rats scrambling over something. I clutched at Adam's arm and screeched.

A man ahead of us spun at the sound. The rats scattered, and Adam pointed to a slow one as it disappeared into a hole.

The man checked his pocket and slapped his thigh.

"I had a heel of bread in here," the stranger said, tapping the pocket. "Must've fallen out."

"I've never seen rats like that," I said. With all the pests we suffered in Terezin—lice, bedbugs, mice—I'd never seen so many rats.

"We haven't fumigated in months," the stranger said. He stomped his feet near the hole where the rats had disappeared. "And now we know where all the Zyklon B went."

The gas chambers of Auschwitz.

I wasn't prepared for the sudden switch in the conversation, and grief barreled into my chest like an outside force. Adam slipped his hand into mine.

The man bowed his head and said in a shaky whisper, "We're the vermin now."

That's how they saw Julia. She was dear to her family and to me, but they had treated her like nothing more than a rat. The man didn't seem to notice the effect his words had on me until I wiped my eyes. When he looked up, there were tears on his cheeks too.

"I'm sorry I upset you, miss," he said, his hand to his heart. "You've lost someone?"

I nodded, thinking mostly of Julia, but remembering the Hens, Isador, and Zoltan too. Hadn't everyone lost someone by now?

"My son, Max," he said. "He was a good boy. Never gave anyone trouble, but he was too simple to work."

"I'm so sorry," I said. That old urge to pull his memory and relieve him of his sorrow leapt up, but I restrained the impulse.

"Nothing could be done. My cousin is an elder. Not even he could save him."

"Who's your cousin?" Adam asked.

"Elder Tesler," he said. "I'm Noah Tesler."

I flinched at the name, and Adam had to elbow me to shake the hand he offered. I'd hated Elder Tesler from the day I arrived, but all his complicity hadn't been enough to keep his family safe.

I grimaced when I considered what Gideon would say about us confiding our theories with the cousin of a ghetto elder. *Well, Gideon isn't here, is he?* I thought.

As with Reiner and Leon, we outlined our theory of the SS plan to liquidate the camp.

"With the railway to Auschwitz blocked, maybe the Zyklon B is being stockpiled here," Adam said.

"If we can find it, we'll know they're building a gas chamber," I said.

"They're not going to store a secret stockpile in a supply room inmates can get into," Mr. Tesler said.

He snapped his fingers and ran, gesturing for us to follow him. He stopped at a door with a sign that read *Do Not Open*. A combination lock hung from it.

"This used to be a supply room for the carpenters," Mr. Tesler said. "A couple of months ago, they ordered us to empty it out, and the next day, they locked it up."

There were no guards in the area, but there were no tools either. "Can we break the lock?"

"They don't let us use any tools without supervision," Mr. Tesler said. "Maybe a rock." He scanned the area for one.

I stood on tiptoe to examine the hinges. Maybe we could take the door off that way.

Mr. Tesler lifted the lock. "This is one of our old ones. I recognize the chipped zero." He held it up to show us the damaged number. He spun the dial in one direction, then the other, back and forth. He yanked down, but it didn't open. He tried several times, swearing each time it didn't work. He banged the lock against the door.

"I can't remember the combination. We used it years ago."

Maybe I could help with that.

I pictured the lock with its nicked zero latched to the rusty hasp of the door and pushed it at the elder's cousin. The familiar rush of strength jolted through me, and Mr. Tesler's hand stiffened for a second before the numbers blurred to the right. The dial stopped abruptly and spun in the opposite direction and back again. After the third number, he jerked down.

The clasp fell out of the lock.

I almost smiled before I remembered what we were looking for.

The door swung wide.

From floor to ceiling, wall to wall, were canisters of Zyklon B.

Chapter Twenty-nine

HEADING TO GIDEON'S CUBBY, I steeled myself for the possibility of confronting him with another girl. Did he have someone up there every waking moment? Possibly. Some unawake too. My insides twisted at the thought, but he needed to know what we'd discovered.

I stomped up the stairs to warn Gideon—and his noisy neighbors—that someone had arrived. It wasn't necessary. The attic was quiet, which made sense at this time of day. Everyone was at work. I knocked on the door. "It's me."

Gideon responded immediately, but he didn't open the door. "You alone?"

"Yes." *How about you, Gideon?*

The door opened, and he stepped aside to let me in.

I took a tentative step forward. Uneven pieces of scrap wood made up the walls like a poorly built tree house. There were no windows in the six-by-eight-foot space, and only a candle lit the room when the door closed behind me. The rafters showed through the ceiling. It must have been freezing this winter.

All this time, he could have been sharing my freshly painted, spacious room with me. That he preferred privacy in this hole hurt more than I liked to admit.

An unmade mattress lay on the floor. The impression of his body in the folds of the blanket made my face flare red. He stepped behind me and shut the door.

I relayed what Adam and I had learned. The extra SS visits, their remarks on the ramparts, and the airtight vegetable storage room. I saved the news about the Zyklon B for last.

"I still say we should blow the site," I said. Gideon sat down on the bed and uncovered a pile of junk in a box from under his blanket. He was always tinkering with something. I kept going to fill the silence Gideon left. "If only Mr. Strauss were alive." I paced in the cramped room. "He'd know how to get word out to the resistance about what's happening here."

Gideon twisted some wire into place and covered it with bits of fabric to hold it together.

"In the meantime, we told the workers to slow the progress on the work site," I said.

He blew some dust from the box.

"We should tell the inmates too. That way, if they call a census out in that field, we can refuse to move. I would rather die in West than out in their fake chicken farm."

"How about not dying at all?" He glanced up from the stupid ball of garbage long enough to smirk at me.

"It's bad enough you aren't listening. Do you have to make fun of me too?"

"Fine." He set the box aside, took my hands and tugged me down to sit next to him on the mattress. "I have to admit something to you, Rachel."

I sat up straighter. Was this happening here? In this cramped poor excuse of a room where he'd done who knows what and with whom?

"It'll be painful to confess, but you'll be happy, I bet." The three words he said next were unfamiliar coming from his mouth, even stranger than the ones I'd hoped for. At least I had imagined him saying "I love you" a thousand times. I never dreamed he would ever say what followed.

"You were right."

"I was...what?"

"This morning. When you said we need each other."

My eyebrows quirked up. Not all hope was lost. I inched closer to him. He watched my hip move toward him.

"I mean the inmates," he said. "We need to trust each other."

That was all it took. His one little confession elicited a flood of my own.

"You were right too, Gideon. It was my fault Julia was transported. I stole something she needed to remember." He opened his mouth to say something, but I couldn't stop. "And I haven't pulled a single memory since I found out, and I'm so sorry I took your memory of Ezra. I can bring it back if you want."

"Rachel..." Gideon was holding both palms out to me. I couldn't stop, but I did slow down a little.

"I brought back my memory of the train." I covered my face with my hands. I don't know if I was hiding my tears or my shame. "I was such a coward."

Gideon peeled my fingers from my face. "You?" he asked. "That's the craziest thing you've ever said. Which is saying something." Gideon smiled so I knew he was kidding.

"The combination lock on the storeroom with the gas...I made him remember."

"What do you mean?"

"You know how you said it would be better if I made sure people never forgot? Well, it looks like I can do that too. I made one of the workers remember the combination for the lock to the supply room."

"Really?" He leaned even closer. "Incredible..."

I touched his hand with the tips of my fingers, lightly enough to be mistaken for an accident. His grazed mine too, and when neither of us tore our hands away, we laced our hands together like the wire in my wedding ring. With his other hand, he lifted the box of junk he had put aside and placed it on my lap like a gift. I lifted it off me before it got dust and grease all over my skirt. "Thanks a lot," I said.

"It's a radio," he whispered.

I gaped at it and placed it gently back onto my lap. A *radio*.

"I've been working on it since I got here. It's been slow going on my own, stealing one piece at a time. But after what you found out, I finished it. Like I said, you were right. I had to trust people. I took a chance and asked someone in Electrical to get the last pieces I needed while you guys checked out the work site." His voice lowered even more. "It's finished."

"Does it work?"

"Yes, but the range isn't great. I got a signal from some Czech partisans. I told them to get word to the Red Cross to request another visit right away, but I can't be sure if they received the whole message."

"You've been working on that thing for more than a year?"

"I should have trusted you." Gideon's eyes were wide, and his gaze kept lowering to my lips. I ran a finger through his hair to the scar on the back of his head. He didn't flinch or back away this time.

"When you came here to tell me about Julia and Ernst, I wanted to comfort you, but the pieces of this thing were all over the room." He squeezed his fists to crack his knuckles but stopped himself. "There wasn't a girl in here, but I couldn't let you in."

I had a feeling we weren't talking about the radio anymore.

"I shouldn't have let you believe the gossip about what I was doing," he said.

"What do you mean? Let me believe what?"

"I needed a good excuse for all the time I spent on this thing." He scooped my hand up in both of his. "So when rumors started flying that I was...entertaining friends up here, I didn't correct them. I needed the privacy."

"That was all a lie?" I tore my hand out of his and stood. "You let me think you were..." The ache in my chest loosened. My voice got very quiet. "You weren't?"

"If you'd known about the radio, you would have given me away. You know you would have, Rachel," he said when I opened my mouth to defend myself. "You were in Terezin five minutes before you got the attention of one of the cruellest men in the place. With the Cauliflower breathing down your neck, I couldn't risk it." He reached up and entwined his fingers with mine. He pulled me down to sit beside him on the edge of the bed again. "I couldn't risk you."

"There were never any girls up here?" I asked for the thousandth time. He was smiling. We both were. "Lena? Esther?"

"There has never been anyone but you."

"You should have told me." I tried to resurrect my right-eous indignation, but it fell flat with the giant grin on my face.

"What if I got caught? You remember how they trans-ported the families of the artists. Little Sophie Haas? You're my Sophie Haas, Rachel."

"You realize if you had been honest about what you were doing..."

"I know. I could've had what I wanted months ago," he said.

"You wasted a lot of time."

His knee skimmed my thigh. "I can't believe you spent the entire day asking questions and not shooting your mouth off."

"Aw, thanks. That's real sweet." I didn't mention that the complete stranger I'd trusted was Elder Tesler's cousin.

"No, I mean"—he took a deep breath—"you've been calmer than me. All I want to do is grab you and fight our way out of here."

"Our way? I like the sound of that."

"Futile attempts ending in our violent deaths?" He elbowed me in the ribs, but grinned. "You're very strange, Mrs. Kaplan."

I pushed him in the chest. "Stop calling me that, Gideon. You know that isn't who I am."

"I hoped." He stared at my mouth again.

He bent his neck to kiss me, but a loud knock echoed through the small room, and we jumped apart. I had images of the SS, the Ghetto Police, and the Cauliflower all gathered in the hallway on the other side of the door. Gideon had trusted the wrong person, and they'd turned him in. He would die, and it would be my fault, just like Julia all over again. I clutched the folds of his shirt. He smiled down at my hands.

"I like the enthusiasm. Save it for later, though." He kissed my forehead and got off the bed. "One minute," he shouted at the door, then lowered his voice. "I didn't like the looks of that big walled-in area, so I asked someone to look into something for us."

He grabbed the radio and stood on the mattress. The ceiling was so low, he didn't need to stretch when he removed the bare light bulb. He didn't unscrew it, only tilted the whole fixture, and it dropped out in one quick movement. There were no wires or electrical connections of any kind. It wasn't a real light.

He shoved the box into the hole it left. His arm disappeared to the elbow. He replaced the fake light and returned to my side on the bed.

"Come in."

The old Lukas would have grinned like a satisfied cat seeing me with Gideon without a chaperone on an unmade bed, but the grin never came. I had a feeling that the old Lukas didn't exist anymore.

I shot a look at Gideon. He put up a hand to stop my tirade, but it still came. "We're going to trust him?" I pointed at the boy who had been my friend when he'd handed the Cauliflower evidence that could have killed me. "You're taking my advice to trust people a bit too far, Gideon."

"Someone needed to find out if the Germans have that many machine guns. Their rifles won't work for this plan." He faced Lukas. "Did you find the guns?"

"Gideon, I don't think..." He looked at me.

"She has the right to know too."

"If I can face the Cauliflower in the Little Fortress—thanks, by the way—I can handle whatever you have to say," I said. Lukas closed his eyes, and I wondered if I meant it.

"You found the machine guns," said Gideon. It wasn't a question. I reached up to take his hand.

"No, no machine guns." Surely, this was wonderful news, but Lukas's face had gone white.

"What did you find, Lukas?" I asked. My voice sounded kinder than I intended.

"Flamethrowers."

Chapter Thirty

GIDEON, ADAM, AND I had to return to work. We planned to meet later that night during leisure time, but Gideon showed up at the Art Department an hour early, sweating and out of breath.

"They raided the project site," he said. He gripped my desk for support. My stomach dropped, but his face broke into a satisfied smile. "They were looking for the radio."

"You're happy about that?" Adam asked.

"Don't you see what it means?" He looked between Adam and me. "One of my messages must have gone through."

"That's fantastic, Gideon." I touched his hand. I'd gotten so used to him pushing me away, it caught me by surprise when he curled his fingers into mine. We couldn't drag our eyes from one another for a few seconds until we remembered a third person—my husband—was in the room.

"They'll come here next, so if you have anything you don't want the SS to find..."

Adam flung open a drawer. He crumpled the postcard with my tearstain into his pocket. It had been there the whole time.

Gideon turned to me. "*You* are what I want to hide." I didn't understand his words. "The Cauliflower is with them."

"Get her out of here," Adam said to Gideon, returning to his desk to unfurl the blueprints. He turned to me. "I'll have to stall them. You shouldn't be here for that."

"Let's go." Gideon tugged on my sleeve. "You know I'm not above carrying you out of here."

"I won't abandon Adam to face them alone," I said.

"I know you're attempting nobility here, but I'd die to protect you." Gideon gestured to Adam. "So will your husband. When both of your admirers are dead, he'll just kill you too. Could we skip all that and just get you out of here?"

I opened my mouth to say no, that I wouldn't leave my friend, when Adam himself grabbed both my shoulders, let out a long breath, and said the only thing that could change my mind.

"I can't lose another family, Rachel."

Through deportations and grisly discoveries, he had hoped for the best for his mother and sisters, but after all this time, he'd accepted they were probably gone.

"I'll go," I said, putting a hand to his pale, nicked face, but I was too late.

Commandant Becker, two Czech gendarmes, and the Cauliflower himself appeared outside the door of the Art Department, cutting off my only means of escape.

Commandant Becker marched straight for Adam. The man who the children had called *Uncle Becker* during the Red Cross visit screamed in Adam's downturned face. "Where is it?"

The three other men charged into the room, over-turning furniture and kicking through the spilled contents. I backed away from the tumult just before the Cauliflower—with more rage than the rest—flipped over a desk. It broke into pieces. He snatched up a splintered leg and swung it at Ernst's lamp. It shattered, and I shielded my eyes from the flying glass. Ernst's desk met the same fate as the other.

When I peeked out from behind my hands, the com-mandant was still screaming at Adam, and the others were ransacking the office, but the Cauliflower stared at the floor, taking in big lungfuls of air. At first, I thought he was catching his breath from overexerting himself, but his gaze fixed on something, and an almost human softness filled his eyes. The floor was littered with papers and debris. From my vantage point, I couldn't see what had elicited the change.

If I intensified whatever image he was looking at, maybe it would calm him enough to keep him from killing us. I pushed the image of the mess on the floor at the Cauliflower. The power strumming through me was familiar and no stronger than expected, although its effect on the Cauliflower was greater than I anticipated. He stumbled and put a hand to the wall.

I took a step closer. I couldn't help it. He seemed less of a danger with that tenderness in his eyes. I had to see what had provoked such a human reaction from him.

A sketch of two men—one of their heads on the shoulder of the other—was in the center of the pile, right in his direct line of sight. The image that had soothed Ernst in his final moments. I looked back up at the Cauliflower's face. He was still struggling to breathe.

I looked down at the sketch again. I'd always focused on the figure that had to be Ernst with his mass of tight black curls.

I had never noticed the other figure—Ernst's Marek—was bald under his cap.

Gideon pulled me backward, and I almost tripped over some of the wreckage, but despite the sounds of the Art Department's destruction around me, I couldn't stop looking at the Cauliflower's expression.

It wasn't disgust. It wasn't rage.

It was grief.

I spoke without thinking. "My God. You're Marek."

His eyes shot to me, and all the aforementioned humanity drained from him in an instant.

His bald head blazed bright red, except for the wrinkles in his forehead, which glowed white with strain. His wooden baton flashed, and I crumpled as he struck my knee. My head hit a desk as I fell to the floor. He brought his foot back, and his boot slammed into my side. A rib snapped, and pain bloomed up my torso. I twisted into a ball.

This is how he killed Mr. Strauss, I thought.

"Please, Commandant Becker!" Adam didn't bother appealing to the Cauliflower. "She's Danish." The Cauliflower's boot continued to pummel my ribs. I tried to wriggle under a chair.

"That will do, Commander," Commandant Becker said casually. The Cauliflower's kicks slowed but didn't stop.

"The radio is in the West Barracks' attic," Gideon said. I couldn't see him from the floor, but his voice sounded strained like he was struggling with someone. His words stopped the kicks. "The fourth room on the left. It's hidden in the rafters above a fake light bulb."

The Cauliflower's face contorted, and he pulled out his pistol and aimed it at Gideon. I tried to reach up at him, but my broken ribs kept me on the floor. I clawed at the cuff of the Cauliflower's pants instead.

"Put it away, Commander Gruber," said Commandant Becker. The Cauliflower glared at his commanding officer, still out of breath from beating me. He slid his gun back into his holster but lunged at Gideon. A crack resounded through the room. Not one of my bones this time, because Gideon grunted.

"Enough," the commandant said again. "Retrieve the radio." The two gendarmes left the Art Department, and the Cauliflower stomped after them without a look back, leaving Commandant Becker alone with the three of us.

"The building project is canceled," Commandant Becker continued. "Be sure to tell them." At first, I thought he referred to the other inmates or the work crew, but that wasn't what he meant. "Don't let them judge me too harshly."

The boys were at my side the moment the commandant was gone. Gideon's nose bled down his chin in thick rivulets.

"Are you all right?" Adam asked.

Gideon lifted me up, sending shock waves of pain up my side. My knee hurt too, but I could walk.

"You should go back to West," Gideon said. "Adam and I will tell the work crew about the radio and what the SS knows."

My mind was reeling, and it wasn't from the blow to my head.

The Cauliflower and Ernst had once been in love.

They had met in Berlin before they had to hide.

Once the Jews were rounded up, the Cauliflower brought Ernst with him to Dachau and transferred him to Terezin to try to keep him safe. For years, he had done just that. Despite his pink triangle, Ernst had a cushy job at the Art Department and plenty of food. Little Sadie's sulfonamide pills and Annalise's honey had all come from him.

My sister was alive because of the Cauliflower.

He'd hidden the painting with Ernst's signature from Lieutenant Colonel Eichmann. He'd killed the man who had beaten Ernst. What else had he done to defend him?

None of it had mattered. Ernst died anyway.

As I limped to the door with Gideon, I couldn't help but mumble to myself, "The Cauliflower is Marek."

"Marek?"

"Ernst's..." I struggled to put a name to what Marek had been to Ernst. Tormentor? Savior? I doubted there was a word for it. Gideon's eyes widened.

"And now he knows you know this?" He pointed his finger into my shoulder. "Rachel, the next time you see him, you pull that memory out of him."

I was too disoriented when he'd stormed out of the Art Department, but the next time I saw him, I would do just that.

"I thought you didn't like it when I used my ability."

"I'm all for it if it keeps you safe." He cupped his hand around my cheek. I leaned my face into him even though it hurt. He yanked his hand away when he saw me wince.

I looked forward to a quiet half hour in my bunk before Annalise came home and worried over me. I wouldn't get a half hour. I wouldn't even get a minute.

The Cauliflower sat on my bed with his gun aimed at my chest.

Chapter Thirty-one

I'D PROMISED GIDEON I'D pull the recognition the next time I saw him, but I worried he'd pull the trigger when his muscles slackened. His hand was already shaking.

"Don't bother running."

My mouth had run dry, but I managed to croak out, "You can't kill me. I'm Danish." It had given the commandant pause in the Art Department a few minutes ago, but it didn't work on the Cauliflower.

"The Third Reich is over," he said. "Becker thinks the Allies will be forgiving, but I know I'm a dead man. One dead Dane won't change that."

I caught sight of Jubilee on my bed and had a wild urge to turn the stuffed horse's glass eyes away so he wouldn't have to watch me die.

Footsteps sounded down the hall, and a pair of women passed my room, chatting. The Cauliflower's eyes darted to the door and back to me. He sprang off the bed and grabbed me by the armpit, setting my side on fire.

"Let's take a walk," he said. He dragged me down the hall past the startled women, digging the gun's muzzle into my side. The hard metal felt like knives twisting between my ribs, and my injured knee buckled on the stairs. Pinpricks of darkness winked in and out before my eyes.

He pulled me into the first alley beside West and flung me to the wall. When I slid down, my hair caught on the rough brick behind me. The edges of my vision went black as I fought to stay upright. I had to remain conscious. As long as I held on, I had a chance. I shook my head to clear it, but it didn't do much good.

"What did he tell you?" He pointed a finger at me with one hand and the gun with the other. "He swore he wouldn't, but I knew. I knew he told you." All those times the Cauliflower came by the Art Department, he wasn't there to keep an eye on me. He was checking on Ernst. Ernst hadn't stayed away to protect himself from the Cauliflower. He'd stayed away to protect me.

The Cauliflower finally lowered the gun, and I had a chance to pull the memory from him, but if I did it now, I'd pass out. I was so weak, I wasn't even sure it would work. But maybe my ability could still save me.

"He told me you played like an angel, that he painted best to your music." I imagined Ernst at an easel, his canvas a riot of color, and Marek with his violin tucked under his chin. I pushed the image at him.

Energy didn't thrum through me this time, but the darkness seeping into my vision cleared and the pain in my ribs lost its edge. He stumbled backward, but the gun stayed at his side.

"Shut your—"

"We both loved him." I pursed my lips together and rallied all my renewed energy to push the image of Ernst, head thrown back in laughter, eyes glistening with joy.

Strength surged through me. This time, the pushed memory allowed me to bear my full weight on my knee. It brought the Cauliflower down to his. He had said Ernst's laugh took his breath away. Today was no exception. He gasped like he'd been held underwater, but he still lifted his gun.

I staggered backward. "He'd never forgive you if you hurt me," I said.

"He was never going to forgive me anyway." He hung his head. "I can hardly blame him." His gun flew to his temple before I could push a reason to live into his mind.

Chapter Thirty-two

I SAT ON THE ground in front of the gates of Terezin and hugged Jubilee to my chest while I waited for the Swedish Red Cross bus that would take me to my family in Sweden. Annalise and I didn't have much to carry, just a single small bag for both of us. We had given away all our clothes and the last of the Red Cross parcels to the people we had to leave behind.

The Danes and their new spouses were the only ones leaving. We waited in the courtyard where we'd had that first lunch in Terezin. I'd gone off by myself to the very place I had stepped off the train a year and a half ago, where the Germans had taunted Leah and ripped my sketchbook, and where we'd met Lukas.

It had been two weeks since I disappeared into an alley with the Cauliflower. No one had seen us go in, so I left him there. His death was never mentioned by any of the guards, as though he had never existed. He might have been one of the first Nazis to take his own life in the spring of 1945, but he was hardly the last.

The Czech resistance had gotten Gideon's message to the Swiss, and the Red Cross announced an immediate return for a second visit to Terezin. The workmen tasked with building the gas chamber were reassigned to a second beautification. This time, the Nazis would have little time to prepare and nowhere to send transports to thin the population. The Soviets had liberated most of eastern Europe by then, and they were getting closer to Terezin every day. They'd be at the gates soon, but we would already be gone.

"You mind some company?" Adam asked. I patted the ground beside me.

Adam took my hand and twirled the wedding ring around my finger. "Remember when I said I wasn't interested in Gideon's love life? It's not really true. There is this one little detail I do find of personal interest." He made a one-inch space between his thumb and forefinger.

"What's that?"

"He's in love with my wife," he said.

I opened my mouth to deny it, wanting to spare his feelings, but I stopped myself. "I'm sorry, Adam."

"I appreciate you saving my life, Rachel. You don't have to pretend to love me too."

I hugged him, so happy he would leave with us today. Too many wouldn't.

"C'mon. Let's go back." He stood and reached a hand out to help me up. My ribs still ached, but my knee was much better. The orchestra played in the park where everyone waited. Annalise stood next to Gideon, Rabbi Hertz, and Hadas.

"Hello, Mr. and Mrs. Shriver," I said to Hadas and Gideon.

"Hello, Mr. and Mrs. Kaplan," he said to Adam and me. Before he could pull me into his arms, Hadas rushed up to hug me instead.

"I never thought to be so happy my husband love another woman," she said in my ear and began to cry.

"I'm sure Gideon did this for you, Hadas."

"I told you, Rachel. You are my guardian angel."

Annalise spun in a flamboyant twirl next to the rabbi. She patted her bobbed hair. Winter had killed the lice, but Annalise had gotten used to her short hair. "When we get home, I'm going to see every one of Cary Grant's movies I've missed since the war started."

"I'm going to eat as much chocolate as I can stand," said Eli.

Leah beamed at her son, ready to give it to him. "I'm going to take the longest, hottest bath in history," she said.

I only wanted to hug each and every one of my family members, but I didn't say that out loud. Adam and Hadas wouldn't be reunited with their families in Sweden. Maybe not ever.

Control was relaxed most of the time in Terezin, but today, that was particularly true. No one worked, and inmates came to hear the music and say their goodbyes. When the music ended and the buses pulled away, they would have to go back to their crowded barracks and eat weak potato soup for dinner.

Annalise nudged me. "I can't stand to see you sad right now," she said.

"It's so unfair we get to leave and they have to stay."

Annalise stroked my arm. "Oh, what the hell." She called over to the knot of non-Danes who'd come by to see us off. "Dr. Golding? Wanna marry me?" The doctor's fifty-year-old face lit with happiness, and he nodded. I hoped his happiness was for escaping Terezin, not his beautiful young bride. "Let's do this, Rabbi," she said.

I mouthed the words "Thank you" to her just as Lukas appeared at the entrance of the courtyard. Ernst's painting had reappeared in my bunk three days ago wrapped in the blue tote Lukas used to bring us food in. He'd returned what he'd stolen. The yellow ribbon had been lost, but I'd bring the painting home. I promised myself I would get it to a museum as soon as the war ended. Ernst's painting would help tell our story.

Lukas hovered by the orchestra stand. Annalise froze when she saw him. He lifted his hand like it weighed a hundred pounds. She glanced back at me. I smiled and nodded, and she returned his wave. Lukas grinned at me as though I'd given him a gift. My forgiveness was a gift for Annalise, not for him.

Gideon joined me. "Congratulations," I said.

"That's right. Married man." He hooked his fingers in his vest. "Don't try anything funny."

"Thank you, Gideon."

"I like Potato Pants." He looked at his new wife across the park. "I didn't do it for you."

"I didn't say—"

"All right, maybe a little for you."

"Gideon..."

"Don't sound so surprised, Abramson." He poked me in the shoulder. "I do have a soft side, you know."

"Yeah, your head." I ran my hand through his hair to show I was kidding or because I wanted an excuse to touch him.

He kissed me, and we didn't even notice when the white buses came through the gate.

The cheering crowd swelled forward as our ferry bumped the dock in Malmö, Sweden, three days later.

"Is that Hans?" Annalise asked on tiptoe, shading her eyes from the sun.

My heart leapt into my throat at my brother's name, even though the child she pointed to was no more than six.

"That can't be him. Hans turned ten last month, Annalise. We don't even know if they'll be here to pick us up," I said, to manage her expectations—and my own.

"There," Gideon said from beside me and pointed to a boy in a tree waving. His hair stuck up like the thatch on Uncle Stellan's fishing cottage. Goose bumps ran down my arm.

"Anders," Annalise said. A man stood at the base of the tree with my brother, squinting at the boat. Seeing him sent a bolt of energy up my spine as if I had just enhanced a memory.

"And Papa," I said. I fought the urge to jump overboard at the sight of my father. Instead, I bounced on my toes, trying to find a gap in the crowd.

"Go," Gideon said. I kissed his cheek, grabbed my sister's hand, and fled to the gangway.

We made our way through the crowd, flailing our arms at our father and brother. Papa caught sight of us. He plucked Anders out of the tree like a fruit and plunged into the mass of people rushing the ship. I didn't see Mama until her arms flung around our necks. We clutched at each other as if someone might try to separate us again.

"My darlings," she said in our ears. The crowd pushed past us trying to reach their own families, and we pitched as if we were still on the ferry. I winced when elbows banged my three broken ribs. Papa pulled on the back of Mama's jacket, leading us out of the way and back toward Anders's tree. Hans, who had grown as tall as me, joined the fray with little Birgitte in his arms. I pulled out of Mama's grip to hug my brother and sister.

"Are you well?" she asked, taking hold of me again.

I tried to speak but nothing came out, so I nodded, jostling a tear or two loose.

"I will never forgive myself for leaving you behind, Rachel," Mama said. A new patch of gray graced her temple. "It should have been me who stayed." She looked down at our feet. "I don't know what I was thinking."

I knew what she had been thinking. She thought we would be safe. I had made her forget the danger.

"It wasn't your fault," I said. I couldn't let her blame herself. Maybe I would explain when I returned her memories of Fafa.

Papa pulled me from Mama and into a hug. "My little warrior," he said. New wrinkles creased the corners of his eyes.

Annalise pulled little Birgitte into her arms. My baby sister could not have remembered her, but she went to the stranger without tears. An outraged gasp came out of Annalise as soon as she got a good look at the toddler. "What happened to you?" Annalise asked with a pout. Birgitte's hair was a tangle, and dirt streaked her dress. "Our terrible brothers have made a tomboy of her," she said. I laughed at her genuine distress. Annalise sucked in her lip and said, "Give me a week. I'll set it right." She rubbed noses with her, and Birgitte shrieked with laughter.

"Are you *low*?" Mama asked Annalise in a whisper, using one of our old code words.

"They had nurses with insulin for me all the time."

Mama started at the word *insulin* spoken aloud but recovered quickly. "Have you eaten?"

I nodded, and Annalise glared at me. The Red Cross had given us plenty of food. I threw most of mine out the bus window at the thousands of refugees that sometimes clogged the roads, but I had eaten enough.

"Did you drive through Germany?" Hans asked with all the curiosity of a person who had never seen war up close.

I nodded but changed the subject. "Where's Erik?" I asked, not wanting to talk about bombed-out cities and abandoned towns.

Papa stepped aside to reveal Erik, not much bigger than when we left him, hiding from the heaving crowd behind the tree Anders had climbed. He was small for a five-year-old.

I unlatched my suitcase, drew out Jubilee, and knelt down to his eye level, hoping the toy would coax him out. "I've brought your Jubilee back, Erik." I held it out so he could grab it away without daring into the pressing throng.

Mama's face lit up. "Look at that, Erik," she said. "Your sisters kept him all this time."

Erik wrinkled his nose at Jubilee with its ratty, faded mane. It never occurred to me he wouldn't remember the toy, although it made sense. He had it for less than a week before he gave it to me.

"Thank your sisters," Mama said, determined to keep the reunion happy. Erik only clung tighter to the tree. I hid the stuffed pony behind my back, thinking maybe the mangy thing frightened him, but he didn't unwrinkle his nose even when Jubilee was out of sight. The expression was for Annalise and me.

"Don't be shy," Mama said, not remembering Erik was only shy with strangers.

"Margrethe," Papa said with the weight of understanding.

Annalise let out a little sob, handed over Birgitte to Mama, and turned away so Erik wouldn't see he'd made her cry.

"It's okay, Erik," I said, seeing his lip begin to quiver.

"No, it's not okay, Rachel," Mama said, her face pinched into a scowl. "None of this is okay." Her expression hadn't been directed at Erik, but he somehow knew everyone was upset because of him and joined Annalise in her tears.

Mama softened her expression, sorry she'd upset him. "You remember your sisters." He looked from Annalise to me, hiccupping. "He cried himself to sleep every night for a week for you," Mama went on. "Wore himself out with crying." She knelt at his feet and wiped his cheeks. "How could he just forget?"

"Margrethe, the boy was four years old," Papa said and turned back to us. "We stopped talking about you. It was too painful. For all of us." He ran his hand through Anders's hair. "We tried to spare them."

That sounded familiar.

Like me, they hadn't meant any harm, but I could fix it this time. I looked at each member of my family. The gray in Mama's hair, the inches on Hans and Anders, Papa's new wrinkles. The Nazis stole so much from us. They couldn't have Erik's memory of us too.

I looked at Annalise for permission. She nodded and whispered, "Please."

A year and a half ago, just a few months before we'd been exiled from Copenhagen, Annalise and I took Erik to Tivoli Gardens. On the walk back, he insisted we swing him high in the air like the Ferris wheel until our arms ached. I pushed that memory into my brother. His eyes widened, and his little back went straight as a soldier. He flung himself into my arms, and I threw him into the air again.

There was hardly any pain in my ribs at all.

We heard a lot of excuses during our months in Stockholm while we waited for the war to end. Governments, organizations, and individuals all said the same thing. *What could we have done?*

Denmark knew.

All but fifty-one Danish Jews returned to Denmark that summer. Most of those who died had been old like Rivka.

Other countries could have sent packages as King Christian did to keep their people alive and their spirits high.

They could have protected Jewish property. When local businessmen, like Papa, came home that June, their livelihoods remained intact.

They could have been like Mrs. Olsen, who, despite her loud dogs, proved herself a better neighbor than we ever gave her credit for and polished Mama's piano every week we were gone.

They could have been like the men and women of the Danish resistance. Glen Lund, who had spirited my family to safety in Sweden on his fishing boat, had spent a year and a half in jail.

After most of my family and more than six thousand Danish Jews had escaped to Sweden, the entire Copenhagen police force had been arrested—including Uncle Stellan. He'd been tied to a pole behind the barracks and shot. He'd never received a single one of our postcards. His widow received them all.

Once we returned to Denmark, I'd enhanced my memories of the last year and a half and filled three sketch pads with drawings of Terezin. Even with all its horrors, I never wanted to forget the place. My parents worried about my morbid inclination, but Annalise understood.

The guards were gone from Tivoli Gardens and City Hall Square. Never in my eighteen years had summer smelled as sweet. It might have been the *wienerbrød* from Muller's bakery or perhaps the blooms overflowing in the window boxes. I plucked a small purple flower from one and twirled it in between my fingers. I tucked it into my hair and slipped my hand into Gideon's.

"C'mon, Gideon. We're already late."

"It's an all-day event, Rachel." Gideon didn't like Cary Grant. The actor didn't do much for me either, truth be told, but it meant a lot to Annalise. "We can miss some of it, can't we?" Annalise had used her feminine wiles to get the theater manager to run a movie marathon of her favorite actor's movies, including *The Philadelphia Story*.

"The Hechts will be there," I said. We'd spent a fair amount of time with the family since Leah had been reunited with her husband, Lars. He didn't look anything like a resistance fighter, more like the postal worker he'd been before the war. "And we shouldn't keep your wife waiting," I said with a serious face.

Gideon rolled his eyes.

Hadas had returned to Copenhagen with us. She had nowhere else to go. She worked in a school while she hoped for word about her family back in Hungary. Her Danish was worse than her German, but it improved every day. Rabbi Hertz's ceremonies had been enough to get twenty other non-Danes out of Terezin. Denmark gave them all citizenship.

Adam had left us a month ago to search for his family in Germany. Like Hadas, no trace of what happened to them remained. Julia's parents had made the worst discovery. I planned to go to her hometown soon to visit the memorial her father was building for her as soon as it was safe to travel.

"Annalise said she would save us seats," Gideon said.

"Glen brought her, you know." I wiggled my eyebrows. The fisherman who had gone to a Nazi prison for bringing my family to safety had earned the date.

"She could do a lot worse than Glen...Hell, she *has* done worse than Glen."

I swatted at him.

Yes, Lukas had betrayed us, but he'd helped us too, more times than I could count. Annalise would have died if he hadn't stolen her medicine back when I'd lost it that first day. I couldn't judge Lukas for protecting his family. How could I hate him? What would I have done to save Annalise and Gideon? I already knew.

Anything.

"I liked Lukas. Admit it. You did too."

"I'm just glad she's moved on," Gideon said, refusing to answer. We waited at a corner for three cars to go by. Gasoline rationing was still in effect, but it wasn't as strict as it had been during the war.

"She says prison made Glen more interesting. Besides, he's much cuter than Dr. Golding."

We crossed and faced the nearly empty lot where our school had been. Our laughter died in our throats as if we passed a graveyard. A British plane had crashed into it during a botched bombing mission of Gestapo headquarters. Peter Jorgensen, the boy who'd betrayed Gideon and the others hidden in the church attic in Rungsted, was badly burned in the fire, but survived. He and his family moved from Copenhagen. Gideon would never have to face him.

"Rebecca would have been better off with us in Terezin," I said, staring at the remains of the half-buried foundation. Rebecca Larsen's two Christian grandparents may have spared her from deportation, but that lineage hadn't kept her safe. She died in the fire.

"We don't know that," Gideon said. He gave me a minute to consider his words before he wrapped an arm around me and whispered, "C'mon."

"I hope Heinrich made it through the war safely," I said as we passed the corner where he used to greet me with his reddened ears.

Gideon stopped short. "That freckled *schmendrick*?" I had passed some of Rivka's Yiddish on to him.

"Jealousy doesn't become you, sweetheart." I kissed his cheek.

"Behave, you two," Ruth Blume called out while sweeping the steps of her cafe.

Gideon tipped his cap, and I waved. "You coming to the festival, Miss Blume?" I asked as we passed.

Ruth shook her head. "We have to keep the cafe open."

Ilse's head popped out of the door, and she waved to us. "Speak for yourself, Ruthie. I'm not missing *Arsenic and Old Lace*." She squeezed Ruth's arm, and Ruth adjusted Ilse's collar.

"Have you heard from Moshe and Victor?" Gideon asked. The Blumes' husbands had moved to America, despite the offer of Danish citizenship. It was just the two of them again.

"They settled in Boston, where they have some family," Ruth said.

We waved goodbye, and I turned to Gideon. "Speaking of fake husbands...would you be upset if Adam came back to Copenhagen?" I used Annalise's wide-eye technique to melt any resistance he might have toward the plan. Adam had mentioned coming to Denmark to go to college for engineering in his last letter.

"Erik will be happy if Adam moves here, the little traitor." My parents had taken in Adam and Dr. Golding as if they were true sons-in-law, but my youngest brother developed an instant and staunch fascination with Adam. In the weeks we waited in Stockholm for the war to end, Erik devoted hours to watching Adam build models and draw designs for buildings.

"You know Adam is not who I want," I said. I curled my arms around Gideon and nestled my head under his chin.

"That's because you're in love with me," Gideon said, kissing the top of my head.

I stood on my tiptoes and whispered into his ear, "And I'll never let you forget it."

Author's Note

Although some details were changed to suit the narrative, *Drawn from Memory* is based on true events. To find out more, check out www.ushmm.org or www.terezinmusic.org.

The Danish Rescue of the Jews
One-third of European Jews died in the Holocaust, but 99 percent of Danish Jews survived.

Although Denmark was a tiny, occupied nation, Germany depended on their meat and butter, so the Third Reich yielded to their demands concerning the treatment of Danish Jews from the beginning of the occupation until the end of the war.

In *Drawn from Memory*, Rachel says King Christian threatened to wear a yellow star if Danish Jews were forced to wear them. This wasn't actually true, but it was a commonly held belief. Even though it never happened, it reflects the trust Danes had in their leader to protect them. Their trust was justified.

Denmark successfully evacuated 7,906 Jews to Sweden. Only 464 people were caught and deported to Terezin (or Theresienstadt in German). While there, no Danish prisoners were executed in the Little Fortress or transported to the death camp Auschwitz. The Danish government insisted their citizens had prominent status, receiving Red Cross parcels and better living conditions. Of the 464 people who set foot in the concentration camp, 90 percent survived. Most of those who died were over the age of sixty-five.

On the other hand, of the 140,000 Germans, Czechs, and Hungarians who walked through Terezin's gates, only 22,000, a mere 16 percent, survived. Conditions were harsher for non-Danes, and 33,000 people died there. The main cause of death, though, was transport to Auschwitz.

LGBT+ Persecution

Along with Jews, the Nazis targeted gay and bi men and trans women. Somewhere between 5,000 and 15,000 people were imprisoned in concentration camps like Terezin and made to wear a pink triangle. They were treated worse than any other group within the camps, and their survival rate was low. Lesbian and bi women and trans men were not arrested based on their sexuality or gender identity alone, although they were targeted for their political beliefs or if their Jewish ancestry.

Defiant Requiem

In reality, the *Requiem* was performed many times, not just for the Red Cross visit in June, 1944. Like in the book, the choir was deported to Auschwitz shortly after the Red Cross visit. Today, the *Defiant Requiem* is a performance that combines the music of Verdi's choral piece and a video testimony of Terezin survivors. It has been presented all over the world as a tribute to their remarkable act of resistance.

Thanks so much for reading. Please consider sharing your thoughts on your favorite review platform like goodreads.com.

Not ready to leave Rachel, Gideon, and Annalise?

Sign up for Laura Hatosy's newsletter and receive a free short story returning you to Rachel's world. It's two years later, and Rachel discovers someone close to her shares her ability! **Scan this QR code to sign up for the newsletter and receive the FREE story!**

About the Author

LAURA IS FROM NEW Jersey, which means she is genetically predisposed to big hair and has a predilection for pork roll sandwiches.

She received her BA in history and education at Rutgers and married her high school sweetheart. She discovered the story of the Danish evacuation of the Jews when she taught the Holocaust to eighth graders. The story was so compelling to her, she wrote her history master's thesis at Harvard on the subject and, later, this novel. Laura has two children, Isabella and Jake.

She lives in Massachusetts and is currently eating a pork roll sandwich.

Get to know her on Twitter, Instagram, and Facebook @LauraHatosy or at www.laurahatosy.com.

Acknowledgments

MANY THANKS TO ALL my friends and family, but especially...

–To my mom. If you like me, it's because of her.

–To my dad. If you like my stories, it's because of him.

–To my husband, Chris. I love you more than Costco.

–To my little star sweepers, Isabella and Jake.

–To the Horde, the Huddle, my RU girls, the Lunch Ladies, and the Cheesers. Your support means the world to me.

–To Rebecca Lanni for all the giggles.

–To indie bookstores and libraries, especially Whitelam Books and the RPL.

–To Facing History and Ourselves. Thank you for promoting compassion and justice through your curriculum to generations of students.

–To my Bulldogs and Rams. I hope you learned from me as much as I learned from you.

–To Kali Hatosy. If I didn't have you as a sister, I'd choose you as my friend.

–To the Wilsons. I have the best in-laws. I don't know what all those comedians are talking about.

–To Jennifer Esselman. If you are looking for honest feedback about your book, she's your girl. If you are looking for someone to fib and tell you that you look great in that hideous bridesmaid dress, you'll need to go elsewhere.

–To every person who put their metaphorical red pen to this book. There are too many to name them all here.

Not only did your comments improve the draft, but the process of discussing it with you made me a better writer for the next one. Special thanks go to Merel, Liz White-lam, and RCG for going above and beyond.

–To Edgar Krasa and Anna Ornstein, for so beautifully representing Elie Wiesel's words, "For the living and the dead, we must bear witness."

Never Forget

Made in the USA
Middletown, DE
10 June 2022

66933846R00154